PRAISE FOR KELLY ROMO

"Romo's chapters with the killer are the most sinister I've ever read. Will the girls survive? Will any of the young women manage to cheat death? The author keeps you riveted throughout."

CRAIG LESLEY, AWARD-WINNING AUTHOR OF *THE SKY FISHERMAN*

"A taut, smothering atmosphere hangs over the novel, casting a pall across every page. *Dead Drift* is a creepy, tense reading experience. From the first pages, this novel hooks you in."

JELENE PYNNONEN, INDEPENDENT BOOK REVIEW

"A fast-paced, disturbing horror story in a gorgeous and dangerous setting."

KIRKUS REVIEWS

DEAD DRIFT

KELLY ROMO

PAPERMOON
PRESS

Copyright © 2022 by Kelly Romo

All rights reserved.

No part of this book may be reproduced in any form or by any electronic or mechanical means, including information storage and retrieval systems, without written permission from the author, except for the use of brief quotations in a book review.

This is a work of fiction. Names, characters, places, and incidents are either products of the author's imagination, or used fictitiously.

❀ Created with Vellum

For my children: Brittany, Brennan, and Ryan

And, for all the lost girls who only want to be loved

Not everyone lost will be saved…

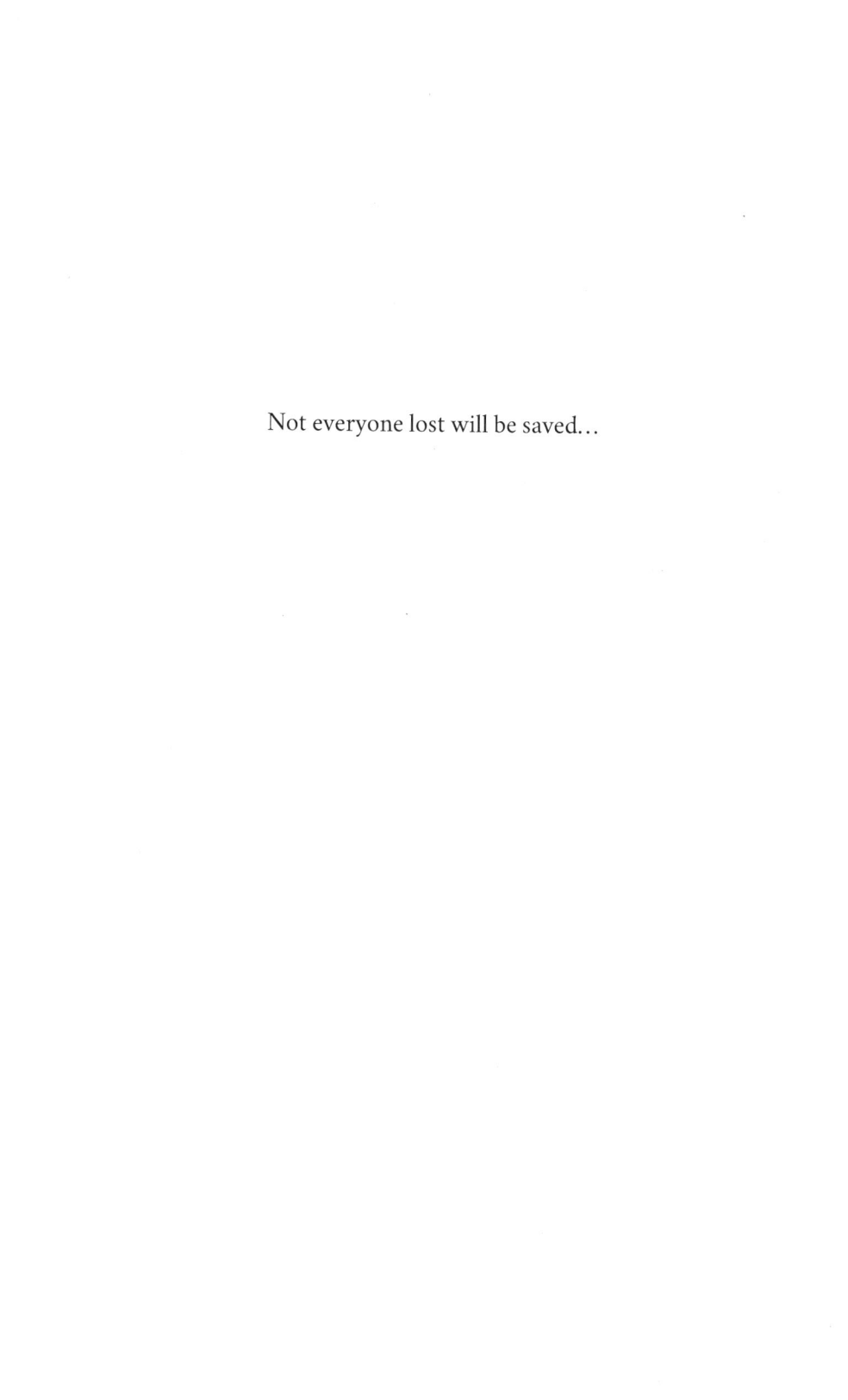

PROLOGUE

HIM

THERE ARE FIVE STAGES OF DROWNING: SURPRISE, INVOLUNTARY breath-holding, unconsciousness, hypoxic convulsions, and finally, death.

Shawna's hair spreads out in a halo of jet-black strands lit by the moon and rippling in the current. There is no fear or panic in her. I spared her of that. Her death is beautiful and silent as I hold her in my arms and cradle her beneath the surface. I put my lips to hers and inhale her very last breath before she gasps and draws my water into her lungs. She becomes heavy then seizes like a fish. My blood surges and thunders inside me. I have never felt so alive. Shawna finally relaxes, surrenders, and becomes mine forever. I hold and comfort her through it all. Binding her to me was easier than I thought. I should have done this years ago.

I raise Shawna up. Her nose, lips, and tits break the surface, all slick and shiny in the moonlight. I give her one last kiss, then take her nipple between my lips and flick it with my tongue. I wish I could keep her longer, but she is losing her warmth. I take a clump of her jet-black hair and wind it tight around my finger until the tip of it goes numb. I yank it from her head. It is surprising how easily it comes out and hangs from my hand, as black and shiny as tar. It will be perfect.

Shawna is mine forever, for I am the river, and the river is me. It is the fluid, and I am the flesh.

CHAPTER ONE

I GUESS I'M TURNING OUT JUST LIKE EVERYONE EXPECTED, BUT AT least I'm not pregnant. Aiding in Amber's escape will be the biggest crime I have ever committed. I don't realize what a death grip I have on my steering wheel until I pull to the curb, put it in park, and turn my headlights off. A million butterflies flutter in my chest and up my throat. It is exactly four-fifteen in the morning, and Amber is not expecting me until four-thirty. She will be shocked that I made it on time.

Everything I own in the world sits in the trunk, which isn't more than a single suitcase. I used to have more until three years ago. I was pissed that I had to leave my foster parents, Scott and Jeanette. I thought they loved me, and their house would be my forever home. I was so tired of packing up and dragging all my shit with me that I threw garbage bags of clothes, photos, notes, and keepsakes into the trash—which I now regret. I thought all the pictures were of former friends who I would never see again. It took me about a month to realize that the only two photos I had of my mom were mixed in with them.

I don't remember much about my mom. She overdosed when I was four. I do remember she had dry hands and a scratchy voice. She used to read to me from a Mother Goose nursery rhyme book with bright watercolor pictures. Other than the two photos, the book was the last thing I had from my mom, but it went missing at my eighth-grade parents' house. I think one of the little kids stole it when they left.

The neon blue numbers on my phone say it is four twenty-five. I step out of my car, press the lock button, and silently push the door until it clicks shut. I lived in this neighborhood—until last November when I turned eighteen. I lived in *that* house. Thanks to the state of Oregon, I've always lived in *that* house in any neighborhood. The one with the foster children—where kids come and go based on their behavior or personality. Sometimes, no matter how good you are, you have to move somewhere new. And you have no idea why.

A few porch lights glow, and some houses have a window or two lit, probably for some child afraid to sleep in the dark—which I never understood. If your light is on, a peeping Tom could stand right outside your window and watch you sleep, even through the smallest gap in the curtains.

My stomach clenches tight, and my heart pounds on the wall of my chest. I broke laws before, like staying out after curfew, drinking underage, egging houses, or stealing things I needed—but nothing like this. I am legally an adult and about to harbor a runaway. I can do hard-time for this. Amber and I have one chance, and we need to get it right.

The group home is a two-story house with a basement, indoor and outdoor security cameras, and motion-activated floodlights—not to keep burglars out but to keep the children in.

The second-story window of the girls' room is dark. Amber better be there, watching for my signal. The girls' room has two sets of bunk beds. Amber and I slept on the upper bunks, letting the two little ones, Willow and Susan, have the lower beds.

The room always reeked like pee, no matter how often Amber and I washed and bleached Willow's sheets. The boys' room also has two sets of bunk beds and stinks like dirty socks and underwear. The three boys are all middle school skater boys with the typical cool-kid attitudes and bad grades to match. I miss them.

I feel like a cat with heightened senses as I creep to the side of the house, avoiding the security lights in the driveway and taking out my phone. I flip it open and hold the glowing screen below my chin, which is our signal, so Amber knows it is me. The curtains in the girls' room flutter, so…just as we planned, I move beneath the bathroom window. It is one of the few without a security sensor and the one we always drop things out of to get them past our foster parents.

Sharon and Mike treated us like inmates. They always patted us down at the door before leaving or entering. We had to sneak everything, except our school books and binders, in or out of the house. We were forbidden from wearing makeup and tank tops, so we kept all that in our lockers during the school year. Amber and I had an entire bag filled with eyeliner, mascara, foundation, our hair straightener, and skimpy tank tops that we would grab and head straight to the girls' restroom every morning. Amber and I had so many tardies to first period we were on permanent after-school detention every Tuesday and Thursday —but we didn't care. Who wanted to go home anyway?

The two tiny basement windows are dark, but that does not mean much. Mike's creepy brother, Ed, could be sitting in there, watching me with his pants down around his ankles. He is in his forties and balding. The little hair he has left on his head is greasy, like he is afraid to wash it and make more fall out. He is the reason Amber is running away. I quit school the day I turned eighteen, so I could get the hell out of the house and make enough money to buy a car and save Amber.

Sharon and Mike went out one time, leaving Ed in charge of all the kids. He lured Amber and me into the basement, where he had a trunk filled with skanky stripper clothes. He said he wanted to take pictures of us to send to a magazine, saying we looked like models. He promised us that we could make a lot of money. As soon as he pulled out the Zip Ties, I freaked out and started screaming—so he let us go back upstairs.

Just before I moved out, Amber and I came home to him watching Willow and Susan play on the swing set. He sat there watching them with a disgusting boner under his jeans. We tried to warn Sharon and Mike, but they called us liars. Lately, Ed had been wiggling his fat purple tongue at Amber like he wanted to stick it inside her. It was only a matter of time before something happened. Last week, Amber heard the bedroom door open and close in the middle of the night. She knew it was Ed, standing there, breathing hard while he jacked off. She lay still, afraid to move until he finished and left the room.

The bathroom window finally slides open, and the screen pops out. Amber's beautiful face peeks through, and she waves. This is the moment. I only need to get her duffle bag and put it in my car. Then, Amber will wait for Sharon to wake up and realize she is out of her French Vanilla coffee creamer. Amber had emptied it down the sink last night, knowing Sharon would send her out to the store for more. Like an addict, Sharon *needs* the creamer for her coffee every single morning.

The end of Amber's purple duffle bag pokes out, filling the entire window frame. I move to where I think it will drop. It wiggles in the opening, inches out, then pops through and falls toward me. I flinch and turn my face away. It hits my arms and slips through, making a thud as it drops onto the dirt. I grab it and flatten myself against the wall. Amber's head sticks out the window, eyes wide and frozen. My breathing is so loud in my ears that I cannot hear anything. I try to hold my breath until my head feels light.

The basement light clicks on. *Shit!* I slowly exhale through my nose. Please, God, don't let Ed come out to check. I draw in a breath and listen. A dog barks a few streets over. Should I go or wait? There is no way in hell I want to face Ed, so I nod up to Amber.

She puts the screen back into place and slides the window shut. I try to listen past the pounding in my ears. The last thing I need is for some nosey neighbor to see me coming from the side of the house with a duffle bag, especially from the side of *that* house. The neighborhood is filled with stay-at-home moms who feel it is their duty to monitor us.

I hurry back around the block, toss Amber's bag into the back seat of my car, and wait for the morning light. Ever since dropping out of school, I have been living with Jill, a single mom with two boys. She gave me a free room for some cleaning and babysitting. Her house isn't much different than foster care, but I can come and go as I please, and I don't have to worry about some pedophile living in the house. I could not tell Jill what we planned, so I didn't get a chance to say goodbye to her or the boys—or thank her for all she did for me. I also could not give two weeks' notice at the Shell Station or Burgertime, leaving them scrambling to fill my shifts.

It feels like I have been sitting here forever, waiting for daylight and sliding down in my seat whenever a car or jogger comes toward me. As the houses come to life with lights, I can almost smell the fried eggs, Pop-Tarts, and toaster waffles. My stomach grumbles. After a while, people start coming out front doors, dressed in business suits. They head to their cars with their leather bags and thermal mugs.

Where is Amber? Sharon must be up by now, throwing F-bombs all around the kitchen, cursing whichever kid touched her creamer, and threatening to ground them all if someone didn't confess.

Finally, Amber appears around the corner, trying not to look nervous but walking faster than normal. She has long, sweeping bangs and amber-colored hair that comes to her shoulders. Amber is delicate, with thin wrists and ankles that always get twisted or wrenched too hard. We are both five-foot-three, but I have stronger bones and thicker hair than her.

I wonder how long it will take for Sharon to realize that Amber isn't dawdling at the store but missing—only to check the girls' room and realize Amber's stuff is gone and she has run away. We thought about Amber leaving everything behind and sharing my clothes, but we decided it would be inhumane to let Sharon and Mike believe she was the victim of a serial killer or something. Plus, we will have less police after us since foster kids run away all the time.

As she gets closer, I can see that her eyes and nose are red and watery. She opens the passenger door and hops in.

"Is everything all right?"

She nods, but tears run down her cheeks.

"Did something happen?"

She shakes her head and takes a few gasping breaths. "I'm worried for Willow and Susan. I feel bad leaving them."

My throat stings. Without Amber or me there to protect them, what will Ed do? But, we cannot take two little girls. They will come after us for sure.

"They're young. I don't think Ed will actually touch them." I reach over and take Amber's hand. "We'll call and report him as soon as we're safe in Canada."

Amber squeezes my fingers and nods.

"We can even lie and say he raped you to make sure there's an investigation."

Her eyes light up. "Can we do that?"

"Why not? We'll be out of the country, and we won't tell them where we are. There will be nothing they can do to us."

She gives me the saddest smile I have ever seen. I squeeze her hand before letting it go, turn the key, put it into drive, and press down on the gas. The engine races, but we don't move. Before I have a chance to let out a curse word or two, the car lurches forward, and we are on our way.

CHAPTER TWO

Unless Amber and I are sitting in the back of a yellow school bus, we are never up at the butt crack of dawn. The sun highlights a thin layer of clouds and turns the sky pink and yellow as we turn down all the familiar side streets, blending in with the herd of cars backing out of driveways on their way to work.

We don't say a word and hardly even breathe as we inch down 99W in my metallic blue Mazda, practically hitting every single red light. We pass at least half a dozen Starbucks, all with long lines of commuters willing to drop three bucks for their morning fix.

As we merge onto Interstate 5 toward Portland, Amber cranks up the radio and rolls her window down. Her hair whips all around her head, and she slides on her sunglasses.

"We did it," Amber says with a big smile.

"We did!" I lower my window and pull my hair tie out.

Soon, Sharon will call the police and post Amber's picture all over Myspace. But by then, we will be all incognito with our fake IDs and partying like twenty-two-year-olds.

The freeway curves around and we have a beautiful view of

the city and the snow-tipped peaks of Mount St. Helens and Mount Hood. We cross over the Willamette River and take the first exit into the city. I always heard that Portland was *weird*. They even have bumper stickers and t-shirts saying so, but I never expected to see a man riding a unicycle in a kilt and playing bagpipes with flames shooting from the pipes.

"Holy shit!" I hit the brakes as a cyclist in red and black spandex makes a left turn right in front of us. "Did you see that? I almost hit him."

I slow down and grip the wheel with both hands. I have never driven in a big city, and people wander everywhere. We pass a homeless woman pushing a shopping cart. I try not to look at her because Amber and I are only one step away from living on the streets. I barely saved enough for the used car, cell phone, and enough money to stay in youth hostels and eat for two weeks. We need to start looking for work the moment we get to Canada.

"You'll have to keep a lookout for the hostel," I say. "I'm playing Frogger with the bicyclists."

Amber keeps glancing down at the map I printed out, then up at the buildings. "Turn right at the next street."

We have a green light but have to wait for a couple dressed as a faun and a woodland fairy to clear the crosswalk. We drive past restaurants with seating on the sidewalks and people with tie-dyed shirts or checkered suit coats and skinny jeans.

"Left at the next light," Amber says, "then right on the street after that. I'm getting hungry."

When I gassed up last night at the end of my shift, I should have packed us some car snacks, but I was so nervous that I didn't think past topping off the tank.

"Turn left at the stop sign, then it will be on the left."

The hostel is an old house with a wide front porch and grass growing on the roof—not moss like most homes in Oregon, but actual blowing in the wind type of grass. I pull down a narrow side street, entirely shaded by the trees on either side of the road, like a magic tunnel ready to transport us to another life.

Amber squeals as I pop the trunk. "We made it! I'm surprised you didn't kill any bicyclists."

"I may have. I felt a thump a few blocks back." I joke, then drop the keys into my pocket. "Once we unload our stuff, want to go browse through all the shops?"

"Yes! And we need to get a beer." Amber loops her arm through mine. "Since we're legal now."

"Define legal."

"True." Amber stops at the bottom of the porch steps. "How about illegally legal to drink."

"Yes, but we will keep that fact to ourselves."

Alcohol will be one of the best parts of the new us. We both bought fake IDs. Amber's was from a girl I worked with at Burgertime, and mine was from a woman who always came into the Shell Station and looked like an older version of me. "Remember…we are no longer Emmy and Amber, but Nicole and Madeline."

I swing open a wooden screen door and about gag. The lobby looks like an old lady's wet dream, filled with overstuffed chairs, pamphlets, crocheted table runners, and scraggly houseplants. Nothing matches. A tacky golden lamp with a fringed shade sits on an end table, and several umbrellas stick up from an empty flowerpot.

A skinny girl with sunglasses and a scarf tied around her blonde curls comes in behind us. She has a gigantic backpack with a sleeping bag strapped to the top and is wearing loose, green khaki pants and a wife-beater T-shirt that is in desperate need of some Clorox bleach. She doesn't have any makeup on and smells like a campfire and other disgusting body odors.

"Are you a backpacker?" Amber asks, always overly friendly and curious.

"I'm hiking the Pacific Crest Trail."

Behind a glass counter, a tiny girl with short black hair and steel bars pierced through her eyebrow and lip, has an old-fashioned pink phone pressed to her ear. A curly pink cord connects her to the part with the dial.

She puts her hand over the mouthpiece. "I'll be right with you."

The girl behind us unbuckles her backpack and lets it drop to the floor. She sighs, stretches her arms, then bends over and touches the floor. Amber grabs my hand and gives it a tight squeeze. "We're going to meet such exciting people!"

"Are you done?" Amber asks the backpacker. "Is this your final stop?"

"No, I'm trying to make it all the way to Canada. I just want to see Portland and get a shower."

The girl behind the counter hangs up the phone by hooking it onto a silver cradle. "You here to check in?"

"Yes, the reservation is under Nicole Keefer."

I feel more confident as Nicole, like I can do anything. Nicole, well my version of Nicole, is a new person and I can make her into whoever I want.

The glass counter is filled with random brochures, books, an old jack-in-the-box, a Sesame Street lunch box, and an old Monopoly game with masking tape on the corners.

"My name is Alexy. As you can see, we are an eco-friendly hostel. That's a compost bin out there in the garden, and I'm sure you noticed the eco-roof."

"You mean the grass?" I ask. "Do you have to mow it?"

"It's a vegetated roof that soaks up rainwater and keeps it from running into the watershed. We harvest the rainwater, store it in cisterns, and use it to flush the toilets and water the garden."

I make a mental note to buy some bottled water.

As Amber fills out the registration slip, I pick up a Magic 8 Ball that sits on the counter. *Will this be an unforgettable vacation?*

I think, sending my brain waves into the ball. I shake it and turn it over. The little white triangle rises to the surface through a blue liquid, revealing my fortune: *Without a doubt.*

Amber slides the completed form back to Alexy and holds her hand out toward the Magic 8 Ball. "My turn."

She shakes the ball, closes her eyes, and puts it to her forehead. After a moment, she opens her eyes then turns it over to wait for an answer. A frown pinches her eyebrows together, and she plunks it down onto the counter. "Those things are stupid anyway."

"What did you ask it?"

"It doesn't matter."

"You should never put your lives in the hands of fate," a tired voice says behind us.

I turn to see the backpacker sitting on the couch with her dirty boots up on top of the coffee table and her hands behind her head, exposing two very hairy armpits.

Alexy sets two room keys on the counter, both attached to green coiled wristbands. "You'll be in the girl's dorm upstairs. There are two sets of bunk beds. So far, the other two beds are empty, but we're expecting more people tonight."

Not that I ever want to sleep in a bunk bed again in my life, but the difference between the dorm and a private room was thirty bucks.

"The kitchen closes at ten o'clock," Alexy continues with her memorized spiel. "Hawthorne Street has shops and restaurants. The Bagdad has cheap movies, and you can eat pizza and drink beer inside the theater."

Up in our room, I throw my suitcase on a bottom bunk. Amber sets her bag on the other bed. We both prefer a bottom bunk because if you ever need privacy, you can drape towels down and make a little fort out of it.

"We could do that…"

"Do what?"

"We can backpack. We can use the rest of our money for camping equipment and backpacks."

Amber's forehead wrinkles. "Neither of us has ever camped, and we both complain if we have to walk up a steep hill."

I drop it for now. If we had a tent, we would always have a place to sleep. But then again, there is the hairy armpit problem.

"Damnit," Amber says and looks down into her shirt. "My bra strap broke, and I don't have another."

We head down to the lobby and get a huge silver safety pin from Alexy. Amber fishes out her strap, and I hold it in place while she pierces the top of the cup and hooks them together. It is her favorite bra, a pink one with light pink embroidered stars.

"Let's see what Portland has other than rainwater harvesting and kamikaze bicyclists."

We link arms and go outside.

We pass the *Awareness Holistic Center* with a white picket fence and stepping stones that barely show through the thick grass. Across the street is *Red Carpet Vintage* and *Roof of the World Tibetan Clothing*, along with an herb and bead shop, a hemp clothing store, and a microbrewery.

"I feel out of place here," Amber says.

"How can you feel out of place?" I sweep my arm past people in camouflage, plaid, ripped jeans, newsy caps, and Rastafarian hats. Some have man-buns, beards, body piercings, or tattoos. "I think just about anything goes."

"I guess I feel out of place with my ordinariness," Amber says. "I feel bland."

"We are bland—just like mushy canned peas. Oh God, remember that time Sharon would not let me leave the table until I finished my peas, and I just sat there for hours until she finally let me go?"

"See, even you would rather be punished than eat canned peas."

A group of naked bicyclists—elderly naked bicyclists—pedal

past us. Amber and I look at each other with raised eyebrows and wide eyes.

"We need to get off the street." I pull her toward a warehouse-sized antique shop. "Let's go in here."

Every inch of the store is crammed with stuffed chairs, Polaroid cameras, trunks, cowboy hats, old clothes, ice skates, naked baby dolls with patches of bare scalp, Jesus figurines, and fake jewelry. Just a bunch of old crap that people bought and got tired of. Or maybe they died, and their kids threw out all their shit.

"This place is awesome." Amber picks up a long strip of fur with an animal head still attached. "Look at this thing."

"Put it down. It probably has fleas." An old Ouija Board sits on top of a stack of board games. I pick it up and shake it, feeling the pieces clunk around inside it. "Should we buy it?"

"Have you ever used one?" Amber asks.

"Yes, I did with Shelly Howell, but I think she moved it just to freak me out. Let's get it. I trust you to not make it move, and we can see if it really works." I flip it over, looking for the price. "It's only five dollars. I'm getting it."

"Hell no," Amber says. "I heard they open doorways for demons, especially if you don't know what you're doing. And we are the poster children for not knowing what we are doing."

"What? Look at us. We are in Portland on the adventure of a lifetime." I set the Ouija Board back on the shelf. "By the way, what did you ask the Magic 8 Ball?"

Amber shakes her head. "It's stupid. I asked it if we'll make it to Canada."

"What did it say?"

She shakes her head again, then answers, "It said, *Outlook not so good.*"

"Maybe you weren't specific enough. Hey, look." I point at a rack of shoes all bent up like tiny crescent moons with their laces hanging out or buckles undone. "They look like elf shoes."

"Oh my God, look at that!" Amber picks up two brand new pairs of lime green Converse tennis shoes. "Both are size six. It's meant to be."

"Sold," I say. I cannot remember the last time I had a pair of new shoes. We usually get hand-me-downs.

"I wish we could take pictures of our adventure and post them on Myspace," Amber says. "Nobody can see our awesomeness."

"We won't feel so awesome if we're caught!"

"True!"

Back at the hostel, we look through stacks of brochures.

"Here's a Bohemian storytelling walking tour," Amber says. "That could be interesting. Or, we could tour a microbrewery. I want to learn more about beer."

"This looks like fun." I hold up a brochure with *Whitewater Rafting Adventure* in big white letters. People in rubber boats and orange and yellow life jackets hold paddles as they splash through whitewater on the cover.

Amber ignores me, studying the brochures in her hand. "Here's a riverboat." She holds up one with a huge triple-decker steamboat with a giant red paddlewheel in the back.

I open the rafting brochure.

"Listen to this," I say. "Thrilling rapids with scenic calm stretches through a rimrock-lined canyon where Native Americans hunted and fished for thousands of years. Experienced guides take visitors through class III and class IV rapids, beautiful swimming holes, and diverse wildlife. The Deschutes River Canyon is home to bighorn sheep, coyotes, eagles, cougars, river otters, and osprey."

"Maybe we should just get to Canada," Amber says.

"We came on this trip for adventure. We need to start living our lives on our own terms."

"I just have a bad feeling," Amber says. "I don't know why."

"Is it that stupid message you got on the Magic 8 Ball? Maybe you should try it again."

Alexy's shift must have finished because a skinny guy, who is all elbows and a huge Adam's apple, comes from a doorway and steps behind the glass counter. He wears thick black-framed glasses like they used to wear in the 1950s.

"You ever been whitewater rafting?" I ask him.

"Oh yeah, it's a blast."

"It looks expensive," Amber says, reading the back of one of the brochures.

"If you're worried about the money, go to Lodell. It's not as popular as Maupin and farther off the main highway, but it's one big whitewater party. The hotel is cheap, the beer is cheap, and the bar is packed. They have a live band on the weekends, and most of the people are young and looking for fun."

"How far away is it?" I ask.

"It's in Central Oregon—just a little over two hours east, on the other side of Mount Hood."

"That's two hours out of our way," Amber says.

"I've never been on the other side of Mount Hood. Have you?"

"No."

"We can't leave Oregon before seeing what's on the other side." Taking on my new persona, I say, "Nicole and Madeline would love to see it."

Amber sighs. "You know I don't like swimming."

"It's not swimming. We will be in a raft with life jackets on." I hold up the brochure. "And look how hot the rafting guides are."

She scans the brochure, and her eyebrows go up. "They are hot."

"What do you say, Madeline?"

"Maddy," Amber says with a smile, finally loosening up. "I go by Maddy."

I knew it wouldn't take her long.

"So…what do you think? One side trip, then straight to Canada?" I take her hand. "I know! We will ask the Magic 8 Ball in the morning and let it decide for us."

"Oh God," Amber rolls her eyes. "Fine, but if it tells us anything negative, it's straight to Canada."

"Deal," I say and give her the biggest hug. "We will never forget this trip."

CHAPTER THREE

Our decision is in the hands of fate or a higher power. However you want to put it. People do that all the time, don't they? And no matter what, it is better than leaving things in *our* hands. Sitting on the lobby couch with both of us feeling badass in our brand new green Converse sneakers, I hold the Magic 8 Ball between us.

"Ready?"

"I guess," Amber says.

We put our foreheads to the cold black plastic. *Should we go whitewater rafting?* I think, then pull it away, shake it, and turn it over. The plastic triangle slowly rises through the liquid, *Concentrate and ask again.*

We do it again and get, *Reply hazy, try again.*

"What did you ask it?"

"If we should go to Canada," Amber says.

"We need to ask the same question. Let's both ask if we should go whitewater rafting."

She nods, and I turn the ball over. We put our foreheads on it again, and I think, *Should we go whitewater rafting?* I shake it and turn it over. The triangle rises with, *Better not tell you now.*

"Seriously?" We do not have time for an indecisive ball. We need to get going. I look around the lobby and don't see anyone, so I drop the Magic 8 Ball into my bag.

"What are you doing?"

"We're burning daylight," I say, just like my fifth-grade foster dad used to, and I start toward the door.

"Emmy…"

I hurry and step out onto the porch in case they have security cameras and are watching us from another room. I pop the trunk and toss my suitcase in. Amber is right behind me, and her purple duffle bag flies into the trunk. I giggle as I jump into the driver's seat and put it in drive. We are rolling forward before Amber even has her seatbelt on.

"What are you doing? Emmy!"

"I'm not Emmy anymore. I'm Nicole! And Nicole wants to leave."

Amber rolls her eyes.

I drive a few blocks, then turn into a gas station and get in line for a pump. I take the Magic 8 Ball from my bag. "Okay, one more time. If it's a direct answer, we'll follow it. Agreed?"

"Agreed," Amber says.

"I will ask alone this time. It may not work with two people."

I put it to my head and ask, *Is it my fate to go whitewater rafting?* I shake the ball, then turn it over. Amber leans toward me, and we watch the triangle rise to the surface. *It is decidedly so.*

I look to Amber. She shrugs and says, "I better not fall into the river."

The car in front of us moves forward, and I pull to the pump. The attendant, all skinny and in a hoodie even though it is not cold out, comes to the window just as I roll it down. When he sees us, a smile comes to his face. "What can I get you?"

"Fill it up," I say. "And can you tell us how to get to Lodell?"

"His eyebrows pinch together."

"Lodell?" He moves to the gas tank and removes the cap. "I never heard of Lodell."

"It's a whitewater rafting town."

"You mean Maupin?"

Amber hands me a brochure. The attendant puts the nozzle into our tank and presses some buttons on the pump. I hold the brochure out the window. "No, it's Lodell."

He takes the brochure and looks at the front cover just as someone at the next pump honks for him. He nods his head. "Oh, yeah, I went there once with my youth group."

The person honks again. He looks over, then back at me. "Take Interstate 84 east all the way to US 197 and go south. Follow the signs to Maupin. Once you're there, you can ask how to get to Lodell."

He walks off just as the nozzle pops and our tank is full.

"That was quick," Amber says.

"We didn't need much, and I want to start with a full tank."

The attendant returns and pumps some more until the numbers round to the nearest fifty cents. "That'll be five-fifty. You want a receipt?"

"No thanks." I hand him the exact amount and put the Mazda into drive. It does that thing again where the engine races, but we don't move for a moment, then it catches and lurches forward. As we roll away, the attendant yells something to us.

"What did he say?" I ask Amber.

She shrugs, "Trans something. Maybe transformation or transportation?"

"Whatever."

We make it to Interstate 84 with Mount Hood just to the right. The peak is covered in snow even in the summer, just like a white-chocolate Hershey's Kiss. The Columbia River is on the left. As we drive into the Columbia River Gorge, steep cliffs rise up with waterfalls pouring down at least six hundred feet. Amber reads the road signs as we go. We zoom past Rooster Rock, Bridal Veil Falls, Multnomah Falls, Bonneville Dam, and the Bridge of the Gods. Windsurfers skim across the choppy river, and fishermen's boats bob up and down on the Columbia.

"Remember that song we learned in elementary school?" I start singing, *Roll on Columbia, roll on*.

Amber joins in, and we sing, mumbling when we forget certain verses but always singing the chorus aloud. The wind picks up, whipping the trees and pushing against our car in gusts. I move to the slow lane and grip the steering wheel.

The gorge, filled with fir trees and wildflowers, eventually fades away to grasslands and rolling hills. Just as we pass The Dalles, a light comes on my dashboard. It looks like a tiny airplane with the word *CHECK* beneath it.

"What does that mean?" I ask Amber, pointing at it.

"I don't know. Did you miss a payment?"

"I don't have payments. Look in the glove box and see if there's something that explains it."

Amber searches, pulling everything out and onto her lap. She sorts through them twice, then picks up a single piece of paper and stares over at me.

"What?"

"Did you steal this car?"

"No! I bought it. You know I did."

"There is nothing here that says you own it. The registration and insurance papers say, *Jennifer Singleton*."

"Duh! I paid for it, but I couldn't register it in my name—especially since we planned to escape. The police could put out an APB on my license plate. Do I look stupid?"

"What about insurance?"

"I can't afford insurance."

"Oh my God!" Amber says.

"What are you worried about? I only paid a thousand dollars

for the car. I could almost buy another one for what I would pay for insurance. If I wreck it, I wreck it. I don't need it replaced."

Amber shrugs. "I thought it is a law that you must have insurance."

"Seriously? You're worried about insurance when you ran away, and I am harboring a minor? You don't go to jail for no insurance."

"True," Amber says. "And Nicole lives as she pleases."

"Right!"

We finally make it onto US 197, which will take us south, behind Mount Hood. Once out of the gorge, the wind dies down, and we speed past nothing but grassland and isolated farms. Every now and then, a truck comes up on our ass, then speeds around us. I stay close to the speed limit. I'm not about to be caught because of a speeding violation.

As we circle around the east of Mount Hood, Amber lowers her window, turns up the stereo, and blasts *Teenage Flight* by Amy James.

Her hair whips around as she sings, "Let's straighten our hair and line our eyes. Don't ever go back, don't ever go back." She glances over at me and smiles.

Now, I know that Amber is all in. She doesn't want to go rafting, but as usual, she never holds a grudge and has a great time once she starts. She isn't like some people who reluctantly go along and then make the entire trip miserable. I love that about her.

I roll my window down and join in singing, "Skinny jeans and boy dreams. Don't ever go back, don't ever go back."

The landscape changes from grassland to high desert covered in dusty green brush and twisted trees, filling the car with a warm and sagey smell. The highway takes us down a canyon into Maupin, and we get our first glimpse of the Deschutes River.

The entire main street is only five blocks of shops, restaurants, a small park, and a school. We pass a service station that looks like it was built in the 1920s with two gas pumps and an old rusty truck parked in front.

The road drops down, winding deeper into the canyon toward the river. Below a bridge, people prepare for a barbecue on a big grassy lawn between the river and a hotel. We cross and drive along the other side of the Deschutes.

Instead of climbing out of the canyon, we take a road that hugs the river. We stop where two cars are pulled over to watch some rafts going through the rapids. The river surges white through dark volcanic rock. On the other side, train tracks and telephone poles hug a ledge, barely squeezing in between the river and cliff.

Several people sit in beach chairs on a big rock close to the rapid. Bright blue and red umbrellas shade them as they snap pictures of the rafts going through the whitewater.

I pull the car off the road, slowly inching closer to the river and feeling panic rise up in my throat. "How close am I?"

"Keep going."

"I'm good." I put the car in park and set the emergency brake.

"We're not completely off the road."

"I don't give a crap. It's too close to the edge for me."

We step from the car and stand at the rim, where the volcanic rock drops straight down into the river. The rapids rumble, and something buzzes like electrical wires in the hot air.

A blue raft with six people in orange life jackets drifts into view, bumping over the whitewater and around the rocks.

The guide in the back yells, "Right side forward," and the people on the right stick their paddles into the water.

Just before the raft drops down into a churning hole, the guide yells, "Stop."

Everyone stops paddling, and the raft plunges through the

rapid. When a big splash of water washes over the front, the rafters shriek and cheer.

"Oh my God," Amber says, but I do not look at her or answer.

Several other rafts go through in a similar way, each taking the rapids at a slightly different angle. But all of them make it through with no difficulty. Right before we leave, an orange raft comes wobbling around the bend with people in mismatched life jackets and paddling wildly with nobody in charge. A man sits on the front of the raft with his legs dangling in the water. He holds onto a strap at the front with one hand with a can of beer raised into the air with the other as he takes the rapids like a bronco buster. A gush of water pushes his upper body back into the raft, but he pulls himself back up and yells, "Yah-hoo!"

Amber looks over at me with her eyebrows raised high.

"We wouldn't go with them," I say.

"Maybe they're from Lodell, and that's why it's so much cheaper."

"Naw, they're just a buncha drunk fucks," a guy behind us says. He looks to be in his thirties and wears a faded orange and black baseball cap with *Beavers* written across the front. "Those are the type of people who flip their rafts or drown. At least these ones have life jackets on."

"People raft with no life jackets?" I ask.

"You'd be surprised," the man says. "I've seen idiots on inner tubes. Some people don't realize how powerful the Deschutes is."

"Can you tell us how to get to Lodell?"

He squints his eyes and gives us a strange look. "You going there alone?"

"No," I say just in case he is a creeper. "We're meeting some people there."

He takes a moment to answer, then points to the top of the canyon wall. It's an hour that way. Take 197 south. It will turn into 97. Watch for signs and follow them to Silverdale. Once you turn off the highway, you will see signs for Lodell.

We climb back into the car and take a steep road up and away from the river. At the top, we have a bird's-eye view of the little town of Maupin tucked against the crevasse of the canyon. We drive away into the lonely nothingness. We are the only car on the road for miles and miles of dry desert brush, driving parallel with the distant mountain range and snow-covered volcano peaks that divide where we grew up with where we are now.

Amber blares the music, and we speed across the desert highway until the radio catches nothing but static.

CHAPTER FOUR

Forty-five minutes south of Maupin, we turn off the highway and start our descent into Lodell. The desert transforms into green pastures filled with black and brown cows. We pass farms with big barns and small wooden houses or trashy trailers with beater cars parked out front. Fields have piles of hay covered with tarps and massive water pipes stretching across them.

"Are you sure this is the right way?"

"There's a sign up ahead."

The road is nothing but blacktop between grass-filled ditches, not even giving us enough room to pull off to the side.

We roll up to a post with a cheap wooden sign with *Lodell* painted in white, and an arrow pointing left. I follow it and drive until we come to another sign that looks like the first, except it has bullet holes shot through it.

"Are you sure about this?" Amber asks, looking out her side window. "I'm getting a creepy feeling that we're driving straight into a Stephen King movie."

She is right. I imagine some beat-up old truck a mile behind us taking down the Lodell signs and following us into the middle of nowhere. We keep driving, and the land turns back into desert with fields of dried grass and abandoned bare-wood shacks that look like old-time pioneer houses.

The blacktop ends at another road sign that points down a dirt road and into a rocky canyon. "Maybe we should just turn around," Amber says.

"Any cell service?"

She shakes her head. "I think we should go back. We can probably make it to Portland before dark."

We promised never to drive in the dark. It would be too dangerous if we got a flat tire or our car broke down.

"We should never have gone off the main road. We are in the middle of fricking Narnia." Amber's voice starts getting that high-pitched whine she gets whenever she works herself into a panic. "We only had to stick to Interstate 5 all the way into Canada, but no, we had to be impulsive. We had to drive completely out of our way to jump onto a raft and risk our lives in a raging river. We should have just stuck with our plan. This is how people get lost, murdered, or die of dehydration…"

Beep, beep, beep. My heart jumps to my throat. An old silver pickup truck pulls up so close it almost takes off my mirror.

"Everything okay? You got car trouble?"

A strong and suntanned arm hangs out the passenger side window. I follow it up to an equally tanned bare chest and face with a smile so big that it makes his eyes squint. A girl with blonde braids and a blue headband, folded and tied around her head like a gangbanger's, sits between him and the driver. The driver's face is in the shadows, but I can see that he is wearing a cowboy hat.

"You need some help?" The girl asks.

"No," Amber says, yelling past me and out the window. "We're fine."

"Where are you headed?" The guy in the passenger seat asks. He has some nice beard stubble and looks like a cross between a mountain man and a firefighter—one of those guys who could shoot you an elk for dinner, then pull you from your burning house when you try to cook it. Oh my God, I might need someone to jumpstart my heart.

I swallow, trying to get the lump out of my throat. "We're going to Lodell to go whitewater rafting."

The guy looks at the sign directly in front of us that reads, *Lodell* in bold white letters, then back at me. "Looks like you're in the right place."

I feel like an idiot.

"That's where we're headed," he says. "Follow us down."

As the truck rumbles past, three guys in the back lower themselves onto piles of orange and yellow life jackets. They hold onto the sides of the bed as it brings up a tail of dirt and turns down into the canyon, dragging a trailer piled high with five blue rubber rafts. An old yellow short bus also bumps past us, filled with sunburned tourists in caps and sunglasses.

I turn toward Amber, then burst into laughter. "Oh my God, they were hot! You in now?"

She does not answer but gives me a nod. I put the car in drive and follow them down into the canyon, hanging far enough back to stay out of their dust cloud. I stop at the entrance to a short cement tunnel beneath some train tracks. It is covered in graffiti. Someone spray-painted a skull with pitchforks instead of crossbones on one side and an owl with giant ringed eyes on the other.

"Ready?" Somehow, this feels like our last chance to turn around.

Amber only shrugs.

I take my foot off the brake and push down on the gas. The engine does that racing thing, but this time, it does not move.

"That doesn't sound right."

I put it in park and then back into drive. When I step on the gas, it races, then catches with a clunk, and we lurch forward into the tunnel.

We roll past more graffiti—not the beautiful graffiti you see on the side of a train or an overpass but artistically challenged graffiti. Sprayed in red, black, blue, or white is *DEATH*. *Jason loves Candie*, and a giant red penis and balls right next to *Becky sucks dick*.

Once through the tunnel, we catch up with the short bus and pass over a creek lined with bright green trees. The road turns left at the base of a giant brownish-red cliff with layers of crumbly dark rock at the top. Everything seems unreal as we cross back and forth over wooden bridges and follow the creek through the canyon.

Just under a gigantic steel railroad bridge, the land flattens out to rock and desert brush. Abandoned bare wood shacks and old rail fences with sagging barbed wire looped between them make the town look like an old pioneer ghost town. A few of the houses seem lived-in, but most have no doors, missing walls, and broken windows.

Amber sits, staring out the window and not saying a word. The only sign of life comes from a one-pump gas station with flapping red, yellow, and blue banners where a man's legs stick out from beneath a car. An old-fashioned sign says, Bud's Garage in large red letters.

"This is Lodell?" Amber asks.

The bus turns left up ahead. "Maybe it gets better."

The road comes to a T at the river. More shacks and a campground with blue, orange, and green tents are to the right. We make a left onto a paved road alongside the river. It curves to the right, and as we round the corner, we come to the town of Lodell.

Cars line the main street, parked in front of mismatched businesses. Most of them have a western look, but some are built with cement blocks or brick with giant store windows.

"It's cute," I say, "for a such a little hick-town."

"It is, but could you imagine living here?"

"Never." We cruise past Lodell Community Church, a small elementary school, and a bunch of shops and restaurants. The silver truck with the hot guys turns at a sign that says Rimrock Outfitters.

"That's where we should book our rafting trip...since they helped us."

"Of course," Amber says like she is in on the conspiracy. "...since they helped us."

The place looks like Valley of the Dogs, with at least a dozen mangy mutts lying around panting under porches or wandering loose in the streets. A brown wiry dog hobbles down the wooden sidewalk and lifts its leg to pee on a light pole. A bunch of dirty-kneed kids run around in groups, chasing each other or playing hide-and-seek behind cars and buildings. They all look like foster kids—the ones without the cool bikes or scooters, the kids who always eat the knockoff brands like *Fruity Os*, *Dorios*, and *Popsi Soda*.

"Guess there aren't any leash laws here," Amber says.

"For the kids?"

"No." She lets out a laugh. "Do you see any hotels?"

I pull over in front of a sign with Carl's Cabins and a giant fish carved into it. A group of tiny buildings that look like they were built with Lincoln Logs are in a U shape around a grassy patch of lawn. "Those are kind of cute."

"Hell no," she says. "The things look like the perfect place to film a slasher movie."

We keep driving, and the road ends at the Whitehorse Inn, a huge yellow two-story hotel with white railings. "I think that's it. We're at the end of town, so it's either Carl's Cabins or the Whitehorse Inn."

"Let's see how much it is," Amber says. "If we blow through all our money, we'll never get to Canada."

The hollow thump of our footsteps on the wooden porch reminds me of the soundtrack whenever two cowboys are about to square off for a shootout. All we need is the chink of spurs. The hotel's front doors stand wide open, with two sets of rocking chairs on either side. It smells of stale cigarette smoke despite the *No Smoking* signs. Three elk heads hang above a rock fireplace, and smaller dead animals stare out from every wall.

I half expect the front desk girl to be in a prairie bonnet—but instead, she has a long face, huge front teeth, and bangs that are two inches too short for her forehead. She looks like a llama. A llama with a massive amount of cleavage springing out the top of her tank top. On her name tag, BECKY is printed in all capital letters. A red and white "Missing" flyer with a girl's picture is trapped beneath the glass on the counter.

"How much are your rooms?" Amber asks.

The missing girl, Shawna Hall, is beautiful with long black hair, big eyes, and a cute smile. Hopefully, she has been found.

"It depends," The girl says in a snotty tone. "Do you have a reservation?"

"No." Amber has that scared guinea pig look she always gets when things are not going the way she expects.

We didn't even think about needing a reservation. The drive back to Maupin isn't too far, but they may not have any rooms either.

The girl shakes her head. "This is a busy weekend. I don't know if we have any rooms. If we do, they range from sixty dollars a night to one hundred and twenty for the bridal suite."

Bridal suite? Who in the hell would get married here? Especially with all the dead animals staring down on everyone.

Becky opens a black binder, licks her pointer finger, and flips through the pages. Don't they have a computer?

"We may have a room, but the housekeeper hasn't turned in her cleaning slips, so I don't know which rooms are available.

Sometimes people don't bother to stop by the desk to let us know they are checking out...or they just stay longer."

Becky slams the binder shut. "I'll be right back. Wait here."

Amber turns toward me and rolls her eyes. We hate girls like that. There is no reason to be rude. Becky locks a drawer with a key attached to her wrist, then drags her llama ass through the lobby as if she has all the time in the world.

"I saw your advertisement," I call to her.

She glances back and gives me a bitchy, tight-lipped glare.

"What advertisement?" Amber asks.

"The one in the tunnel, *Becky sucks dick*."

Amber's eyes pop wide open, and she slaps her hand over her mouth, but the laugh still escapes, causing Becky to look back one more time before turning down a hallway.

"We can do sixty a night, but no more," I say. "We may end up at Carl's Cabins after all."

All the color evaporates from Amber's face.

I gather my hair into my hand and twist it up. "It's like an oven in here. I'm going outside for a minute. If the llama girl ever comes back, and it's reasonable, will you check us in?"

"I guess," Amber says, looking around at all the dead animal heads.

From the front porch, I have a great view of Rimrock Outfitters and the hot guys from the truck. Two of them stand talking to a group of people from the bus while the other four lift rafts down from the pile on the trailer. The girl with the blonde braids pulls life jackets from the back of the truck and drapes them over chairs and a chain-link fence.

The hot guy from the passenger seat grabs the front half of a raft while the driver in the cowboy hat takes hold of the rear. The hot guy is bare-chested and wears nothing but swim trunks, sandals, and a khaki baseball cap.

They disappear behind the building but come right back to get another raft. He freezes and looks straight at me. He smiles, and I could swear that he winks at me—but it is too far away to be sure.

A group of middle-aged women in polo shirts, golf visors, and *skorts* make their way toward the inn, laughing and making excited gestures with their arms, "You should have seen your face!"

"I was shocked. One moment we were approaching the rapids, and the next, I was in the water."

"Let's go see if they caught that on camera."

The women turn toward a tiny brown building with white trim and a *Shooting the Rapids Photography* sign on the front. Thank God! I do not need Amber hearing about anyone falling out of a raft.

Back at the outfitters, a group of six girls in string bikinis, half-up their asses, hang around the outfitters, obviously waiting for the guides to be free. A burning feeling starts in my chest, and I want to scream at them. I don't even know the name of that guide, but I do not want those girls anywhere near him.

"Hey," Amber says, stepping out onto the porch.

"Did she give us a room?" I ask.

"No. She hasn't come back yet."

"Oh my God," I whisper as the guide starts walking toward us. "Dibs on him."

"Hey, ladies," he says. "You get all checked in?"

"No," I try to keep the frustration out of my voice. "The front desk girl seems to have disappeared."

"Yeah, I'm not surprised." He circles around us. "Come on, let me give you a hand."

He taps the bell on the desk six times. Oh my God, he is hot.

"Becky, you have customers out here," he calls out toward the rooms.

Becky emerges from the hallway.

"Hey, Brian." Her voice sounds much different than it did before—in a sickening, syrupy way.

"You got room for these girls?"

"Sure I do. I was just checking to see if Mary cleaned it yet." She slides back behind the counter, pulls out a form, and forces a smile at us. "We got a sixty-dollar room and the bridal suite."

"We'll take the sixty-dollar one," Amber says.

"Please fill this out." She slides the form toward me.

I push it to Amber.

Brian's muscles are so ripped I want to run my hand through his chest hair and down his happy trail.

"If you don't already have a rafting trip booked, come on over to Rimrock, and I'll hook you up. I gotta get back to help."

My throat feels so thick that I can hardly speak. "All right," is all that comes out.

Just before he walks out the door, he turns around. "Hopefully, I'll see you at Buckskin Mary's tonight."

All I can do is stare.

"We'll be there," Amber says, helping me out like a good friend.

He walks out, disappearing into the bright sunlight. When I turn back, I catch Becky glaring at me, but she quickly turns it into a fake smile and hands us the keys to room 114.

CHAPTER FIVE

The hallways are yellow with white trim and old red carpeting. Luckily, our room has some sort of an air conditioner. The brown plastic thing fills one of the two windows with slivers of Styrofoam wedged in the gaps around the sides.

"How do you turn this thing on?" Amber asks, peering around it.

I cannot see any knobs or switches—just solid fake wood and a yellowed grate. "Maybe it flips down."

She pulls at the top, the sides, and the bottom, but nothing moves.

"I'll call the front desk and ask," Amber says, looking around. "Do you see a phone?"

Surprise, surprise, no phone—and no cell service. The room has the smell and atmosphere of a Goodwill store. Two twin beds, covered in thin red-striped bedspreads, are pushed against opposite sides of the room, each with a cheap nightstand next to it. A bulky silver television set takes up the entire surface of a three-drawer dresser.

Finally, the front section of the air conditioner slides to the right, exposing three plastic dials labeled *Cooling*, *JET-AIRE Vent*, and *Thermostat*. When Amber turns the dials to *High Cool* and *Max Vent*, a rush of warm and dusty air blows out.

"Okay," she coughs. "That should do it."

"Where do you think this door goes?" Amber turns the knob and swings the back door open. It leads to a porch with a wooden railing that overlooks a tangle of blackberry bushes and trees between us and the river. The porch runs along the entire river side of the hotel, with chairs outside each door. Every air conditioner along the patio hums, and a mess of towels and swimsuits hang drying on the rail.

Amber stares off through the tangle of brush. A fisherman stands in the river. Not on the bank but in the water with a long fishing pole. He swings it back, making his line fly through the air in giant loops.

"What's wrong?" I lean toward Amber until our shoulders touch.

"I don't know. I have a bad feeling about this."

"You never like change." Every time Amber is sent to a new foster home, she goes through a depression. She will never admit it, but I can tell when it happens.

"Do you think they have a BOLO out on us yet?"

I shrug. "Honestly, I don't think the police even care about two runaway foster girls."

Amber's smile disappears, and I instantly regret saying it.

"I bet the Piersons are really worried."

"Yeah…worried their check will be smaller."

"We can ask if there's a computer somewhere and check Myspace."

Amber gives me a bit of a smile. "Can we report Ed so he won't touch Willow or Susan?"

"I think we should wait until we're in Canada. If we do it from here, they'll know where we are."

"I'll never forgive myself if he does anything to the girls."

"He won't. I'm sure the police have been to the house questioning the kids and the Piersons about your disappearance. He'll wait until he knows the cops won't be back."

Amber nods and leans her head onto my shoulder.

CHAPTER SIX

STILL BARE-CHESTED AND TOTALLY GORGEOUS, BRIAN LEANS UP against the silver truck with a can of beer tipped up to his mouth. The dude in the cowboy hat sits on a cement ledge with the blonde girl sitting between his legs. Some sort of a gray and white spaniel mix dozes in the shade of the building, and two more dogs lay in the shade of the truck. A skinny dude with messy dark-blonde hair and a scraggly beard squats down with a stick, dragging it through the dirt and drawing some sort of an illustration to go with his story.

Feeling like we are intruding, I consider turning around—but it seems as if they were only half-listening to the guy with the stick anyway. The guide on the cement whispers something to the blonde. She turns her head up to him, and they start making out. Brian notices us. He smiles and walks away from the group, leaving the skinny guide still talking with nobody paying any attention.

"How's the room?" he asks.

Good God, I cannot take my eyes from Brian's tanned body and tight abs. Two well defined sex-lines *V* down and disappear into his swim trunks.

"It took a while to figure out the air conditioner, but it's all good," Amber says.

"Cool, cool. You here to book a rafting trip?"

"Yep."

"Come have a beer with us, then I'll set you up."

The scrappy guide stands above his diagram in the dirt with the stick hanging limp in his hand.

"This is Skid," Brian says, "I'm sorry, did you tell me your names?"

"No," I say. "I'm Emmy, and this is Amber."

Shit! We are supposed to be Nicole and Madeline. We suck at being fugitives.

Brian motions to the guide in the cowboy hat and the girl. "This is Jake and his girlfriend, Erin."

Jake looks like a wrestler—thick, with a full-moon face and mutton-chop sideburns. He glances down at our feet. "Those are some bright green kicks you got there."

I'm not sure, but based on Jake's smirk, he just made fun of us.

Erin gives him a look, then stands like she's pissed at him. She towers over Amber and me. I bet she is at least five-foot-nine. There is something about Erin that I like. She looks strong and German—like the ladies in tight bodices at the Oktoberfest. She comes across as someone who does not put up with anyone's crap.

Skid yanks the last two cans of Rainier beer from a six-pack ring and holds one out to Amber. She takes it, gives him a forced smile, then backs a few steps away from him. Not that Amber and I are telepathic or anything, but I can practically hear her mind screaming at me that I better not leave her alone with him. Ever.

Skid offers the other beer to me. I take it and crack it open. "Are you girls alone or here with more people?" he asks.

"Alone," I say, going against every single *Stranger Danger* lecture ever given to me.

"We're on a road trip," Amber starts blabbing her mouth. I try to catch her eye to tell her to stop, but she doesn't look my way. "We were headed to Canada, but we took a detour to come rafting…"

"What's with all the dogs?" I interrupt Amber before she starts giving them her social security number and date of birth.

"What do you mean?" Brian asks, looking down at the two wiry mutts, one gray and one yellow, in the shade of the truck.

"There are stray dogs all over town."

He shrugs. "They aren't strays." His forehead wrinkles like he doesn't understand why I would think that.

Two of the town kids, a shirtless boy in cutoff jeans and a girl in a T-shirt and bathing suit bottoms, run up to Skid.

"Wanna go fishing?" the boy asks. He has one giant adult tooth growing in and a gap where he just lost a baby tooth. He opens his hand, and sitting in his grimy palm is a wad of something that looks like bright-colored and tan dandelion fluff. "I got some of my daddy's flies. He ties them himself."

"Did he give them to you?" Skid asks.

The boy looks down into his hand and does not answer.

"You should never touch a man's flies without his permission. Go put those back, and I'll bring some that you can keep."

The boy smiles in a goofy big tooth grin.

"I'll meet you at the spot in about an hour." Skid takes a long gulp of his beer.

"Will you bring us some rods to use?"

"You bet," Skid says before the two run off.

"Time to finish up." Jake drinks the rest of his beer and crushes the can with his hand. Everyone goes into motion, except for the dogs, who barely twitch their ears while everyone moves around them.

"I'll help in a minute," Brian says. "I'm gonna take these girls to Jan."

We follow Brian toward the guide shop.

"Are the rapids dangerous?" Amber asks.

"Yes. That is why you should always go with a guide and follow all safety instructions. The biggest water we will go through is a class IV. There is a class VI rapid further downstream, but it is unrunnable."

Amber's face is white.

"It's called Mullins Falls, and we will not go near it. Our two-day trips portage around it."

"How high do they go?"

Brian opens the door to the shop and steps aside for us to enter. "How high does what go?"

"The numbers for the rapids?"

"Class VI is as high as they go. They are considered too extreme, even for the most skilled guides."

Amber grabs my hand as we pass by Brian and into the shop. The display racks are filled with T-shirts, caps, water shoes, suntan lotion, water bottles, and water cannons. The T-shirts have sayings on them: *Rimrock Outfitters, I Skipped School to go Rafting, Daddy's Little Rafter,* and *Paddle Faster, I Hear Banjos*.

Amber takes a hanging T-shirt from the rack and holds it against her body. "We should get one that says, *I skipped Canada to go Rafting*."

An older lady with graying hair stands behind a counter and cash register. Behind her are two retro-looking travel posters with people paddling through rapids. One says, *Whitewater Rafting. Lodell, Oregon.* The other says, *If I'm Missing, I Am Probably Whitewater Rafting. Lodell, Oregon.*

"Hey Jan," Brian reaches an arm around her shoulder for a side hug. "Can you get these girls set up to go rafting tomorrow?"

"On your raft?" she asks, raising her eyebrows at Brian.

"That's up to them." Brian turns to us. "I'll see you at the Buckskin tonight."

We book our trip using our fake names since there will be a written record of us being here. Jan tells us that lunch will be provided and gives us a list of things to bring, including hats, sunscreen, and straps for our sunglasses—none of which we have.

Back at the hotel and inside our room, the door to the back patio is cracked open.

"Did we leave the back door open?" Amber asks.

"No. I locked it before we left."

Amber goes to the door and looks out. She stands silent for a moment, then says, "Do you hear that?"

I cross the room and join her at the open door, listening. A soft, haunting coo comes from the side of the hotel.

"What is it?" Amber whispers. "It sounds like a ghost."

"Maybe it's some kind of a flute or a bird." I step out onto the porch. It sounds again. "Or that fisherman."

"He isn't there anymore."

I turn to Amber and put a finger to my lips, trying to listen above the hum of the air conditioners.

I take Amber's hand, and we tip-toe all the way to the end of the patio. Down a path to the river, a thin man with a possum-like face squats on the bank with something in his hand. He slowly turns his head toward us, and when our eyes meet, a chill washes through me.

Amber and I take the three steps from the patio to the dirt and peek around the corner. Just as we do, a bird flaps out of a tree, making my heart leap to my throat. "Holy shit!"

Its wings whistle, beating their way into the sky as a high-pitched and hysterical laugh comes from the man on the bank.

"What's that?" At first glance, it looks like a dead tree filled with lifeless birds hanging by their necks. Still hand-in-hand, we stare at the leafless tree—not filled with birds, but with shoes. Dozens and dozens of sun-bleached Nike, Converse, Adidas, Puma, and Vans dangle by their laces—twisting in the breeze.

CHAPTER SEVEN

HIM

SHE IS HERE. AMBER WITH AMBER-COLORED HAIR.

It is parted to the side, sweeping over one eye and down, shimmering in waves across her shoulders. I want to wrap my fingers in the strands and feel their silkiness—winding tighter and tighter, turning the tips of my fingers red.

My chest aches as I tap out a smoke from the pack of Camels, light it, and set it in the ashtray to burn itself out like a stick of incense. It fills me with the scent of tying, fishing, and riding in the old Torino with the windows down and the baseball game on the radio.

I set my tackle box on my desk and lift the lid. The trays rise up, filled with hooks, spools of thread, yarn, wire, beads, head cement, and the remaining strands of Shawna's jet-black hair. I take out a size fourteen dry fly hook and clamp it in my vice.

My adrenaline spiked the moment I saw the color of Amber's hair. She will be mine forever, just like Shawna. I will breathe in her last breath and hold it within me until her lungs fill with my water, binding us together forever.

I slip the end of a thread through my bobbin and wrap the hook's shank, creating a base for the dry fly wings.

Amber is staying in the same hotel room as Shawna, maybe even sleeping in the same bed.

I choose the perfect brown grizzly hackle feathers, strip off the extra fibers, and bind them to my hook.

Shawna helped me discover how to satisfy the raging and the thunder. Now, it is for Amber to keep down the flow.

I lift the hackle feathers, wrap the base, so they stand up from the shank like wings, and separate them with a figure eight. I wrap backward toward the curve and tie on some brown and grizzly hackle fibers for the tail.

Amber will be at the Buckskin tonight—a pure soul in the surge of teasing, slutty, drunk-ass girls. I wrap the bobbin thread with gray dubbing and wind it around the shank, creating a thick thorax behind the wings.

The lock of Shawna's hair still has the scent of her shampoo and dried river moss. I slip a single long and silky strand from the copper wrap. It tickles my lips as I run it through them and picture her tits rising up from the water. I bind her hair down, then wind it all the way from the tail, through the wings, and to the hook eye with evenly spaced wraps.

I finish my fly with a brown grizzly hackle feather and a drop of head cement behind the eye. Trout will always take an Adam's dry fly, for it mimics the whirring wings and frenzied legs of an insect struggling to shed its nymph shuck.

I lay out my hair color charts and run my hand over the photos of the shiny ash brown, ginger, burgundy, tan, auburn, copper, bronze, golden blonde, honey blonde, ginger, and platinum strands. My fingertips run over the indentation of the X over the jet-black color sample.

Soon, I will have Amber's amber hair for my flies. She will be mine. I surge. I rage. I tremble, and I pulse. I give or take what I want, for I am the river. It is the fluid, and I am the flesh.

CHAPTER EIGHT

L̲ive music, a jumble of voices, and the sound of clinking bottles come from behind the bouncer at Buckskin Mary's. He holds our fake IDs in his hand like two playing cards. He is humongous with arms as big as my thighs and a full sleeve tattoo of raging water, and a skull. He wears a plain black shirt with a backward baseball cap and has a puffy red chin beard.

He looks at us with eyes so light blue, they seem almost white, then back at the photos. I stand there, trying to look confident. He could confiscate our IDs, call the police, or toss our butts out the door. I'm afraid to look at the expression on Amber's face.

The bouncer does not look convinced, but he lets us in, giving us a red stamp in the shape of a star on the back of our hands. We squeeze through the crowd. People cram around the bar while the bartenders move like crazy, filling glasses and clinking beer bottles down on the counter. Where in the hell did all these people come from?"

On the dance floor, the three middle-aged ladies, still in their golf visors, dance together to *I Love Rock and Roll*. Next to them, a guy in a leprechaun suit sway-dances with his beer, losing his rhythm every time he tips it to his lips. A tall man in a red soccer jersey and Mardi Gras beads jumps straight up and down, popping above the crowd like a whack-a-mole carnival game. In a red vinyl booth along the wall, two girls push their boobs up with their hands and catch ice cubes being thrown at their cleavage by a guy at the table next to them. I do not see Brian anywhere.

Amber puts her mouth so close to my ear that I can feel the warmth of her breath. "My shoes are sticking to the floor."

"Mine too. This is awesome. Let's get a drink."

The bartenders, an older woman with gray hair and an exceptionally large man with a thick mat of hair that may or may not be a wig, work like a Nascar pit crew—scooping ice, pouring booze, clinking glasses and bottles on the bar, and making change. I wave, trying to get the attention of one of the bartenders, but neither of them even look my way. A beer-bellied man, who looks a bit too old for the crowd, stands at the bar next to us.

"Is this the line?"

"I hope so," he says.

The lady bartender clunks three beers on the bar, then turns and looks into the eyes of the man. Just as he begins to tell her what he wants, a girl squeezes in front of him. She shouts an order for six Purple Hooter shots.

"I was next," the man says.

"That's okay." She waves an unsteady hand. "You can be after me."

The girl, young enough to be the man's daughter, smiles up at him—unsuccessfully.

"You need to wait your turn," he says.

A guy comes up next to the girl and grabs one of her half-exposed butt cheeks. She turns her head, and they French kiss so close to me that I can see their tongues.

The bartender returns and lines the bar with six shot glasses.

She tips a bottle of vodka to fill each shot glass halfway, then pours in lime juice and some raspberry liqueur. The girl waves a fan of fives and ones at the bartender, who takes them and slides the line of shots toward her. She cups three of them into her hands, passes them off to her boyfriend, and scoops up the last three. The liquid slips over the lip of the shot glasses and drips across her fingers.

Once the man next to me gets his Coors, I order two Bud Lights as the band starts playing *Achy Breaky Heart.* I glance around but do not see Brian or any of his friends.

"Where should we go?" Amber asks.

Every seat is taken. "Let's go stand by the dance floor."

I stop up my beer bottle with my thumb as we squeeze and bump our way through the crowd. A middle-aged woman dances by herself around the perimeter of the dance floor, brushing against men on the sidelines. One after the other, they turn their backs to her, walk away, or step aside. A couple dances, attached at the pelvis, writhing and making out in the middle of the floor.

As the lead singer starts singing, *She's a brick house,* a tiny girl with short dark hair and wearing a newsy cap, baggie pants, and a wife-beater shirt zeroes in on Amber. That's when I notice two girls pulling Brian onto the dance floor. Seriously? They aren't even that cute. Maybe that's why they are offering a twofer.

Oh God, Brian is hot but not necessarily the best dancer. He moves stiff and out of sync with the two girls running their hands all over him—one in the front and one in the back. His awkwardness makes me like him even more.

The girl in the newsy cap struts up to Amber, half dancing, half walking. "Hey girl, wanna dance?"

Amber stands stunned for a second, then says, "Uhhhh, no thanks."

"It's all good." The girl winks at Amber, then reaches out and touches her hair. "Is this your natural color?"

I pull Amber away from her and out onto the dance floor, where we become part of the mass of people, some moving to the music, others just moving. Amber leans in, singing along. *She's mighty-mighty.* Her eyes sparkle, and her mouth sweeps up into a huge smile. I join her, singing, laughing, and shaking our shoulders together—acting out the lyrics like we have our shit together—which we do not.

When the song ends and the band starts playing, *Come Away With Me,* I feel someone touch my back. Before I have a chance to turn around, a deep and warm voice whispers into my ear, "So, you made it."

I turn around. Brian. I cannot speak.

"How about a dance?" He holds his hand out, and I take it.

I swing my beer toward Amber. For one moment, as Amber takes my bottle and Brian pulls me toward the dance floor, I am connected to both of them. Until I let go and leave Amber standing there with my beer. Once we make it to the very center of the floor, Brian slides his arm around my back and pulls me to him. His body feels solid, and he smells like soap and the earthy smell of the desert. I relax and fall into his rhythm. His awkwardness on the dance floor evaporates—he was meant to be a slow dancer.

"So," he whispers in my ear, "tell me about yourself."

"What do you want to know?"

"Everything."

Something in his voice makes me want to forget everything—to just be here, right now, on the dance floor with him. I don't want to think about leaving for Canada in two days. Right now, right here, I am dancing with Brian, and I do not want to think of anything else.

"Okay," he says, "everything's a lot. How about telling me how you ended up in Lodell?"

"We found your brochures at a youth hostel in Portland, and we were looking for adventure—the rest is history."

His beard stubble rubs against my face.

"What about you? How did you end up in Lodell?"

"Nothing exciting. I was born here."

The song ends, but I do not want to stop dancing with him. He releases the pressure on my back as the band begins playing *Sweet Home Alabama*.

"We have a booth over there," he says, standing still in the crowd of jumping, swaying, gyrating people. "You and Amber want to sit with us?"

"Sure."

Amber stands by herself, holding two bottles of Bud Light and trying not to look at the girl in the newsy cap who keeps inching closer and closer to her. I wave Amber over.

The same guides we met earlier, Jake, Erin, and Skid, sit in one of the red booths with ten empty beer bottles for a centerpiece. "You guys remember Emmy and Amber?"

Skid scoots around the u-shaped seat, making room for us. Amber gives me a pleading look before sitting down. Taking one for the team, she slides toward Skid and makes room for Brian and me. Hopefully, more people will join us. When the band starts singing *Mustang Sally*, Erin jumps up and pulls Jake toward the dance floor.

Besides the unfortunate name, Skid has the look of one of the stray dogs—definitely not Amber's type. She goes more for the preppy, football player, or future salesman type. Poor Skid does not have a chance. I figure he knows it, and that is why he orders rounds of whiskey shots for the table. The first one goes down like little sips of lighter fluid. Brian and Skid laugh at us, explaining that we are not supposed to sip a shot.

"Hold your breath and take it all at once." Brian demonstrates the technique. He dumps it into his mouth, swallows, and exhales.

We try it again, and I feel like throwing up.

"Here, chase it with this." Brian pushes my beer toward me.

By the time Amber and I take the second shot, everything seems easier, funnier, and less focused.

"I think it's time to get you girls back to your room," Brian says. "You don't want to be feeling like shit on the river tomorrow."

He scoots out of the booth and holds his hand out to me.

I would love Brian to walk us back, but I'm sure it is a two-for-one deal, and Amber will kill me if I let Skid into our room. "We're okay. We can make it by ourselves."

"I'm not letting you walk back alone."

"We're fine." I scoot out and stand. The room sways, but Brian steadies me.

"You sure?" Brian asks.

"Oh, yes." I take hold of Amber's arm. "We're troopers."

We sway through the crowd and stumble out, past the bouncer.

"You ladies shouldn't be out alone in the dark." He comes toward us. "I'll walk you back."

"We're good," I say.

"He's scary," Amber whispers as we step out onto the porch and down the wooden steps. "He has zombie-eyes."

A train whistle blows in the distance, and groups of people stand outside the tavern smoking cigarettes.

"You okay?" I ask.

"Yes. Thanks for...for...," Amber giggles, "...for not letting Skid walk me home. Who would name their kid Skid? Hey, that rhymes."

We step away from the bar and into the darkness. The hotel lights glow in front of us, but we cannot see the road beneath our feet.

"Look at the stars," I say.

As we stop and gaze up, Amber loses her balance. She grabs

hold of me, and we both crumple to the ground, laughing. The sound of the train chugging grows louder. Its wheels screech, and the whistle blows again.

"Star light, star bright, first star I…" The entire sky is filled with stars but no moon. "Which one did I see first?"

Amber giggles. "Maybe you can make a million wishes."

"Do you hear that?"

"The train?"

"No. Sshhh." I put my finger to Amber's mouth and whisper, "footsteps."

We sit silently on the edge of the pavement and dirt but only hear the distant sounds of the train and the music from the bar. I start to push myself up when I hear a slight scuffing sound. Amber hears it, too, because she freezes. A growling noise comes from behind a dumpster.

"The dogs," I whisper. "We forgot about the dogs."

The town's stray dogs trot lazily down the street or pant beneath trees in the daytime, but now it is night. We are on their turf. Another growl comes, deeper than the first.

"Should we run?" Amber whispers.

"What if they chase us?"

Amber grabs hold of my arm, and we cling together. The scuffing comes from all around us. All I can think about is that scene in Wild Mountain when the wolves attack a lost man, tearing him to shreds. They are so close, I hear them sniffing.

"Stay still," I whisper. Something wet touches my face, and a loud snorting sound blows in my ear. The dogs surround us, prodding and poking with their noses.

"Put your head down," I say to Amber. "Protect your face."

"Should we play dead?" Amber asks.

"That's for bears."

"Shoo," a deep voice yells—half-laughing from above us. "You girls need help?"

"Depends," Amber says. "Are you cute?"

I recognize Brian's laugh. "Not really, but we can make sure the dogs don't bother you."

Brian and Skid help us to our feet.

"Were you following us?" I ask.

"Of course. I'm not about to let you walk back by yourselves."

The rest of the way to the hotel, I can hear Amber and Skid's feet shuffling behind us—and I can feel her eyes boring into my back, cursing me for Brian's choice of friend. Once through the lobby and to our door, I feel around in my pocket for my hotel key and slide it into the lock. The door opens, and Amber pushes past me, leaving Skid alone behind us.

"Thanks," I say to Brian, turning toward him and pausing long enough for him to kiss me.

"No problem. Make sure you set your alarm. You need to be at the outfitters by ten o'clock." He winks and turns to leave—without a kiss.

CHAPTER NINE

"Emmy." A hand touches my shoulder.

"Emmy," the whisper comes again.

Where am I? Oh yeah, the hotel. It is still dark, and Amber kneels at the side of my bed. "What's wrong?"

"Did you hear that?"

I listen but cannot hear anything but the loud hum of the air conditioner. "No."

"Someone was at the patio door, putting a key into our lock."

"Are you sure?"

"Yes."

"Someone probably got the wrong room."

"Can I sleep by you?"

I scoot over. It is not the first time we have shared a twin bed. In third grade, we were in the same foster home and frequently crawled in with one another because of nightmares or worry.

"You okay?" I ask. The bed sags and creaks as Amber climbs on. Since we have grown, we put our heads at the opposite ends of the mattress in order to fit.

"This place creeps me out."

Amber's pillow falls across my feet, so I move them closer to the wall.

"You know in movies when the bad guy is right around the corner, and you want to warn the character?"

She does not give me time to answer.

"That is how I feel...only, it's us." Amber slides her feet under the covers, all the way up to my shoulder.

"Do you want to leave?" I adjust my pillow.

"Now? In the middle of the night?"

"Or in the morning," I say.

"Maybe."

Amber doesn't say anything more. I stare up at the ceiling, listening to the squeak of footsteps from the room above and the constant hum of the air conditioner. The bed creaks as Amber shifts onto her side, and together, we drift back off to sleep.

CHAPTER TEN

We wake to my phone alarm blaring Latin music from somewhere across the room.

"Oh my God," Amber says.

I cover my head with the pillow. "Hit the snooze."

The bed shifts, Amber's footsteps pad across the wooden floor, and the alarm goes silent. I roll over and doze. The toilet flushes.

"It's time to get up." Amber shakes my shoulder.

My mouth feels like sandpaper. "Do we have any water?"

When she returns with a cup of water, I push myself up and sit on the edge of the bed. "Why can't we sleep in?"

"We need to be there at ten."

"I thought you wanted to leave."

"That was last night. We're here, so we might as well…"

"Your bad feeling is gone?" I head toward the bathroom.

"No, but I don't want to be the one who ruins our fun."

I wash my face and pull on a pair of shorts and a tank top over my bathing suit. When I come out, Amber is tying the laces of her Converse.

Outside, the street is crowded with people headed to the

different rafting companies. Several stray dogs already lay curled in pools of shade, and the kids are already out and playing. Everyone walks around in combinations of bathing suits, shorts, and tank tops. Most wear baseball caps or visors and carry water bottles.

A Harley, with some forty-year-old man dressed in steampunk, comes rumbling up the street. He stops in front of Carl's Cabins, and a horde of street children run over to him. Two of the red-headed ones climb onto the bike with him.

Outside Rimrock Outfitters, a group of girls in string bikinis wander around outside the guide shop, obviously trying to get as much attention as they can. Two parents sit in white plastic chairs outside a shack in the back of the yard while their boys play in a hammock strung between two trees. And, what seems like a church group of middle school boys and their youth pastor stand in the center. I look around for Brian but don't see him.

"I hope we're not put in the same raft with the bikini girls," I say. "That would be annoying."

Jan trudges out of the guide shop with a clipboard. "Everyone over here, please." She waves her arm in the air.

The customers, all slathered in sunscreen, cluster around her. "Y'all need to head over to the boat launch just out front. You'll see our rafts to the left. The guides have your names, and they will find you."

The launch lay just outside the outfitters and directly across from Buckskin Mary's. Vans and trucks from other outfitters back trailers toward the river with rafts piled four and five high. Barrels of paddles and piles of life jackets fill the truck beds.

Brian raises his hand up when he sees us, waving us over to him. He is wearing camouflage swim trunks, water sandals, a khaki baseball cap, and sunglasses. Unfortunately, he has a life jacket over his bare chest.

Two guys and a girl, all in their early twenties, also move

toward Brian. The tall guy, with a look of a computer programmer, is obviously the girl's boyfriend by the way he stands protectively close to her and eye-balls Brian. Brian introduces himself and points to each of his passengers to make sure he has their names down. He points at the couple, "Ian and Katie?"

They nod their heads.

He moves his finger over to their friend, "and Mason."

Brian lightly taps his fingers on my and Amber's heads, almost as if he were playing duck-duck-goose. "Emmy and Amber..." His hand freezes, hovering inches from my head, and his smile disappears. "Or is it Nicole and Madeline?"

I look over at Amber, remembering that we registered for the trip under our fake names. She shrugs, so I say, "Emmy and Amber."

"Emmy, as in M and Emmy?" Mason says. "Would you melt in my mouth and not in my hands?"

I roll my eyes and ignore him. It's not like I have not heard that a hundred times before from all the jerks in high school.

A little barefoot boy with a shaved head helps Brian pass out the orange life jackets. He looks about eight years old, and Brian introduces him as Dustin. Hopefully, he is not Brian's son. He could be his brother.

Amber and I buckle our life jackets and pull the straps to tighten them. Mason cannot buckle it over his stomach, so Brian pulls at the straps to loosen them. Mason forces the clasp together on the highest strap, but there is no way he will ever get the other ones hooked over his belly.

"Looks like you'll need the big-man life jacket." Brian steps over to the truck bed, digs through the pile of life jackets, and tosses a large blue one in Mason's direction.

Brian steps up behind me, sticks his thumbs under the shoulder portion, and lifts up. "You need to be tightened." He grabs the loose ends of the straps and cinches them, standing a few inches closer to me than he needs...and he keeps his hands on me a few seconds longer as he checks the shoulders of my life jacket. My tummy flutters like it is filled with butterflies, beating their wings and rising up into my throat.

I stand there, possessed and breathless. Good God. Brian checks Amber's and moves on to Ian.

"Emmy," Amber says, putting her hand on my arm. "You okay?"

I lean over toward Amber and whisper as Brian checks Mason. "Did you feel that?"

"What?"

"When Brian touched you, did you feel anything?"

"I felt my life jacket tighten."

I have had cute boys touch me…many times, but it always felt forced and mechanical. Nothing like Brian's touch. Nothing that caused shivers to wash over my entire body, especially between my legs. Thankfully, he adjusted mine first, giving me a moment to calm myself. Like my school counselor taught me, I take deep breaths and try to focus on the moment.

Brian's voice breaks through my breathing. "All right then. Everyone grab a paddle."

We all move toward a plastic barrel filled with blue and yellow paddles. As Ian grabs one out of the barrel, Brian asks, "You left-handed?"

Ian shakes his head.

"That's a left-handed paddle."

Ian starts to put it back but pauses with the paddle hanging over the barrel. He looks at it, and with a big smile, realizes it was a joke.

"Guide jokes are the equivalent of dad jokes," Brian says, "You've been warned. Now, everyone grab a paddle and follow me."

Amber lifts two from the barrel, looking a bit pale.

Our group follows Brian, with Dustin right at his side, to one of the blue rubber rafts.

"First things first," he says, opening a small ice chest strapped inside. "You can put your drinks in here. I have some water and soda, so if you want any, help yourself."

Ian pulls an Arizona Iced Tea and a bottle of cranberry juice from a plastic sack and drops them in. Mason pulls two Rockstars from either pocket of his swim trunks and tosses them onto the ice. Amber and I have nothing.

All the bikini girls group around Jake's raft. One of the girls runs her hand across Jake's bicep, "Ummm, look at these arms." She's wearing a tiny impractical brown bikini tied in two little bows at her hips.

Skid has the group of six boys and their youth pastor, and Erin has the family with two boys.

Brian pushes the raft farther into the river but still onshore. "Okay, everyone likes a different experience, so please choose your adventure! The front of the boat is the splashiest, and the back is the bounciest. Those blown-up things that look like seats are called thwarts. They are used to keep the raft from folding in half. They are not meant for you to sit on. You are supposed to sit on the big blue tubing on each side.

"Will we fall out?" Amber asks.

"You can slip your foot in the corner of the thwart for extra support and hold on to the safety straps here." Brian holds up a blue loop cinched around the inflatable seat.

"When we are going through the rapids, you can also hold onto the chicken line." Brian slips his hand under a rope looped around the outside of the raft through some black plastic rings.

Amber's eyes are wide, and she puts her fingertips to her temples.

"If you fall out and find yourself under the boat, we call this wearing the big blue sombrero. Use your hands to walk yourself out from beneath it. Pick a direction and stay in that direction."

The girls in Jake's raft screech and giggle at something he said.

"The paddle commands are simple," Brian continues. "I'll say 'right side forward,' 'right side back,' 'left side forward,' 'left side back,' or 'all forward.' If I say 'three forward,' paddle three times forward. 'Stop' means to not paddle at all, and 'all back' means to paddle backward."

"Hey Brian," one of the bikini girls calls over, "I had fun last night."

She has perfectly curled shoulder-length brown hair and a red bikini that isn't much more than three triangles and a bit of string.

Brian gives her a wave then turns back to our group. "Rafting is safe as long as you respect the river's power and avoid making any major mistakes."

Brian must have gone back to Buckskin Mary's after walking us to our hotel room. Why am I so jealous? It feels like I swallowed a rock. Brian doesn't have any commitment to me. He didn't even kiss me goodnight when he had the chance…and we are leaving in the morning anyway.

"I need you all to pay close attention," Brian says.

I feel my cheeks flush red as if his comment was meant for me.

"This is my safety talk. It could save your life. Number one, never tie or secure yourself to the raft in any way. If the raft flips, you need to get free where you can float to the surface and breathe."

Amber grabs my hand and squeezes it tight.

"You must also keep your footwear on and tightly tied or strapped all day. Foot injuries are the most common injury on rafting trips."

I look down at our matching pairs of green Converse, tightly laced and already rimmed with dirt.

"Always wear your life jackets and do not loosen them. If you think your jacket is too tight and you cannot breathe, then it fits properly. If you cannot breathe, then you cannot drown."

Amber's grip on my hand tightens until I start to lose feeling in my fingers as Brian goes on with what to do in emergencies, from collisions with rocks, a flipped raft, a person overboard, self-rescue, to various river hazards,

"It will be okay," I say to her. "Hundreds, maybe even thousands of people do this every year."

"We're armed," Brian says. "See those water cannons there next to the seats? Once we're on the river, it's an all-out war with other rafts. Please do not aim for anyone's face. Shoot above their heads and let the water rain down."

I know exactly who I will shoot, making her curled hair stick flat to her head.

"What if I don't want to get wet?" Katie asks.

"You're going to get wet. There's no way around it—whether it's from the rapids or a water fight, you'll be soaking wet."

Katie glares at Ian, but he tries to smile it off.

"Please dip your feet in the water to wash off the sand before putting them into the raft."

Ian and Mason sit on opposite sides in the front, with Katie behind Ian.

"Emmy and Amber can be back here by me," Brian says with a wink. We climb in and sit on the tubing, which is firmer and thicker than I imagined. I expected it to feel like one of those rubbery red school balls the boys always hurled at our heads whenever we played dodge ball.

Brian pushes the raft into the water and jumps in. Once we are afloat, Dustin gives us the last little shove to deeper water.

"Thanks, Dude," Brian says before turning to us. "Okay, all forward. Good. Left side paddle toward the eddy."

"Is he your brother?" I ask.

"Nope. Just one of the town kids. He likes to hang around and help us."

The raft glides into a large pool of calm water right beside the main current that rushes past. It looks ready to grab hold of our raft and catapult us downriver.

Jake's raft launches with the girls screaming and their paddles in the air. He calls out paddle commands, but they obviously didn't listen to his directions. "Paddle, paddle, paddle," he calls.

They finally dip their paddles in and lamely steer the raft toward the eddy, with Jake standing in the back, doing most of the work.

"What are we waiting for?" Ian asks.

I had that same question, hoping we could get going and leave Jake's raft behind.

"We're waiting for Erin and Skid, then we'll head out," Brian says. "We go down together as a pod."

"Why's that?" I ask.

"It's safer. We'll go through the rapids one at a time and pull to the side so we can help catch swimmers."

"Swimmers?" Amber asks, gripping her paddle with one hand and the chicken line with the other.

"Yeah, anyone who falls out is a swimmer." Brian reaches down beside his leg and pulls up an orange canvas bag. "This is the throw bag. If anyone goes in, I'll throw it. Don't grab the bag. Grab the rope. If you grab the bag, there is seventy feet of rope in there, and you will go all seventy feet before we can pull you in. If any of you fall out in a rapid, lean back in your life jacket and go down feet first so you can use your legs like shock absorbers to push yourself off of rocks. Just relax and go with the flow of the river. The water naturally takes the easiest route, so don't try to swim against it."

A blast of water shoots across the eddy and douses Katie. A blonde girl in Jake's raft screeches and holds her water cannon up in triumph. Katie's face pinches, and she gives Ian the dirtiest look I have ever seen.

"Throw me a gun," I say.

Mason tosses one back and keeps one for himself. I hold my tip into the water, pull the plunger back, then take aim right at the brunette in the red bikini. My aim is perfect, and I blast her right in the face. It plasters her hair to her head and makes her look like a ferret in a bikini. Mason gets revenge on the blonde, and as it hits her, he lets out a war-whoop. Ian reaches for the third gun, but Katie snaps a few words at him, and he withdraws.

"Pass it back," Amber says.

Mason hands the third gun to Amber, and we all gang up on the screeching girls. When Skid's raft drifts in, we turn the guns on them, immediately soaking every kid. Unfortunately, they are unarmed and can only splash back with their paddles. When Erin's raft finally joins us, nobody fires—it doesn't feel right to shoot at a family with two kids.

As soon as Erin's raft enters the eddy, all four guides call out their paddle commands, and we head for the swift-moving water.

CHAPTER ELEVEN

As the raft enters the current, Brian stops the paddle commands. Long grasses, gray rocks, and lush green trees line the river that cuts a gash through the dry brown desert. Across the river, a herd of white, brown, black, and painted horses graze on a small grass field between the river and the steep slopes of a bluff. Three of them drink at the water's edge. A brown horse with a black mane stands chest-deep in the river. As we drift by, several horses lift their heads and watch.

I don't have many memories of my mom, but one time we were at a store for a carton of Marlboros, and I wanted a Barbie doll. She said, *If wishes were horses, then beggars would ride.* Which I realized meant that I wasn't getting the doll.

"Are they wild?" Ian asks.

"Yep. That entire side of the river is the Confederated Tribes of Warm Springs," Brian says. "We call it the Rez."

"They're beautiful." Katie rests her paddle across her lap.

A train whistle blows, and the rhythmic power of steel wheels thundering across the tracks rumbles deep inside my chest. Two orange locomotives with BNSF in large black letters pull a long chain of graffitied boxcars and black tankers between the base of the cliff and the river. On the other side, the horses raise their heads. Some shake their manes or swish their tails as the rumble and screech of steel echoes through the canyon.

Brian guides the raft with his oar as we drift alongside the moving train. Two fishermen stand thigh-deep in the river, casting their lines. Amber raises a hand to them, and they wave back. The barren hills and railroad make me miss my fifth-grade foster dad, Rod. He would love this place. I should contact him one day to see how they are doing. An old tumbledown shack sits on the hill just past the fisherman.

"That's cool," I say. "Do you think pioneers lived there? I'd love to explore that."

"You need to be careful going into old buildings," Brian says. "Last year, a cougar poked its head out the door and watched us float past."

This place is so remote. I could not imagine living here back in the pioneer days, especially as a woman with children.

"Would any of you like to hear a bit of history? If so, I have a few local stories to share. If not, I'll spare you."

"I'd like to hear," Ian says.

The rest of us nod.

"Further down, you'll notice the train will be on the other side of the river," Brian motions downriver with his chin, "but there's a railroad grade on both sides. Back in the early 1900s, when they were laying the tracks, two companies fought to get from the Columbia River to the city of Bend first. The winner would be able to tie up the shipping contracts and operate the railroad."

Brian opens the cooler and grabs a bottle of water. "Anyone want a drink? It's easy to get dehydrated on the river."

"I'll have one of my Rockstars," Mason says.

I pull a water bottle from the ice, open it, and hold it out to Amber. We can share one.

Brian continues. "The railroad crews worked simultaneously on either side of the river. They would sneak into the other camp at night, blow up their black powder stores, dump boulders down on them, and steal their supplies."

"There's another story about how, after a powder blast, one side found a den of hibernating rattlesnakes all balled together." Brian takes a gulp of water. "They put them in burlap sacks, rowed across the river, and put them near the sleeping men's wood stoves, hoping the heat would make the snakes come out of hibernation."

"There are rattlesnakes here?" Amber asks.

"Yes," Brian answers. "Every now and then, when we beach, a baby rattler will cool itself in one of the self-bailing holes of the rafts—then when we shove off, they crawl into the raft and up your legs."

Amber yanks her feet up from the bottom of the raft, tips backward into the river, and grabs the chicken line just as she slips off. Brian grabs the shoulders of her jacket, leans back, and slides Amber back into the raft.

"I'll make sure we're clear of snakes if you're that worried about it," Brian says.

"You okay?" I ask.

Amber nods, but her pale face says differently. Thanks to her grabbing the chicken line, she never went completely under the water—just the ends of her hair got wet. She sits back on the edge of the tube with goosebumps covering her arms and legs—even though it is at least eighty-five degrees out already. I shouldn't have made Amber come rafting.

"If I go in, there's no way you'll be able to pull me back in like that," Mason says, pulling his overly tight life jacket down to cover all of his belly.

"I've gotten bigger boys than you back in," Brian says.

Brian takes hold of his paddle again, sinks it into the water behind the raft, and steers it back to the center of the river. It's as if Brian is physically a part of the landscape. His hair and skin are as brownish-red as the steep canyon walls, and his eyes are the same deep greenish-blue and white as the churning river.

"We'll be coming up to our first rapids soon," Brian says. "It's only a class II and should be no problem at all."

Amber adjusts her grip on the chicken line. Up ahead, the river churns, causing white-tipped waves. I wedge the toe of my shoe under the thwart and hope I won't have to grab hold of the chicken line or the safety strap. Two rafts ahead of us bob and bounce over the rapids. Behind us, the girls in Jake's raft cheer at the sight of the whitewater, wolf-calling and holding up their paddles.

Our raft rises and falls, rocking side to side over the rapids. Water splashes over the tube, soaking my shorts. Amber clings to the chicken line but looks like she is having fun. Toward the end of the rapids, the river narrows, causing the waves to reach higher. The front of the raft pops up, then down. Katie holds tight to the blue safety strap as the front end rides high on a wave then plunges down. A cascade of water rushes in over the bow.

Katie must have breathed in just as it washed over her because she chokes and gags, glaring at Ian. I do not understand why she is so upset about getting wet—what did she expect?

Jake's raft slides up behind us.

"Whoo, hoo," the girl in the red bikini yells. "Hey Brian, you're sure looking hot. Save a dance for me tonight."

Then, one of the girls sticks the tip of her water cannon in the river and pulls back the plunger. She shoots a stream of water directly at Katie again.

"Ahhhh." Katie clenches her fists and shakes them at Ian. "Make them stop."

"You can't get any wetter than you already are," Mason says.

"I don't," Katie says, slowly pronouncing every word through her tight lips, "like getting hit with water."

Brian nods at Jake and then downriver. I assume he is telling Jake to go on ahead of us.

"All forward," Jake calls to the girls in his raft. One by one, they put their drinks between their thighs, dip their paddles into the water, and float away.

A group of deer stand in the grass across the river heads up and staring at us like they are frozen in a game of Simon Says.

"This is a great place to swim. You can just float alongside the raft or hold onto the chicken line if you want," Brian says. "And Mason, I can show you how to get back into the raft."

Ian stands up and flings himself off the side of the raft—probably glad to have a bit of freedom from Katie. Mason leans back and slides into the water with his feet up in the air. I want to give it a try, plus I need to take a pee. I slide off the raft on my belly and lower myself into the river by the chicken line. The cold water makes it difficult to pee, so I float next to the raft, waiting.

Mason and Ian splash around in their life jackets and float belly-up with their arms outstretched. Katie watches, her hair finally drying in strips that make her look like a dog with matted fur. I pull on the chicken line and try to swing my leg over the tube but just slide back into the water. Then, I try going down and kicking my legs to propel myself up and onto my belly, but I slip back in.

"Need help?" Brian asks.

I grasp his outstretched hand, and he pulls as I kick my feet in the water. Brian yanks me in like I am no more than a rag doll.

A hand comes over the edge of the tubing, and Ian tries to pull himself up. "Holy shit, this is tougher than it looks," he says as he slides back into the water.

"Yeah, there's not much leverage, and the tube is too thick to get your arm around," Brian says. "Here, let me give you a hand."

He reaches a muscled arm to Ian. It flexes into tight knots as he pulls. Ian gets a leg up and flops into the raft.

"Ahoy," Skid calls from his raft filled with boys as it floats up behind us.

Mason's hands palm the tube and squeegee down it, back into the water. "I don't think I can get in. Could you beach the boat?"

"Naw, I got you." Brian goes to the side where Mason's head bobs above the water and takes hold of both shoulders of his life jacket. "Okay, just relax. I'm going to dunk you under, then as your life jacket pushes you back up, I'll yank you into the raft."

Brian shoves him down, then leans back. Like a giant slug, Mason slips over the tube and out of his swim trunks. The force of his weight drops Brian to the bottom of the raft with Mason, butt naked, right on top of him.

After one moment of shocked silence, everyone breaks out in hysterical laughter as Brian wiggles under Mason, trying to scoot himself out.

"Damn," is all that Brian says from beneath Mason's naked bulk.

Mason pushes himself up, letting Brian wiggle out. Brian goes to his spot at the back of the raft with his mouth tight and jaw clenched, looking like he is trying to control his laughter.

When Mason raises himself up into a kneel, he cups his hands over his junk. What is he going to do for the rest of the trip?

"Dude!" Ian says between laughs. "Does anyone have a towel or anything?"

"Ahoy," Skid calls out. The boys paddle toward us. One boy stands in the bow with his paddle extended and Mason's swim trunks dangling from the end.

"Here are some trunks for your booty," the boy calls as amused and sarcastic as only a middle-school boy can be.

Skid's raft bumps up against ours, and the paddle with the

shorts appears between Amber and Katie's heads, but neither girl touches them.

"Holy shit, they're not going to bite you," Mason says. Still cupping his junk with one hand, he reaches across the raft and snatches his shorts.

CHAPTER TWELVE

BRIAN STEERS THE RAFT TO THE RIGHT BANK OF THE RIVER. A dark cliff rises up behind the railroad tracks—all cracked and jagged as if it can crumble into a million pieces at any moment.

Jake's raft already rests alone on the rocks, piled with discarded life jackets, paddles, and empty bottles. As we slide up beside it, the last girl's bare legs and blonde hair disappear into the bushes. High pitched voices and giggles echo in the remote quiet. Jake and the girls appear again, scrambling up the grade and onto the railroad tracks.

"Just around the corner, we can scout Lava Canyon Rapids," Brian says, pointing in the direction Jake and the girls are headed. He jumps out into knee-deep water and beaches the raft. Ian climbs over the tube and onto a large rock on the shore, then holds his hand out for Katie.

I sit on the edge of the tubing, and Brian helps me out. I don't need it like Katie does, but I'm not about to lose any chance to touch Brian. Amber does the same but comes up a little short and steps one foot into the river. Once everyone climbs out, Brian pulls the raft further onto the dry land. The boys in Skid's raft paddle toward us, followed closely by Erin's with the family.

"You can take your life jackets off for our little hike if you want," Brian says. "And watch where you put your feet. You don't want to be stepping on any rattlesnakes."

Amber jumps to the top of a boulder, glancing around the rocks.

I unbuckle my life jacket and toss it into the raft. I didn't realize how tight it squeezed my chest until I can actually breathe again. My wet shorts and tank top cling to my body. I think about taking them off but don't want to climb through the bushes and up the bank in nothing but my bathing suit like the stupid girls in Jake's raft.

"Lava Canyon is the most challenging rapids we'll go through. It's a class IV, so we always scout it ahead of time." Brian starts up a dirt path toward the railroad tracks. I turn to follow him but notice Amber not moving. Ian, Katie, and Mason circle around her and fall in line behind Brian.

"What's up?" I ask. Amber stares at a tree just on the other side of Jake's raft. Three crosses rest in the shade beneath it—two white and one plain, unpainted wood. She moves toward them, ducks under the hanging branches, and stands in a cavern of shade.

A wreath of faded pink plastic flowers hangs over one of the white crosses. Below it, a plastic frame holds a water-warped photograph of a teenage girl—probably her senior portrait. Etched in the wood is the name Ashley Grebe 1984-2002. A pile of river rocks stabilizes the base of the other white cross with the name Victor Pineda 1978-2004 burnt into the wood. The third cross has a set of antlers tied to the base, and the bottom section of a fishing rod lies on the crossbar. Mickey Brandt, 1947-1999, is hand-carved into the cross below the fly rod.

"Emmy and Amber, you coming?" Brian calls. He stands above us on the railroad tracks with the towering black cliff behind him. The boys climb up behind Skid like a squad of soldiers, marching across the tracks behind him. Maybe they are a Boy Scout troop rather than a church group.

"Let's go," I say. I need to get Amber away from the crosses. We are on the river, with no way out but through the rapids.

"Everything okay?" Brian calls, still waiting up above us.

"Yeah, we're coming." I put my arm around Amber. Her skin feels cold and clammy.

As we climb up the bank, the air becomes noticeably warmer. Rocks and gravel cover the last few feet to the top of the grade. Brown dirt clings to our wet shoes, making the lime green look more of a puke green. We step up onto the railroad ties, where Brian waits for us. The warm air smells oily, like tar and dried sage.

"You okay?" Brian asks.

"We saw the crosses."

Brian nods with his lips tight, then turns and steps from tie to tie. I hear the family coming behind us, with the dad instructing his boys to get off the rails and the mom asking how often trains come by.

I catch up with Brian. "How many people have drowned here?"

"Not many," Brian says. "It's usually people who aren't wearing life jackets or are wearing the wrong kind. The people who drown usually don't respect the river's power. Some people just rent a raft, plop it into the water, and don't know what the hell they're doing."

Amber takes a deep breath and slides her hand into mine.

Once we round the bend, Jake, his group of bikini girls, and Skid with his group of boys all stand looking down at the river. The water surges through the gorge in turbulent waves. They smash into each other, rising up into frothy whitewater and cascading over giant rocks for as far as I can see—until the river disappears around a bend.

"So, this is Lava Canyon," Brian says. "We always scout it because the river changes. A log or branch could be caught up in it—or a boat that hasn't been recovered yet."

Brian points to where we will enter the rapids. "We need to avoid three big rocks. The first one there," he moves his finger toward a gigantic boulder with water cascading over it.

"That's Troll's Back. The next one—see the jagged rock there? That's the Fish Fin, and the last one is Holy Crap rock. They call it that because you don't realize it's there until you're on top of it, then it's like, *holy crap!*"

Amber squeezes my hand. I don't want to look at her face.

All the way down the tracks and at the end of the rapids, two people sit in chairs under a big blue and white striped umbrella on a rock ledge.

"Who are they?" Ian asks Brian.

"They're from *Shooting the Rapids Photography*. They take pictures of everyone going over the rapids. They have a shop in town, and you can look at the pictures when we get back and buy them if you want. They take pictures at Steelhead Rapids too."

"How long does it take for them to print the photos?" Ian asks. "We may be leaving town as soon as we get back."

"They'll be there before you. Runners go back and forth between Lodell and here, dropping off the memory cards."

"We could try to get a ride back with one of the runners if you want," I say to Amber. "I'm sure they wouldn't mind."

It takes Amber a moment to respond, but then she says, "No. I don't want to wimp out."

Jake lets out a whistle, and everyone turns toward him. He nods his head upriver at an orange raft just about to enter the rapids.

"That's what I was talking about. It's a rental, and those dudes are obviously not familiar with the river, or they would have scouted the rapids first."

Four shirtless guys, who look in their mid-twenties, sit in a boat loaded down with a huge cooler and camping gear stuffed into black plastic bags. They miss Trolls's Back, bouncing up and down through the rapids like they are riding a bucking bronco. Their boat tips and bobs as it takes the waves with them, paddling like crazy. They bump against Fish Fin and luckily miss going over the top, but they are headed straight for Holy Crap rock.

"Stay to the right," Brian screams through cupped hands, but I doubt they can hear him above the roar of the water.

The river forces them on top of Holy Crap. All four of them and their gear lurch forward as the boat grinds across the top of the rock. The current pushes them off sideways. Everything shifts to the right as the rafters lean left to keep the boat from flipping. The right side drops off the boulder, and the current shoves them back downstream, out of the rapids.

They let out whoops, shouting, *Oh yeah!* And *Woo, hell yeah!*

Brian shakes his head. "They got lucky."

Their excited cries of *Bro, I thought we were going to flip for sure,* and *Holy shit!* fade as they disappear around the bend.

Erin stands with one of those disposable waterproof cameras, taking a picture of the family with the rapids raging through the gorge behind them. She counts, "One, two, three, cheese," then snaps the picture and hands the camera back to the mom.

The girls follow Jake around like ducklings as they make their way along the tracks toward the rest of us. Their boobs bounce and their hair, now in ponytails and messy buns, swing as they hop from railroad tie to railroad tie. Skid and the boys stop tossing rocks down into the river to watch the girls pass by.

Jake has a lump of chew in the lower right corner of his jaw and spits brown liquid into the dirt as he passes us. Two of the girls catch up to him and slide their skinny arms under his, laughing and flirting with him. How can Erin stand seeing those girls all over her boyfriend? She must be one secure woman or just very professional—who knows how she handles it once they are back home. Nobody knows what really happens once people close the doors of their house.

Back at the rafts, Brian checks the self-bailing holes for snakes by pushing the raft into the water to flush them out, then pulls the raft back to shore for everyone to get in.

As the girls load into Jake's raft and lock their life jackets over their boobs, he calls out to Brian, Skid, and Erin. "I'll go first and set safety, then Brian, Skid, and Erin."

Everyone nods and the guides check the life jackets of the rafters in their boats. Jake rearranges the order of the girls in his raft. Erin has the littlest boy sit on the floor of her raft, between her feet, and tells him to take hold of the blue safety strap.

"Katie, how about if you come back here with Emmy and Amber and let Ian and Mason take the front," Brian says.

Jake pushes out first, and for the first time, it looks like the girls in his raft understand the danger they face because they finally keep their mouths shut. They paddle toward the rapids with Jake's commands, "Three forward," and disappear around the bend.

"Remember, if you go in, get your feet downriver so you can push yourself away from the rocks." Brian waits a few minutes before calling out any paddle commands. "Okay, here we go, all forward."

We enter the rapids, staying to the right of Troll's Back. Our raft rises and falls over the tall waves, everyone silently paddling and holding on command. Brian keeps his paddle planted like a rudder at the rear of the raft.

Brian's commands can barely be heard over the roar of the water in the gorge. "All forward until I yell stop." The raft bucks and sways. It rises up and plunges down with water washing in over the bow and the sides. Amber paddles hard in front of me.

Her skinny arms plunge and pull, plunge and pull. The pointy tip of Fish Fin appears to the front left of the raft. Ian and Mason work hard in the bow, with water gushing in at every dip as the current pushes the raft dangerously close to the boulder.

"Stop," Brian shouts, but Amber doesn't react quickly enough. She dips her paddle in just as a wave shoves us into the rock. Her paddle hits and flings her into the river.

One moment she is there, and the next, she is not.

"Amber," I scream. "Amber fell in."

"I see her," Brian yells. "She will need to ride the rapids in her life jacket."

I see Amber's orange jacket in the waves. She isn't feet first. Oh my God. One of Amber's arms shoots into the air just before she cascades over a boulder and disappears. I scan the river, watching for her to come up. Oh my God. Why did I bring her here?

"Where is she?" I scream. "Where is she?"

Katie drops to the bottom of the raft and grabs onto the safety strap. Oh God, please let Amber live. Please. The damned Magic 8 ball. The raft rises and falls with the powerful current in complete control of our lives. A flash of orange appears downstream, then disappears beneath a wave again.

"Ian, if we get close enough, hold out your paddle for her to grab. If we don't, Jake will get her."

Jake's raft appears close to the bank ahead. His eyes watch where I had last seen Amber's life jacket. What if she is unconscious? She can't grab the safety rope. Jake stands while the girls sit still and solemn in his raft. The whole scene appears and disappears with the waves splashing over the bow and us bouncing through rapids.

Jake tosses the orange throw bag. It arcs through the air, straight at Amber's face. Amber's arm flies out of the water and latches onto the rope. Jake pulls. Our raft stills as we come out of the rapids. I stand, watching Amber's orange jacket move across the river toward Jake.

"All forward," Brian calls.

I sit back down on the tubing, heavy as if my body has been filled with rocks. Breathe. I paddle as hard as I can toward Amber. We drift in next to Jake's raft just as Jake grabs Amber's life jacket and pulls her onto the tube. The girls gather around Amber, blocking my view of her. Once our raft touches Jake's, I scramble over both tubes and into his raft. "Amber!"

She lies across one of the seats, face down, and hugging it to her. Her entire body shivers. "Are you okay?"

I lie over Amber and wrap my arms around her, pinning her to the inflatable seat. Amber's body trembles beneath me. "I'm sorry. I'm so sorry."

The image of the Magic 8 Ball with the white triangle rising through the blue liquid with its damned predictions comes to my mind. *Concentrate and ask again.* Maybe Amber and I do not have the same fate. And we decided to come here based only on mine.

I feel a hand on my back. I turn to see Mason standing over us.

"Let's get her to shore," he says.

I don't let go. Mason's hands try to pry me from Amber. "I need to get her warm."

"Your skinny little wet body isn't going to do much good. I'm a paramedic. We need to get her to shore. She'll be okay. She's probably just in shock."

I need to let go, but I cannot. I don't ever want to let Amber go again. Amber is all I have. She is the closest thing to family. Mason pulls me off and lifts Amber over the tube to Brian, who stands waist-deep in the water. Brian cradles Amber in his arms and climbs onto the shore.

Mason slides over the side and wades over to the other raft. "Throw me my backpack," he says to Ian.

Ian tosses him the black bag, and Mason heads for the bank. I scramble over the seats, pushing past the girls to the front, and jump to the shore.

Brian sits on the ground with Amber hugged to his chest. Mason unzips his backpack and pulls out a first aid kit. He digs through it and removes a shiny silver packet.

"Take her life jacket and clothes off," Mason says. "You can leave the swimsuit on, but take off the wet shorts and top."

I drop to my knees in front of Brian, "I'll do it," I say.

"You doing okay?" I ask Amber.

"Yeah," Amber says with her teeth chattering. "Just cold."

Once I strip her down to her bathing suit and they wrap the space blanket around her, Mason checks her head for blood or bumps. He checks her pupils and feels for any broken bones.

"She has a couple of small bruises and lumps on the side of her head. It looks like she's just in shock, but she may have a concussion."

"I'm sorry," I say again.

Amber smiles a thin blue-lipped smile. "I'm fine."

"We only have about ten more minutes of a float to get to where we're having lunch," Brian says. He must have noticed the fear on Amber's face because he adds, "There aren't any rapids between here and there, and you can get a ride back to Lodell with one of the cooks."

Mason hands me the wet clothes as he gets Amber back into her life jacket. The float down to the campground is easy. Nobody shoots water between rafts or jumps into the calm water. Amber and I sit in the middle of the raft with her wrapped in the space blanket.

The campground is hard-packed earth, scaly trees, and brush at the base of a steep cliff of crumbly layers of rock. Cooks stand over barbecues that were obviously brought in by the pickup trucks with their tailgates down.

Brian points at a massive man flipping chicken breasts and burgers with a spatula. "Our lunch is to the right."

"Isn't he one of the bartenders at Buckskin Mary's," I ask, noticing the thick wig-like hair.

"Yep," Brian says, "Big Doug is camp cook by day and bartender by night."

Hamburger buns, hot dog buns, and aluminum trays filled with pasta salad, chicken breasts, hamburger patties, hot dogs, and brownies cover one of the picnic tables.

Brian guides Amber to one of the picnic tables with the blanket still wrapped around her, then heads straight to the front of the food line.

"Want me to get you some lunch?" I ask.

"I'm not really hungry."

Brian returns with two plates loaded with chicken breasts and pasta salad, followed by Katie holding two cups of lemonade. They set them in front of us before going back for their own.

"Just try to nibble a little," I say.

The boys and their pastor or scoutmaster, whoever he is, load their plates high with food. Each boy takes several brownies. Mason, Ian, and Katie sit down at our table with their plates. Brian, Jake, Erin, and Skid sit together with other guides.

"How're you feeling," Mason asks. He reaches across the table and puts his hand on Amber's forehead. "Your body temperature is coming back up."

"I feel pretty good," Amber says.

"Are you heading back with one of the cooks?"

"Yes," I say at the exact same time that Amber says, "No."

"I think we should."

"I don't want to spoil our trip." Amber forks a spiral of pasta and sticks it into her mouth. "See, I'm eating. I'll be fine."

"I think it would be best to go back and take a hot shower and a nap," Mason says.

"I'm heading back," I say, making the decision for us. "It was fun, but I'd love to take a shower and nap myself."

The girls from Jake's raft finish lunch, and two of them come over to check and see how Amber is feeling, then bounce off to where the guides sit. The girl in the red bikini squeezes in between Brian and Erin, practically rubbing herself all over him like a cat wanting to be pet. Brian gets up and leaves her sitting in his spot.

"So, how's our swimmer doing?" he asks, joining Amber and me.

"I'm feeling much better."

"You want me to ask Big Doug to give you a ride back to town?"

Amber starts to shrug her shoulders, so I answer for her, "Yes, she needs to get a shower and a nap." I badly want to stay with Brian, but Amber needs to get back to the hotel.

"Hopefully, she'll be feeling better by this evening so you two can come out to the Buckskin again," Brian says. "Can I talk to you for a minute?"

I look over at Amber, not wanting to leave her side.

"I'm fine. I'll wait right here."

I follow Brian down to the river where all the rafts line the bank, beached on the river rock. We stand at the edge and listen to the voices of the rafters behind us.

Brian turns to me.

"There's something I forgot last night. Well, I didn't forget. I chickened out." He puts his arm around my waist and pulls me close, causing shivers to wash all over me. "You've been driving me nuts since the moment I saw you in your car."

And before he has a chance to kiss me, I kiss him.

CHAPTER THIRTEEN

WE RIDE BACK TO TOWN IN THE FRONT CAB OF BIG DOUG'S TRUCK with the barbecue strapped into the bed, the windows down, and dust swirling in. He is awkward and keeps sneaking glances at us—as if we wouldn't notice some forty-year-old dude creeping on us. Without a word, he slides a CD into the player and places his big hand on the seat next to Amber with his pinky finger almost touching her leg.

The entire way back to Lodell, Ozzy Osbourne blares through the speakers, pounding in my chest and piercing my ears. Every time Big Doug looks over at us, Amber inches closer and closer to me until we are practically hanging out the window. By the time he pulls up to the Whitehorse Inn, I can't wait to jump out of his truck.

"I'm ready to leave this town," Amber says.

"Now?"

She shrugs. "It doesn't feel right. Every nerve in my body is screaming to leave."

I am not ready to leave. I cannot get Brian out of my mind, and every nerve in *my* body wants him. "We will not make it to the border before dark. It is too dangerous for two girls to drive at night."

I don't know if it is still the shock of falling in the river or the beginning of an anxiety attack, but Amber's body starts shivering again.

"Let's ask if there is a computer we can use, and we'll print the directions to Canada. We will leave first thing in the morning," I say. "I promise."

The hotel has one computer, and Becky begrudgingly leads us into a back office to use it. The office reeks of stale cigarette smoke and has a mustard yellow couch that looks like it is made of some sort of fake velvet with questionable stains on it. The wall to the left of the desk is covered in photographs of the people of Lodell. It looks as if someone has pinned the entire town to the wall.

There are pictures of all the different river guides, posing in their rafts or with beers in Buckskin Mary's. One of the pictures looks like it could be Brian and Jake when they were about ten years old. Their heads are shaved, just like they do to the foster boys to save on haircuts, and they are sitting on a porch smiling toothless grins.

Just think…that little boy grew into Brian. And he kissed me today. I can still feel the little electrical charges in my nerve endings from his touch.

Becky heads around the desk and starts up the ancient computer, causing all sorts of electronic noises and static and beeping. Good God, it is dial-up! Amber and I shoot each other looks and eye-rolls.

Hundreds of brightly colored origami birds, all strung together like strings of fish, hang from a hook in the wall. They remind me of the story of the little girl who folded the paper cranes, thinking she could beat cancer if she made a thousand of them. We read that book in middle school, and the whole class folded origami for weeks, trying to get to a thousand.

Five-by-seven school pictures of a boy, showing a complete age progression, hang in rows of cheap plastic frames on the opposite wall. His round smiling kindergarten face all the way through his serious senior photo stare out. Dozens of snapshots of the same boy are stuck to the wall with thumbtacks. There are photos of him in a Boy Scout uniform, riding a pony, whacking a piñata, and fishing. And as he got older, in a wrestling singlet, football uniform, and standing in front of a sign that reads, Rimrock Outfitters.

"Is that Jake?" I ask Becky.

"The one and only," she answers, her voice dripping with sarcasm.

Jake's face hasn't changed much over the years—always a round moon-face—but as he aged, it took on mutton-chop sideburns and a mean glare.

"There you go," Becky says, standing up and leaving the room. "Don't bother anything."

Amber goes around to the chair.

I wonder if the raggedy little boy in the background of some of little Jake's pictures are Brian. One photo shows three little boys and a blonde girl—two of the boys and the girl hold up fish, while the third boy pouts next to them with his arms crossed and no fish.

"You think that's Brian, Jake, Erin, and Skid?" I point to the picture.

Amber leans over the desk for a closer look. "It's definitely Jake and Erin. I think that's Brian and Skid too."

Brian holds a fish by the lip with a huge smile on his face. "Can you imagine growing up with the same people and knowing them your whole life?"

Amber sits, scanning the computer screen with her hand on the mouse. "I think it would be cool. You would really know the person."

I go around the desk to help Amber. She starts to sign into her Yahoo account.

"No!" I grab her wrist. "They can track us. Just go to MapQuest."

Amber types *MapQuest* in the search bar and clicks the directions button. For the starting point, she types in *Lodell, Oregon*, and for the destination, *Canada border*.

"Six hours and forty-five minutes." Her shoulders drop, and she starts shivering again.

"And that's just to the border," I say. "We need to get to Vancouver."

She changes the destination. "Seven and a half hours."

"That's not too bad if we leave in the morning," I say. "Print the directions, and we'll go get our showers."

Amber hits *print*. "I want to check Myspace so bad…What do you think people from school are saying about us?" The printer starts making all sorts of grinding noises.

Becky peeks her llama face into the room. "Nobody said you can print. This ain't no Internet cafe. If you want to camp out at a computer and print, you can go to Worldlink. It's right behind the photography shop."

"Is that Brian and Skid there?" I point at the photograph of the group with the fish. The printer keeps making a bunch of grinding noises.

"Yep," Becky says. "Those boys were terrors, always getting into mischief. And Erin was always right there with 'em."

"Whose office is this?" If I have to guess, it is someone related to Jake since his face is plastered everywhere.

"You two sure are nosey. I got work to do." Before she turns to leave, she puckers her lips and says, "As soon as that's done printing, you need to get out of this office. And that will be one dollar per page for the printing."

A dollar per page? I open my mouth to put the bitch in her

place, but we need those directions. The printer keeps grinding and clicking.

"And I need to see your IDs. You're not the only ones who know how to use a computer. Nicole and Madeline, my ass."

A cold chill sweeps over my chest.

Amber looks over at me.

"What a bitch. We need to get out of here, now," Amber says, grabbing the papers from the printer. "Before she figures out exactly who we are."

I put three dollars on the counter, and as we hurry out past Becky, I feel her eyes on our backs. We go straight to our room and throw all our clothes, makeup, shampoos, hairdryer, and straightener into our suitcases.

"Let's go out the back," I say, "If I have to see her smug look one more time, I may slap her."

Becky will be the reason I do not get more time with Brian or get a chance to say goodbye.

With our suitcases in hand, we sneak out the back door and across the patio. We climb down the steps, right to the shoe tree, startling two of the stray dogs. They jump to their feet, snarling.

"It's okay…good doggie," I say.

The shoes dangle in the dead tree, looking like a hundred executed birds, hanging by the neck and swaying in the breeze.

I slowly bend down, picking up a rock while Amber huddles behind me.

"You want a ball? Come on, you know how to fetch?" I throw the rock. The dogs watch it thud onto the ground with a small puff of dust. They don't seem impressed, but their hackles go down, and they slink away from us.

"That tree gives me the creeps," Amber says, making a wide circle around it like one of the dead branches will reach down and grab her.

We circle around the parking lot to the Mazda, wedged between a jeep and a jacked-up Ford truck with giant wheels and flying an American flag behind the cab. I put the key in the trunk, and something seems off.

"Oh my God!" Amber says. "The tire is flat."

It isn't just one tire. Both back tires are completely flat as if someone had slashed them.

CHAPTER FOURTEEN

We wake up so late, I'm afraid that Brian will already be hooked-up with another girl. After seeing the flat tires on our car, we went straight back to our room, dropped our suitcases, and walked all the way through town to the old ghost town part of Lodell where Bud's Garage is.

We rode in the tow truck back to our car, where he inspected it and said the punctures could be patched, but he recommended two new tires, so we didn't end up having a blowout later. Of course he wants to sell us new tires. That is how he makes a living.

At one-hundred-thirty dollars per tire and seventy-five dollars for the towing, we had no choice but to go for the patches. Patches and a prayer. After the exhaustion of all that, we went back to the room and collapsed on the beds, instantly falling asleep and not waking up until dark.

By the time we get to the Buckskin, everyone is already half-trashed, and our hair is still damp from our showers. The bouncer must recognize us from the night before because he just stamps our hands and lets us in.

"Ready for our last night on U.S. soil?" I ask Amber.

"Or…if Becky calls the cops, our last night of freedom," she says. "Either way, bring it on."

The girls on the dance floor move their asses, grinding and rubbing against the guys' crotches, and a beer pong tournament is full-tilt at a back table. The spaghetti strap of a barely conscious girl at the bar has fallen off her shoulder, and her bare boob hangs out. She seems completely unaware that the creepy old man next to her is cradling it in his hand, bouncing it up and down.

Erin waves at us from a booth across the room and starts toward us. "Hey, how are you feeling?" she asks Amber.

"Better than her," Amber points at the girl with the boob hanging out.

Erin shakes her head and steps up beside the girl. She pushes between her and the old man, knocking his hand away.

"Looks like you have a blowout there," Erin says, tucking the girl's boob back into her halter top and lifting the strap onto her shoulder.

"Why'd you do that?' Jake asks.

His voice makes me jump. I had no idea he was behind us. He stands so close I can almost feel the heat from his body. "You ruined the poor guy's fun."

"You're such a dick," is all Erin says to him.

Two of the girls who had been on Jake's raft approach the bar, wait for Big Doug to notice them, then lift their shirts, flashing their bare boobs at him. He clunks two shot glasses down on the bar, filling them with booze. They lower their shirts and giggle before walking off with the drinks. I look over at Erin to see if she noticed.

She shrugs her shoulders as if it isn't anything new. "If you flash your tits at Big Doug, you get free drinks."

What a perv! He had to be at least forty or fifty years old. Thank God he didn't make us flash our tits at him when he gave us a ride back to town. Come to think of it, he could have pulled over onto the side of the road at any point and did whatever he wanted to us.

Several bras hang from the antlers of the deer heads mounted on the wall. "Is it boob night tonight?"

"Most nights are boob nights," Erin says. "Want to come sit with us?"

I look over at the booth, where only Skid sits, staring toward the dance floor with about a dozen beer bottles on the table. "Where's Brian?"

"You just missed him. He was worried about you and went to the hotel to see if you're all right."

He is looking for us? Oh my God! My heart starts beating so fast I can feel my pulse in my throat. I have never believed in love at first sight. And I still may not—it may only be lust at first sight, but whatever it is, I am on board. It sucks that we are leaving in the morning.

I look over at Amber, who has a gloomy look on her face. I know she does not want to be left to fall on the *Skid grenade* just so I can be with Brian.

"I won't leave you alone with him," I whisper in her ear. "I promise."

She nods, and we follow Erin and Jake to the booth. Seeing us coming, Skid perks up and scoots out to let us in. "Let me get you ladies a couple of beers."

"What a dumbshit," Jake says. "Don't waste your money. They'll probably spread their legs for free."

Skid's shoulders droop, and his smile disappears.

Before I have the chance to tell Jake to go take a flying leap, Erin punches him in the arm, saying, "Seriously?"

She turns to us. "Ignore him. He's still in the anger stage. He lost his mom to cancer last year, and he was very close to her."

A chill washes over me. All the photos in the office, especially of Jake through the years...and the paper cranes. I bet that was her office. And we sat in her chair. We touched her things.

The things of a dead woman who folded paper cranes thinking they would save her. I need a drink.

I look over at Skid, who stands there looking sad.

"Thank you, Skid," I say, making sure to use his name. "We would love two Bud Lights."

As he hurries off toward the bar, I let Amber into the booth first so she will not have to sit next to Skid when he returns. I keep looking toward the door for Brian. Jake seems ADHD or something, constantly scanning the room or tapping his hand on the table.

"I thought maybe you had already left," Erin says to us.

Jake lifts his chin at someone at the beer pong table before walking away without a word.

"Someone slashed our tires," Amber says.

Erin's eyebrows pinch together. "Slashed? Are you sure you didn't just run over something?"

Amber shrugs. "Bud said they were slashed."

"Bud?"

"From Bud's Garage."

"His name is Todd. Bud was his grandfather," Erin says, "but if Todd says they were slashed, they were slashed."

"Why would someone do that to us?" Amber still has that hurt look on her face, devastated that someone would violate us like that. She had actually used the word *violate* when Todd confirmed they were slashed.

Skid comes back with our beers and scoots in next to me. Brian appears in the doorway, stopping to talk with the bouncer. Just the sight of him makes my heart go straight to my throat again. He tosses his head back in a laugh, then nods at something the bouncer says. Then, he turns toward us, making eye contact with me, and giving me his big, eye-squinting smile. I try to play it cool, taking a gulp of my beer to help my nerves. Yes, this is what I need. I need to get tipsy, mellow out, and relax. I take another drink.

"Glad you made it," Brian says with a wink to me, then looks at Amber. "How's your head feeling?"

"Better now," she holds up her beer.

"Need another one?"

"Why not?" She says. "This one is already two sips down. It's our last night, so we might as well get trashed."

It will not only be our last night in Lodell. Tomorrow night, we will be Canadians. As Brian walks off, it feels like a hole is opening in my chest. Too bad he isn't a Canadian. Maybe he would like to come with us. But why would he leave his job and his home for a girl he just met? For all I know, we would be at each other's throats in a month, then what would I do? Maybe this is what he does to all girls coming through town for a bit of fun.

Brian plunks our beers on the table, then holds his hand out to me for a dance. Skid scoots around to let me out, then slides back in next to Amber. She looks miserable. Brian pulls me to the middle of the floor, sinking us deep into the crowd. He swings me around and pulls me against him. I can hardly breathe as he puts his mouth to mine. All I can feel is his body, his mouth, and the beat of my thumping heart.

Amber and Skid join us. She has a fake smile. Poor Amber. Poor awkward Skid. As the song ends, one of the guides we had seen earlier comes up behind Amber. He has shoulder-length curly blonde hair and a chin beard—looking more like a surfer dude than a river guide. He leans over her shoulder and whispers something in her ear. Amber flinches, then turns, and a wide smile of relief comes to her face.

"Who's that?" I ask Brian.

"Matt," Brian kisses my neck, causing shivers to sprinkle down my spine. "He's a good guy."

After Matt hones in on Amber, pulling her away from Skid, I relax. She will be fine. She will have a great time. I slide my hand into Brian's back pocket and pull him against me.

I so badly want to have sex with Brian. In our hotel room or his house, I do not care. I want to see his naked body and feel it against mine. I want to have him inside me.

Song after song, we make out on the dance floor, only coming up for air to have another sip of our beers. We spend the rest of the evening dancing, kissing, and drinking. Everything blurs. People turn into nothing but a single moving mass. It feels as if I have slipped beneath the surface of the river. It swirls around me, but I still stand here breathing.

Brian and I float in the center of a whirlpool. The lights and music rotate around us. Until I rise up above Brian. Out of my body. The mass of people smears together like melted crayons.

CHAPTER FIFTEEN

HIM

HER AMBER HAIR SPREADS OUT OVER THE PILLOW. EACH SILKY strand is the same color as her eyelashes and eyebrows. The first moment I saw her, a tingle started in my gut that grew and grew every time I looked at her—until I could not stand it anymore. When I heard her name, I knew. Amber with amber-colored hair.

I trace my finger down her tiny and perfect nose. When I get to the fine tip, her eyes flutter, and she sighs. I put my mouth to hers, not quite touching, and inhale the breath that comes from deep within her. I feel her warmth on my lips, then the coolness as her breath recedes, then the warmth again. In and out. I open my mouth, breathe deep, and inhale her. I wish this could last forever. She will never know how much she means to me.

I roll her onto her back. She lets out a groggy moan but does not wake. Sliding my hand beneath her neck, I lift and fan her hair out over the pillow until she looks like she is floating on water.

Her breasts are the perfect size to cup in my palms. I run my hands over them, down to her belly and down, past her perfectly trimmed amber pubic hair. My hands separate her thighs then run down each soft and hairless leg. I take her again. She is mine.

Afterward, I stand over her, never wanting to forget her pale skin against the sheets. I wrap my finger around the strands, winding it tighter and tighter until I lose circulation and yank them free from her scalp.

I knew she was the one.

Amber is naked and cradled in my arms as I step into the moonlit river. It rises up my calves and thighs until I am waist-deep. She gasps as I dip her into the water, but she is limp and does not resist. I immerse her, and just as it rises to her ears, she opens her eyes. They stay open beneath the surface. She is realizing that something is wrong, and when she screams, I put my mouth to hers. As I take it into my lungs, it vibrates in my throat. I hold her under as she takes a breath, filling herself with me. She is mine forever, for I am the river. It is the fluid, and I am the flesh.

CHAPTER SIXTEEN

What is that sound? *Thwack, thwack, thwack.* I open my eyes. Each thwack feels like a blow to my head. Where the hell am I? The room is sweltering hot and dim. Strips of light push through the slats of some blinds. The bed has a rail on it. A heavy tube is taped to the back of my hand. I follow it up to a fat plastic IV sack of clear liquid. I'm in a hospital. I need some Tylenol—something. My head.

"Hello?..." I call, but the pulsating noise drowns me out. It vibrates and pounds the walls like I am trapped inside a stereo speaker.

My thighs slide together, slippery with sweat. What idiot put a blanket on me in this oven? I sit up. Holy shit, I am sore down there. Did I hook up with someone last night? Nothing is bandaged or broken. Just a sore crotch, thick head, and pounding headache. Oh...and bruises, good God.

I am wearing a dingy green hospital gown. I slide it up my legs. Dozens of purple bruises tattoo my thighs. And there are more on the soft underside of my arms. I need out of this bed. The damned rail. I scoot to the end. A pain stabs the top of my hand. My IV. The tubing. I'm at the end of my line. I drop my legs over the side.

My stomach spasms. I grab the hair at the back of my neck and vomit where I had been lying. What the hell? There are knots all the way from my scalp down to the tips of my hair. It is one giant tangle and damp at my scalp. What the hell happened? Where am I?

"Hello," I call again to nothing but that noise throbbing the walls. It has to be a helicopter. I pull a cord to call the nurse.

The room has a 1980's decor with a row of dingy, mud-brown triangles painted halfway up mustard-yellow walls. And now it reeks of vomit.

Where is the nurse? I slide off the bed. My legs quiver under my weight. Good God, my privates hurt, and whatever is making that noise is sucking the air from the room.

Beneath the IV needle is a red star stamp. There are two red stars, one faded more than the other. What the hell?

A muffled voice yells outside. I cannot make out what it said. I grab the IV tubing to yank it off but think better of it and lift the sack of liquid from the hook. The sac jiggles, heavy in my hand, and I step toward the window. How in the hell did I end up in a redneck hospital room?

I split open a gap in the blinds but see nothing but a whirl of dust and the dark shape of a helicopter with whirling blades. Is that how I got here? Was I in a car accident?

I need to find a nurse. My bare feet scuff across the dusty linoleum floor as I step toward the door. I grab for the knob. My bare-ass sticks out the back of the gown. I scan the room. Where are my clothes? I could not have come here naked and barefoot.

I step into the hallway holding the back of my gown closed. Every door but mine stands wide open to vacant rooms. A different muscle aches or shoots with pain with each step down the hall.

"Hello. Is anybody here?"

The waiting room is also empty, with nothing but black padded armchairs facing a massive dark coffee table. Where is the receptionist? Or the nurse? Who would leave someone alone in a hospital? What the hell happened? I vaguely remember something about the desert and driving with…who?

I have a nasty taste in my mouth. "Somebody…I need some water. And some goddamned Tylenol."

The intensity of the thwacking grows as I step closer and closer to the front door. It pulsates deep in my chest and throbs in my head. I want to cover my ears to block out the noise slicing through them, but I have the IV bag in my hand. As I reach for the knob and turn it, the door blows in and pounds me square in the shoulder, almost knocking me to the floor.

"Shit," I yell, but my word is swallowed up by the pulsing blades of the helicopter. Tiny needles of dust pierce my face, arms, and bare shins.

The blurred shape of a tall and thin man hurries, crouching beneath the blades and holding a cowboy hat down on his head. A bulging black bag hangs from one shoulder, and he holds what looks like a scuba tank in his other hand. He climbs up into the passenger seat of the helicopter and pulls the door shut.

The chopper slowly rises up off the ground in an immense swirl of choking heat, dust, and noise. It climbs, hovers like a giant blue and white hummingbird, then turns away. It flies low and slow, taking the pulsating noise with it.

The place looks familiar. The dried-up blue-green shrubs, run-down buildings, dirt-stained children, and the river. It all comes back. The desert. The Deschutes River. Whitewater rafting. Green shoes.

Where in the hell is Amber? She isn't in the hospital. All the rooms are empty. Where is she? Why isn't she sitting in the chair by my bed waiting for me to wake up? She would never leave me alone.

"What in the Sam Hill are you doin' out here?" a woman's voice pierces through my head like a knitting needle.

She has thick red hair feathered back in a big 80's hairdo and teeth that stick out so far I doubt she can even close her lips over them. She looks like a ginger llama. Something familiar. Her overly tight T-shirt has two jugs of whiskey printed right over each huge boob.

"What's going on? Why am I in the hospital? Did that helicopter bring me here?"

"You didn't ride in no helicopter. You need to get back in bed. If Doc sees you out here, he'll have my hide." In large red letters, her T-shirt says, *Keep Your Hands Off My Jugs*.

"What happened to me…and where's my friend, Amber?"

"I'll answer all your questions as soon as you're back in bed." The woman reaches for the IV bag. "And we need to call your family and let them know what happened."

I swing the bag away from her. "There's nobody to call."

She narrows her eyes at me. "Now give me that bag. It's supposed to be above your head. Ain't doin' you no good like that."

"No." I swat at the woman's arm. "Where's Amber?"

"No need for you to be a pain in my patootie now. We're helping you out. You 'bout drowned last night."

Drown? I remember being in a bar and partying with Amber. Neon lights, pool tables, darts, a band, dancing, free beer if you flash your boobs at the pervert bartender. "Where's Amber?"

The woman tries to grab me, but I step back.

"Where's Amber?"

The woman pauses, then speaks softly like you would to calm a child. "They haven't found her yet."

"What do you mean?"

"She's in the river."

"What do you mean? She can't be. She doesn't even like to

swim." I remember. I helped Amber escape the group home, and we were headed to Canada. We wanted out of the country for a fresh start. We stopped in Portland and bought matching pairs of lime green Converse…and I talked Amber into coming whitewater rafting…We are still in Oregon. Shit.

"Honey, you need to go lie down now. We have experts lookin' for her. That man in the helicopter is Rooster Powers, and he's the best at recovering bodies. If he can't find her, nobody…"

Recovering bodies? I clasp the IV bag to my chest and run. The liquid jiggles each time my feet hit the dirt, and the plastic tubing swings, tapping against my leg.

"You get your ass back here," the woman screams behind me.

Groups of people cluster around the river, watching and talking like people do when there's an accident or a fire. A white trailer with *Canyon County Sheriff Incident Command* written on it is parked by a boat launch and next to a sign. *Rimrock Outfitters*. Whitewater rafting. Brian. Did he do this to me? A white sheriff truck has a trailer piled with red rafts. Men in helmets and bright red, yellow, and orange life jackets unload the gear.

Dozens of people trudge over rocks, combing through the grass and willow along the shore.

"She's not in there," I scream. "Stop it…she's not there."

"Oh my goodness. Honey, calm down." A woman with long brown hair pulled into a skinny ponytail comes toward me. The woman's eyes are such a pale blue that they make her look dead. A bouncer with a skull tattoo and the same eyes. Zombie eyes. Amber said he had zombie-eyes.

"She's not there. They're wasting their time."

"You must be the other girl—the one that Brian saved," the woman says. "Let me help you with your gown. Your whole backside is peeking out."

Brian. It feels as if a bird is trapped in my chest, frantically flapping and unable to get out.

"She's not there. Amber doesn't like water. She wouldn't be in the water. Stop it!"

Something catches the woman's attention. I turn to see the llama lady and a strong old man with steely gray hair coming toward me.

I look to the right and to the left. The hotel. Amber will be in our hotel room. Asleep on one of the beds. The llama lady and old man are almost to me. I run. Pain pierces my head as if it is cracking open.

"Stop her," a deep voice rumbles behind me.

I run past the bar where Amber and I had used our fake IDs. That is where I got the red stars stamped on my hand. I remember the pool tables and dancing with Brian. That is the last place I remember being with Amber. We were shit-faced. Amber must be passed-out in our hotel room…or in another room with some guy she met. They are wasting their time in the river.

I run into the entrance of the Whitehorse Inn. Becky. The llama lady looks like Becky. Only older. The lobby is empty. I run past the big fireplace with the dead elk heads and down the hallway. I run past closed doors, all the way to room 114—my and Amber's room.

The door stands wide open. I slow down and stop before entering. Why is the door open? I peek in. It is completely empty, and the beds are made. Where are our suitcases? And all of our clothes that we left strewn on the beds? And our make-up and blow drier? Where is my hair straightener? Someone has cleared out all of our stuff.

My stomach turns. I need to throw up again, but I don't want to be trapped inside the bathroom by the llama lady and old man. I run for the other door—the one that leads to the long patio outside our room. I go for it and burst through just in time to barf over the railing.

I close the door and step around the back corner. Leaning

against the dry yellow siding, I yank off the tape, pull the IV needle from my hand, and drop the bag into the dust. I grab hold of my temples. My head feels like it is cracking open. This has to be a mistake. Amber did not drown in this dusty little hell-hole of a town.

I hear a soft throat-cooing sound that, for a split second, I think is my own cry escaping my chest. A light gray-brown bird perches in the top of a tree filled with shoes. I remember the tree, except now, toward the top, and swaying in the breeze are two brand new pairs of lime green Converse—size six. The bird coos again, the same moaning cry.

Oh my God, Amber! I cannot lose Amber.

The llama lady and old man appear on the edge of the patio.

"You gotta stop running and let people take care of you," she says, just as the strong hand of the man closes around my arm.

CHAPTER SEVENTEEN

I REFUSED TO ANSWER THEIR QUESTIONS UNTIL THEY TOOK ME TO see what was happening in the search for Amber. Doc Unger loads me into his dirty old pickup truck, and we follow Chief Unger in his police car all the way through town, finally stopping at the top of a cliff.

I stand at the edge, all weak and trembly. A strong and hot wind whips up the canyon, blowing my hair and making me feel as if I will crumple up and blow off the edge—just like a dried-up spider.

Something scratches at my bare leg. I look down. A grayish-green bush, all dry and spiky, rubs against a blue and black bruise on my calf. These are not my clothes.

Down below the crumbly rock ledge, the men in bright-colored gear float in red rafts tethered to ropes strung across the river like telephone lines. Men on the bank pull them tight or tie them to the trees. They stick long poles into the water, prodding the bottom where the river rushes white, churning, and boiling against boulders. Their voices rise up, calling to one another or asking for more line.

"She's not in there," I say to Doc and Chief Unger, who stand on either side of me. "Unless someone put her in there. Amber hates the water. She would never go near it."

Wouldn't I feel it if Amber had drowned? Wouldn't I feel as if I could not breathe instead of this light, blowing-away sensation I can not get rid of?

I think of Mason, the big slug who slipped out of his swim trunks, and wonder if he had scooped Amber up and drove off with her. He was big enough. Or I think of that bartender, Big Doug, who gave us a ride. He gave us both the creeps blasting his Ozzy Osbourne and inching his hand closer and closer to Amber's leg. Or the bouncer with the zombie-eyes.

"She needs to sit down," Doc says, taking me by the arm and leading me toward his pickup.

Chief Unger drops the tailgate. Doc lifts me and plunks me down on the hot metal.

"All right," Chief Unger says. "We brought you here. Now you need to answer some questions like we agreed."

The chief of police has the same last name as the doctor. I doubt they are a couple. Maybe brothers. They both have the same shape to their eyes and thick hair for men their age, but Doc is tall and gray, while the chief is short with light brown hair dyed the same flat color as my second-grade dad.

Chief Unger takes a small notepad from his back pocket. He slides out a pen attached to the side.

"Your full name, please."

Oh, God. Will he put my name through a database? *Emmy Jenkins. Be on the lookout. Wanted for harboring a minor.*

"Hello? Your name, please." He looks irritated. "Your name, please."

"Emmy May Snarfenberger." Oh, God. Is that even a real name? It sounds straight from Sesame Street. I need time to think. How should I answer him? Dammit. I knew they were going to interrogate me. I should have prepared.

"We have your driver's licenses." He stares at me like all men in authority do, with absolutely no sense of humor and talking to me as if I am a worthless piece of shit. "We found four driver's licenses for you and your friend. If you are Emmy, I am assuming you are Emmy Renee Jenkins."

I nod.

"And who do we have missing? Is it Madeline Lane, Amber Ward, or Nicole Keefer?"

I swallow, trying not to throw up. My chest hurts, and tears run down my cheeks. I look down. These are Amber's shorts. And her tank top with the tiny pink and yellow flowers. They went through our things, not knowing which were mine. But the shoes are not ours. Ours are in the tree.

The sound of a train coming closer rumbles in my chest. It thumps over the tracks and lets out one long blow of the whistle. Amber and I drove beneath that trestle on our way into town. There was a cement tunnel with graffiti and then the huge metal trestle. Amber had a bad feeling. I should have turned around.

"Who is missing?"

How long have they been staring at me, waiting? "What?"

"Who is missing?"

"Amber. Amber Ward." She used to joke that she was Amber Ward, a ward of the court.

"And what is your relation to Amber?"

"We're sisters."

He raises his eyebrows, giving me that *cut the bullshit* stare that all adults give to foster children.

"You don't need to have the same last name to be sisters."

He doesn't say a word. He just waits like he has nothing in the world better to do, and he will wait me out no matter how long it takes.

"We had the same foster parents."

"All right." He scratches some words into his notebook. "I see that she is still a minor."

"Emancipated minor," I say, just as Amber and I had decided in case we were asked—mainly to keep me out of jail and her from going straight back to the Pierson's.

"Who can we call to come get you?"

"There is nobody to call." My head starts to spin. "I'm not feeling well."

"Surely there is a family member we can call."

"Find Amber. She's the only one."

More footsteps crunch on the ground. I don't look up. I don't care who it is. I suddenly feel cold in the sweltering heat, and a million tiny pinpricks sting my cheeks. Everything becomes hazy, and the next thing I know, someone is laying me down in the bed of the truck.

"Here, take a drink." The hard plastic rim of a water bottle presses against my lips. I open my eyes to see Brian. His eyebrows pinch together, and he looks pained. Water fills my mouth and dribbles down my jaw. I swallow.

"Doesn't she need to be in the hospital?" Brian asks.

"She insisted," Doc says, "but, yes, we need to get her out of the heat."

"We need to ask her some questions," the chief says.

"Can it wait? Look at her."

I feel myself being lifted and the sound of boots crunching on dirt and twigs. Brian sets me onto the bench seat of Doc's old truck, straps the seatbelt over me, and climbs in beside me. The cab smells of cigarette smoke and dust. As we jostle over a hard rutted road, a rip in the seat rubs against my bare leg with every bump.

Should I tell the chief I want a lawyer? He cannot question me if I ask for a lawyer.

Doc and Brian talk with me between them. Their words volley back and forth over my head like a ping pong ball.

"You already gave a statement?"

"Yes. We all did," Brian says.

"You didn't see the other girl?"

"Not since Matt and I took them to their room."

My privates still sting. Had Brian and I…? Had he?

"Now, I'm gonna ask you something. I'm only asking as her doctor."

A long silence with nothing but the creaking of the old truck on the dirt road fills the cab.

"Did either of you boys take advantage of these girls?"

"No. They were drunk. We walked them back to make sure they were safe. I personally locked their door before pulling it shut. I told them to lock the bolt, but I did not hear it slide. Matt and I separated, and I went home. I don't know if he went to the guide shack or back to the Buckskin."

"Are you sure he left the hotel?"

"I'm positive. But he could have gone back."

"How did you come to rescue this one?"

"Well, you know how I cannot sleep and take walks at night?"

"Yep."

"I couldn't sleep, and I went to the river. It was a clear night, and I lay down to look up at the stars. That was when I heard something strange, like the lapping of water against a raft. I sat up and saw the shadow of a raft with someone laying across one of the pontoons, about to fall in. I called out, but the figure didn't move. I waded into the river, then swam toward the raft. It hit against something, and she slipped off. I made it to her and pulled her to shore."

"Did you have sex with her then?"

"No. Did something happen to her? Did someone?"

"You know I can't say anything because of patient confidentiality…I just need to know."

The pressure in the truck builds up. Even with the windows down, it squeezes the air from my lungs. "Someone raped me," I say.

"Damnit!" Brian punches the dashboard. "I'll beat the shit out of…"

"I took a rape kit. Didn't know if anything consensual…It may not work because of her being in the water, but I'll send it off. We have one more problem." The doctor says. "She said she has nobody to come get her, and I cannot keep her in the hospital."

"She can stay at my place. I'll sleep on the couch." Brian looks down at me with his greenish-blue eyes. "That okay with you?"

My entire body begins to shake, and just like a dumb-ass child, the moment someone shows me any sympathy, it breaks me.

CHAPTER EIGHTEEN

HIM

I LOVE THE EXCITEMENT OF A DROWNING.

Just like church. My church. The people come to my banks, humbled by my power. They study me and try to uncover my mysteries—praying that I will release my victim even though they know it is too late. Their strongest men come with their physical strength, their skill, and technology, trying to overcome the raw power that nature gave to me.

In me, their strongest men doubt themselves, fear their own weakness and powerlessness. In the end, whether I reveal the body or not, everyone gathers to pay tribute, leaving their crosses and flowers, marking each occasion along my banks.

They realize that they have taken me for granted. They had fun at my expense, not knowing the thunder that rages beneath my surface. They float around in their artificial bubbles, thinking they are safe and invincible and not realizing that at any minute, I could rage and snatch whoever I want.

Now, they know better. And that excites me.

The crowd parts. We all move aside, stepping closer together as the ambulance backs toward my bank with its high-pitched, *beep-beep-beep-beep.* Have they found Amber or Shawna? She must not have floated down very far.

A purely white dog, so white I can see the pinkness of its skin beneath, turns and stares at me. It knows me. They all know it is me, for they are always lurking around in the dark, smelling things, sensing things.

I need to think happy little thoughts. I need to calm myself. If it was night, I would sedate the white dog with the pink skin, take it into the water, and hold it under until it lets out its last little bubbles of air—until it is nothing but meat and bone and water.

I stand here surrounded by my people and the flatlanders, all of us waiting for the excitement of the great reveal. Waiting to get a glimpse of the body. In their fear and reverence, I bring out the best in people, giving them a mission and a purpose. They cook food, minister to the family of the victims, and come out of their houses and bars to do something positive—something that makes them feel good.

The rescue boat, the only motorized boat allowed on my surface, can barely make headway in my current, even with the motor whining at full throttle. We all wait, watching it come toward us in slow motion, waiting for a glimpse of my nymph. I have brought purpose to our town. I take who I want and release who I want. For, I am the river. It is the fluid, and I am the flesh.

CHAPTER NINETEEN

NINE MONTHS LATER

BRIAN BOLTS UP IN BED, GASPING. SWEAT COVERS HIS BODY, AND he breathes hard.

"You all right?" I ask.

He pants and then lies down with his back to me. "Just a bad dream. That's all."

I scoot closer until my breasts touch his bare back. That usually calms him. I wrap my arm over his waist and whisper, "I love you."

He reaches back and places his hand on my hip. "I love you, Emmy…with all my heart."

The curtains glow with moonlight and hang flat over the open bedroom window. The wind has finally stilled. Every night, it gusts through the canyon, starting and stopping like someone hit a switch. A train chugs and screeches in the distance. Brian's breath slows down as he falls back to sleep, staying in bed with me.

Many nights, when Brian cannot sleep, he slips out into the darkness to walk or sit by the river. He has been doing that ever since his mother died when he was eight years old. It is the only thing that gives him peace—until now. Because of me, he is able to slide back into sleep more often. I dread the nights when he cannot. I hate being left alone in our bed. I cannot resent it, though. If not for his nightmares and insomnia, I would be dead.

A nightmare had woken Brian and brought him to the river the night Amber disappeared. I still do not remember Brian saving me, nor the details of what happened. It is as if my mind has deleted it. Brian never saw Amber in the river that night. And nobody has ever seen her since. They recovered the other girl, Shawna, and took down her missing posters, but Amber still has not been found. Her suitcase, still packed with her things, sits outside in the trunk of my car. The thought of opening it and smelling her scent is too much for me.

Brian told me that bodies usually surface within two weeks, but the river has never returned her. The search and rescue team believes Amber is still in the river, trapped in a lava cave or pinned beneath a boulder by the current.

I cannot stop thinking about how frightened Amber was when she fell out of the raft and into the rapids on our rafting trip. I see her wrapped in that thin silver space blanket with her teeth chattering and her lips blue whenever I close my eyes. The biggest mystery to me is how we ended up in the river. I wonder if Amber had been on the other side of the raft from me and slipped into the water before Brian got to me.

Brian is all I have in the world. He took me in when I felt so lost and alone, and he has let me stay. We have spent the Fall and Winter together, fly fishing or hibernating in his one-bedroom house—curled in the nest of his bed or snuggling on the couch watching *Dr. Who* or *Man Vs. Wild* and getting to know one another. Thanks to my father, I have changed homes my entire life, living with whoever would take me. This time is different. I am loved, and I am loved by the man who saved my life.

Brian's breathing slows, and I can feel his muscles relax as he falls back to sleep. I breathe in his salty river and juniper scent as I close my eyes and feel my brain drifting back to sleep. I love Brian so much it hurts.

THE DAMNED ALARM clock blares its missile-warning siren. The worst thing about going fishing is the inhumane early mornings.

Brian slaps the top of the clock, putting it on snooze. I hate the thing. It is one of those plastic clocks with red digital numbers that glow all night long, lasering the time onto my eyeballs every time I look at it.

The morning twilight lights the window, revealing the cracked and patched surface of our bedroom wall and the dusty stuffed bobcat that Brian keeps on top of the dresser. If not for the pointy tips of his ears and thick stubby tail, he would look just like a giant house cat. I made fun of it the first time I saw it, which upset Brian. His mother bought it for him from a second-hand shop when he was a child. She had cancer and knew she was dying, so she told him that he would always be protected and watched over by the bobcat. His name is Otis. And the ashes of Brian's mom are in the wooden box right next to it.

Outside, the mourning dove calls its daily and haunting coo. It is a deep pillowy sound that makes me think of Amber. The first time I ever heard a mourning dove, Amber and I thought it was a ghost outside our hotel room—and now, it has followed me to Brian's. Every morning it coos, like my own little spook reminding me that Amber is still missing.

Brian reaches over and switches off the alarm before turning onto his side and snuggling up to me. His morning boner presses hard against my back, and he kisses my neck—tickling and causing shivers to run through my body.

"Want me to stop?" He breathes into my hair.

"No."

He runs his hand up my belly, pulling me tighter against him as he takes hold of my breast, still kissing my neck and all along my shoulder.

"You never tell me to stop," he says.

"Because I never want you to stop."

Brian's hands and mouth are loving and giving like he wants to feel and taste every part of my body—not hurt or demand. He is so different from other guys. There is a difference between making love and having sex. And this is it.

"Are you sure?" Brian slides his hand over my hip and between my legs.

"I'm sure."

He slips his fingers inside me. "Mmmm. You're already wet."

He slides inside me, and we move together, wrapped in the sheets, the early morning cool, and the scent of juniper coming in the window. Nothing feels more natural to me than making love to Brian—we are wild and primitive, just like the land, the river, the canyon, and the wind.

I pull away and roll onto my back. I want to watch him when he cums—to see his intense gaze like I am the only person on this earth for him. Brian pushes himself up and rolls on top of me, smiling. I can never resist his smile. There is a sadness to it that pulls me in and holds me under so deep I cannot breathe. Brian puts his mouth to mine. He kisses me before moving down to my breasts, my belly, and between my legs.

A hollow aluminum knock comes from the front door screen.

Brian rises up on his knees and glances over at the clock. "Shit!"

I grab the edge of the bedsheet and pull it over myself.

"Damn him!" Brian kisses me on the forehead and whispers, "To be continued..."

"Maybe we can meet Skid at his house next time," I say. "Then, we can go when we're ready."

Brian sits on the edge of the bed with his back to me, bending to pick something up from the floor. "You ever see someone's house so filled with junk that there are pathways? That's Skid's house."

Brian stands, pulling up his shorts just before the doorknob squeals.

"Hello…" Skid's voice calls into the house. "I'm not interrupting anything, am I?"

I get a peek of Skid's messy blonde hair and angled face just before Brian pulls our bedroom door shut behind him.

"What the hell?" Brian says. "You weren't supposed to be here for another twenty minutes."

"Thought maybe I could be in time to have breakfast with you."

"Did you bring any food?"

I get out of bed, pull on my waders and a T-shirt before going to the bathroom to pee, and take my birth control pill. I'm still working on the lunch sack full of pill packs that Doc gave me when I moved in with Brian. At first, I thought it was a comment of my character, then just him being a practical doctor type, but now I wonder if he was just looking out for Brian.

Out in the kitchen, Brian and Skid are setting out bowls, spoons, Cheerios, and the plastic milk container, down to its last two inches.

"Good morning," Skid says to me. "We made you breakfast."

Skid stands there in his khaki green waders and fly vest with his net on a quick-release clip and hanging down his back.

Skid means well, but he is one of those naturally annoying people—like showing up at our house early and interrupting our lovemaking. He is squirrelly and impulsive, which rubs people the wrong way. I feel sorry for him.

"Good morning," I say, sitting down and waving a fly from

the lid of the sugar bowl. "You looking forward to rafting season?"

Until Jake and Erin return from college in the middle of June, Brian and Skid will run Rimrock Outfitters. For days, the three of us have been getting the outfitters ready by cleaning out the guide shack, inflating the rafts, dusting off the life jackets, and restocking the gift shop.

Skid shrugs. "It's got its ups and downs. I am looking forward to all the hot girls."

My stomach turns to acid. I try not to let my mind rush down that path. Soon, Brian will be on the river all day. And sometimes, he will be guiding hot girls in bikinis.

Brian reaches over and puts his hand on my lower back. "No girls are hotter than my girl."

That is bullshit, but I appreciate his effort. There are plenty of beautiful girls who will be all over Brian. Damn Skid, why can't he keep his mouth shut? I don't want things to change. All winter, Brian has wrapped me up in his love, only leaving to do odd jobs lifting, hauling, or mending fences on the farms in the area. He has helped me feel like I can breathe again after losing Amber. Soon, our life will be nothing but him guiding and us hanging out at the Buckskin or with Jake and Erin every single waking moment.

I have to move and stop thinking about it. My chair makes a loud scraping noise as I stand. "Let's get going while the fish are still biting."

"What about breakfast?" Brian asks.

"You two can eat. I'll meet you at the river."

Just as I turn, I see Brian throwing a punch at Skid's shoulder with a distinct knuckle-to-skin thump.

"Ow! Shit! What's that for?" Skid whines, totally clueless.

I grab my fly vest and rod and head out the door. One of the town's stray dogs, a brown, white, and black shepherd-beagle mix, lies on the porch chewing on one of my flip flops.

"Drop that," I yell, swinging the tip of my boot toward the dog. "Stupid mutt."

It drops my shoe and scampers off with its tail between its legs. The dog ducks behind my car that sits gathering dust in the driveway. I worked hard for that car. It was my and Amber's chariot to a better life. What a joke. Now, it sits in the driveway coated with rain-splattered dust and tiny hand-shaped raccoon tracks. I should see if it still starts. If it wasn't for Brian, that is where I would be living.

The morning twilight casts a pale glow over the canyon's east rim as most of the townspeople still sleep in their tiny houses, shacks, and trailers. Brian's street is off the main road. The backs of Whiskey Dick's Bar, Louis Hardware, and Happy Cow Hamburger, which reminds me of *Hey diddle, diddle the cat, and the fiddle*, can be seen from our backyard. Like most streets in Lodell, ours is filled with small one or two-bedroom homes.

Across the street are two white bungalows with dark green trim and fake shutters nailed to the side of the windows. The paint is peeling, and there is gravel on either side where several cars are parked. They are two of Doc's rentals with new people coming and going all the time. The house on the corner is one of the nicer homes with a white picket fence and green lawn. Louis and Nora Perry, the owners of Louis Hardware, live there. Their kids are grown, but they keep a blue kiddie pool in the front yard for their grandchildren.

In a few days, the streets will be filled with cars, rafters, and old yellow and blue school busses shuttling rafters back to town and dragging trailers of bright-colored rafts behind. The shops will all be open and filled with customers buying sunscreen, snacks, and t-shirts. The hospital will treat people for poison ivy, insect bites, sunburn, and dehydration.

In the evenings, Buckskin Mary's will be overrun with drunks, lost souls, and wild girls with their butt cheeks hanging out the bottom of their shorts—everyone looking for a good time. And none of them caring that Brian is mine.

"Hey there, Emmy." Carla, one of the red-headed Stewart girls, raises a hand in hello. It is hard to believe that she is Becky's sister and the daughter of Tina, the receptionist at the hospital who wears the skanky t-shirts.

"Morning," I say, praying they are not headed to our normal fishing spot.

The fishing guides have a longer season than the whitewater guides with all the different runs and bug hatches.

Carla and Jeremy Dixon, her fiancé, whose family owns Railroad Canyon Fly Shop, lead two old fishermen toward the river. The men are completely decked-out in gear, and they probably loaded their fly boxes with newly bought flies tied right there in the shop by Mr. Dixon. The fly shop is filled with bins and bins of flies and fly tying supplies like feathers and fur, thread and wire, scissors and hooks, and bags of fluff and beads. The flies are so tiny that it seems like overkill to me.

"Where's Brian?" Carla has her hair bound in a short red ponytail that sticks out the bottom of her fishing hat like a frayed rope.

"He's still getting his ass in gear."

"He's never been a morning person," Carla says, giving me a jealous flutter in my belly.

How would Carla know Brian's sleeping habits?

Carla's hat is loaded with dry flies, hooked all around the band—I guess when you're having sex with the shop owner's son, you get all the free flies you want.

Buckskin Mary's and the Whitehorse Inn are on the bend in the river—right where it horseshoes around the town. Unfortunately, the best place to fish is just past the Whitehorse Inn by the shoe tree. Or the sole tree, as many people call it. In other spots, I have to wade out past my calves and stand in the rushing current or hang onto willow branches to keep from falling into the river.

The twisted gray trunk of the shoe tree looks as if it has been charred by fire. A horrible feeling of dread washes over me—like I am on the edge of the rimrock with my toes hanging over the side. Over a hundred pairs of tennis shoes hang in its lifeless branches, dangling in the wind. Our two pairs of lime green converse still hang toward the top, above the biggest mass of shoes, twisting and bumping in the breeze. After almost a year of exposure to the heat, wind, and freezing cold, our shoes have started to fade. One day, they will be as dusty gray as the tree itself.

Another thing that never made sense about that night is that neither Amber nor I could have thrown our shoes so high into the tree. We were the worst softball players in gym class, and the odds that two girls from foster care who hardly ever got brand new shoes would throw them away is about nil—drunk or not. Not to mention that Amber had this thing about dirty feet. She even wore flip-flops in the shower, so there is no way that she would ever throw her shoes into a tree and walk back to the room in bare feet.

I head down the dirt path toward our favorite fishing spot and stop at Amber's cross. We put it right where they think Amber and I had gone into the river. When Brian first brought the cross home, I started hyperventilating to see her name stenciled in black on the white wood. He had to take it away and hide it from me for a week, giving me time for it all to sink in.

I still sometimes think that she will magically come driving into town or make her way up the bank of the river. I still look for her. Deep down, I know that she is gone, but there is that small spark of hope that maybe she pulled herself from the river and has amnesia.

A thin morning fog rises up from the river. I squat down and watch, seeing if any fish are rising—looking for any tiny rings, boils, or surface swirls to appear through the mist. Sometimes they rise in a gulp, or they jump and splash. For every ten fish Brian can spot, I may see one.

Willow, tall grass, and smooth gray boulders line the river's edge. Around Mother's Day, during the salmonfly hatch, the bugs, which are the size of grasshoppers, are so thick they swarm the trees and grasses. The town kids stand there and let the clumsy insects crawl all over them, making them look like creatures in a horror film called Day of the Crawling Dead. It is one of the best times to fish, so we went out. They crept all over my waders and arms, even around my hat brim. Every now and then, one would drop off and plunk into the water.

I open my fly box. I don't own many flies. I have two Woolly Buggers, three Elk Hair Caddis', one Golden Stone, and a Pheasant Tail Nymph. That is it.

This is my first time fishing alone. Brian always reads the river for me, telling me which fly to use. He always says that an Elk Hair Caddis is a great go-to, so I take it from my box, thread my rod, and tie it to the tippet.

That tingling feeling of dread comes to me again, except this time, it feels as if I am being watched. I turn to see if Brian and Skid are sneaking up, ready to grab and startle me, but no one is there. A horse whinnies across the river. A big man in a cowboy hat sits on top of a horse on the opposite bank, watching me.

"Catch anything?" he calls across the water.

Oh shit. I forgot. The reservation partially regulates the use of the river, and I don't have a fishing license.

"What're you using?" he asks.

"Elk Hair Caddis."

"That should work," he says, "Unless you want to use a nymph and dredge the bottom."

A chill sweeps across my shoulders. The bottom with mossy rocks, sludge, lava caves, and the dark churning pressure of the water that has my Amber trapped.

"Hey," Brian says, coming up with Skid following right behind. "Who are you talking to?"

"The man on the horse." I point across the river, but nobody is there—just a bunch of brush, willow, and bare land.

"Seeing ghosts?" Brian asks, kissing me on top of the head before making his way into the river.

The man had been there, and he spoke to me.

I'm surprised Skid doesn't have a town kid or two trailing behind. He's like the pied piper but with a fishing rod. My stomach grumbles as the morning warms up. I should have eaten breakfast and not let Skid affect me like that. Brian loves me, and I need to trust that.

Brian catches a nice eighteen-inch rainbow trout, and Skid lands a sixteen-inch one. I had two fish rise for my fly, but I prematurely yanked it out before they had a chance to hook themselves. I drop my fly into the drying powder and give it a shake. On my backcast, I catch a willow and snap the fly off.

"Damnit!" I yell. I don't have many flies to spare.

"If you wade out, you won't get snagged as often," Brian calls over to me.

I cannot step past the shore. It is not because I am afraid of the current or being swept downstream. I am a good swimmer. Amber is down there somewhere, and I know it is irrational, but I picture my wading boot stepping onto her and sinking into her chest cavity.

Probably as a peace offering, Skid sets his rod down and comes toward me. He slides his fly box from his vest pocket. He has an old wooden box with a lid that slides open like a cigar box. Instead of foam for the hooks, it has dividers with compartments, each filled with a different type of fly.

"Is that an antique fly box?" I ask.

"It was my grandfather's."

Skid was in middle school when his grandfather died of a heart attack. He died standing in the middle of the river casting his line. It made him a hero with all the fly fishermen in town. It seems like Skid wants to be like his grandfather. Whenever he is not guiding or hanging out with Brian or Jake, he is fishing. Sometimes alone. He usually brings two rods and teaches the town kids how to fly fish.

Skid lifts out a fluffy orange, white, and brown fly then reaches for my line. "Give this one a try."

"That's all right. I've got my own." I swing my rod, moving the tippet out of his reach. "I would rather you just tell me that you're sorry."

"I am sorry," he says. "I say things without thinking. I always have."

"I accept your apology. You don't need to give me one of your flies."

"I want to."

When I'm not mad at Skid, I feel sorry for him. He has a kind heart. Brian and Jake are the alpha dogs, and Skid is the scrawny mutt who rolls onto his back or tucks his tail between his legs when they are near. I swing my rod, causing the line to sweep right in front of him.

He ties on the fly and lifts the line until it dangles between us. "This is called a Stimulator. You should catch a nice big rainbow with it."

Skid turns and watches Brian cast his line. He nods as the fly floats down a seam in the current. "That is a perfect dead drift."

I'm not exactly sure what that means. It has something to do with the fly floating naturally in the current without any tension or drag from the line. It is supposed to trick the fish into thinking it is a real bug, not an artificial one tied to a fisherman's line.

"Nobody can dead drift like Brian." Skid watches as Brian pops his fly off the water and throws his line back upstream.

"You know," I say. "You don't need to kiss people's asses to get them to like you."

The smile fades from his face, causing a lump in my throat. I did not mean to hurt him. "I'm sorry. It's just that…Brian loves you. You don't need to try so hard."

"Hey, dipshit," Brian calls from the middle of the river, where he stands casting into the current. "Stop hitting on my girl."

Skid flings me an *I-told-you-so* smirk, picks up his rod, and wades out into the river. "Dude, I wasn't hitting on her…she lost her fly in the willows and…."

Brian isn't even listening to him.

CHAPTER TWENTY

With rafting season beginning on May first, Brian and Skid need to get paddle-ready, so we head toward the river with a raft and all the gear. I follow Brian and Skid, with each carrying a side of the raft and talking with excitement. Brian has been getting in shape by hiking and scouting the reachable sections of the river from the shore.

The anticipation has been running through Brian like a current of electricity. Even our lovemaking has changed, becoming high energy rather than slow and hibernating like it was all winter.

The guide shack is empty, but soon it will be filled with the seasonal guides and their gear. The higher temperatures warm the juniper and sage and give the entire town an earthy scent. It is the same scent that had filled our car as Amber and I drove around to the backside of Mount Hood singing *Teenage Flight*. We were so stupid. No...*I* was stupid. Amber did not want to come in the first place.

Now, I see one of Amber's red and white missing posters everywhere I turn. They are in the windows of the mercantile and all the restaurants and shops. We had so few memories in this town that I cannot forget a single one, and they play on a loop inside my head.

In the background, I hear Brian and Skid laughing, sharing a story. I'm not following it, but their words float toward me. *Flatlander, couldn't paddle worth shit, hit the hole.*

The guys set the raft down, half in the water and half on the bank. Brian tosses me a life jacket. As I slide my arms in, sweat starts to form on my neck and forehead even though it is only about seventy-five degrees out. Before I even pull the straps to tighten it, it feels like a giant hand is squeezing all the air from my lungs.

My last time on the river was the trip with Amber. I breathe in deep but cannot get enough air. It wasn't my last time. I had been on the river another time that I have no memory of. My head feels fuzzy, so I bend over and take some deep breaths.

"What's wrong?" Brian asks.

"Nothing." I do not want to be *that* type of girlfriend—the type too prissy or scared to have fun. Rafting is Brian's passion, and I want to be a part of it. I have always been brave, but I can feel the fear rising in me, and it feels like a swarm of moths circling in my chest. I am not myself anymore. Somewhere behind me, a mourning dove coos its haunting call—that soft throat-cooing soulful sound that follows me wherever I go in this town.

Brian comes to check my vest. He tugs on the straps and talks to me about river safety. Skid stands behind him, watching, blurred into the background. Brian's voice is muffled as if he is talking through a pillow. I need to get myself together. Breathe.

I am with two of the best guides on the river. They will not let anything happen to me. I need to let the fear wash over me. I am safe. The fear is only in my mind.

"You okay?" Brian asks. "You don't have to come."

"I'm fine." I force a smile up to Brian, but I can tell he does not believe me.

"I won't let anything happen to you." He pulls me close with our life jackets creating a barrier between us. I wish we were skin-to-skin in our bed with his arms wrapped around me.

"I'm good. Let's go."

Brian releases me and heads toward the raft. He pushes it further into the water, holding it steady for me to climb in. As I lift my leg to swing it over the tube, Skid reaches a hand out for me to take. I grab it, and just as my leg touches the hard rubber of the raft, everything goes black. My eyes are wide open, but there is no light.

The next thing I know, I am in Brian's arms, and he is carrying me. I have a flash of memory from that night. I remember floating with Brian's arm wrapped around my chest, moving backward through the water in the dark. He swam with me, reaching out in strokes, jerky, and pulling me toward the shore.

"I remember," I say into Brian's chest as he carries me. "I remember you saving me."

CHAPTER TWENTY-ONE

Rafting season has been ramping up. The sidewalks and shop windows are clean. Happy Cow Hamburger opened yesterday, filling the air with the scent of grilled meat and deep fryer oil. A new display of used clothes decorates the window of the What-Not-Shop. And a new faded red beater car is parked outside the guide shack of Wild River Rafting. Now, with the schools and universities out and all the guides arriving, it will be one long party, and I don't know if I am up for it.

I walk into the Lodell Mercantile, an old-fashioned white country store with a big covered porch. It has a huge ice machine out front and smells like lunch meat and sour milk inside. The mercantile is just like any country store with basic food items. It's nothing fancy. It has aisles of paper goods, cleaning products, boxed and bagged foods, a refrigerator with cold stuff, and a meat counter.

I grab a bag of Fritos and take them to the counter, thankful that Shelly is behind the register instead of Ted. He always cracks jokes about Brian and me "shacking up" or asking me when we are getting married.

My throat tightens at the sight of Amber's missing poster

taped to the side of the cash register. They used her Myspace profile picture, the one I took of her the day we skipped school to hang out in the woods behind the skate park.

"Anything else?" Shelly asks as she scans the chips and sticks them in a bag for me.

"No." I pay her, take the bag, and head back to the house where Brian is cooking a welcome home dinner for Jake and Erin.

I hope, but I'm also afraid that rafting season will bring back the memories of that night. Maybe something, even something small, will crack it all open, and I will know what happened to Amber. I hope she is still alive. I don't know what that will mean—maybe that she was kidnapped and is someone's sex slave. Or…I don't know what to hope for. I just want Amber.

In the distance, a cloud of dust rises beneath the railroad trestle. Any car, truck, or guide bus coming along the dirt road through Old Lodell drags a tail of dirt behind them all the way until they reach the pavement of town. It is probably another guide returning from their winter gig as ski patrol on Mount Hood or Mount Bachelor—or, as in Jake and Erin's case, college.

When I get home, the front door is standing wide open. I'm surprised to see Jake and Erin sitting at our kitchen table since we didn't expect them for another half an hour. Brian stands at the stove, bareback and beautiful. The house smells of baked beans and marijuana.

I set the bag on the counter next to Brian.

Jake flicks his lighter over the bowl of his pipe and takes a deep drag. He holds the smoke in, then chokes out, "You're still here?" as he exhales.

"Knock it off," Erin says to Jake, taking the pipe from him and putting it to her own mouth.

Brian turns and looks at me with an apologetic smile.

All last summer, I never once saw Erin without her blonde braids and a tan that seemed impossible for a girl with such light hair and blue eyes. Now, she looks more suitable for giving ski lessons in the Swiss Alps than guiding in a tiny desert rafting town—until she speaks or punches someone in the arm.

"You look beautiful," I say to her.

"Thanks. It won't last long. I've been in university mode, wasting away behind my laptop screen and trying to blend in with the city girls."

I give Brian a kiss and run my hand down his naked back.

"Have they found your friend yet?" Jake asks. "What's her name?"

"Amber," I say. My cheeks begin to tingle, and I can feel a quivering in my nerves. I kiss Brian on the arm and head toward the bathroom.

"Knock that shit off," I hear Erin say as I close the bathroom door. "You know they didn't. Why do you always flick her so much shit?"

"Just having fun," Jake says.

"No, you're giving her shit," Erin says, "and you know it."

I sit on the edge of the bathtub and close my eyes. This is going to be a long summer. I am the outsider. I am the one who needs to adapt and fit in—or I will lose Brian. I've dealt with dicks like Jake my whole life. I'm just grateful I don't have to live in the same house as him. I do have to say, though, it feels good to have Erin stick up for me.

I splash water on my face and step back into the kitchen just as Skid comes in with a twelve-pack of Rainier beer. The case already has a hole torn into the top, and he has a beer in his hand. "Anyone want some Vitamin R?" He plunks the pack onto the table.

"Need any help?" I ask Brian, who stands stirring the beans.

He turns and gives me a kiss. "It's just about done."

I lean over the steaming pot. The baked beans bubble with chunks of hot dog rounds floating in the liquid. Brian opens the oven door and sticks a toothpick into the center of a pan of cornbread. "About ten more minutes."

"Brian…" Skid calls, causing Brian to turn around just in time to catch a can of beer hurtling through the air at his face.

"Thanks." Brian cracks it open, then puts his hand around my waist, pulling me to him. "The Buckskin should be fun tonight."

I force a smile at Brian. To tell the truth, going to the Buckskin is getting old. At first, playing pool, throwing darts, or bullshitting with everyone was new and a way to get to know everyone in town. But the downside to that is that everyone knows me, and I cannot use my fake ID. Being the only sober one in our group is annoying. And now, with all the rafters arriving, it will be packed—one big loud music, boob flashing, drunk, stumbling party.

"Beer?" Skid asks, holding a can out to me.

"Contributing to the delinquency of a minor," Jake says.

It's hard to believe that Jake and Skid are cousins. They are nothing alike. Skid can't even manage to work as a guide and keep his front yard clean. Jake just finished his sophomore year at Oregon State. He is majoring in agricultural economics, whatever that is, then going to law school. So he freely offers legal advice to everyone.

Ignoring Jake, I take the beer and crack it open.

Brian slides the pan of cornbread out of the oven. He tosses a potholder on the table and sets the cornbread on top of it. He throws down the other potholder and clunks the pot of beans and hot dogs on top of that one. I take five plates from the cupboard and pass them around as Erin gets the silverware.

"Did you see those two girls who checked into the Whitehorse?" Skid asks.

"Yep." Jake says, "Did you see the ass on the blondie?"

Erin punches him in the arm so hard I bet it will leave a knot. Jake is lucky to have Erin. I have no idea why she stays with him, other than they grew up together—and that Jake's dad, Doc, is helping her pay for college. She wants to be a veterinarian, and that is expensive.

"I'd like to get a piece of that brunette," Skid says, shoveling a giant spoonful of beans and hot dog into his mouth. "Her tits were practically popping out of her shirt."

Brian's lips are pressed tight. He drags a butter knife through the cornbread, mutilating it into crumbly yellow squares.

Skid gives his food a couple of open-mouthed chews, then before swallowing, he says, "I think I need to break me off a piece of that!"

There is instant silence. I look up, and Jake has an odd, almost primal spark in his eyes as he nods at Skid. Brian shakes his head without looking up from his plate.

"Why don't you shut the hell up," Brian says to Skid. "You are the biggest dumb ass."

I look over at Brian, and he gives me an apologetic shrug, but there is something deeper and boiling that he is holding down.

As usual, as the sun starts to go down, the wind kicks up through the gorge. A swirling gust slams the front door shut so hard we all flinch. One second later, the squeal of tires screech from outside, followed by the frantic yipping of an injured dog.

We all jump up and run to the door to see a little brown mini truck stopped in the middle of the road. Both doors stand wide open, and a guy with curly blonde hair kneels down beside a yelping Jack Russell mix. The poor thing tries to get up, but its two back legs won't move. Another guy stands on the dog's other side, looking pale and in shock.

"Dude, it just ran out in front of us," the guy raises his head and looks up.

It feels as if someone punched me in the stomach. It is Matt, the guide who had been with Amber that night. I stare at him, trying to see if he remembers me—to see if he will flinch or look guilty.

Erin runs to the dog, taking charge. Brian told me that she has always doctored the dogs in town, even as a child. People start crowding around. All the little ragged Lodell children wiggle through to the front. I recognize Dustin, the boy who always comes to visit Brian, and a few of the Stewart children.

Dustin turns to a little girl in a blue dress with band-aids on her knees. "Go get Doc."

"Dude, is this your dog?" Matt asks Skid, who is now kneeling beside Erin and trying to comfort the poor animal by stroking its head.

Matt does not show that he recognizes me at all. If he had taken Amber away with him, wouldn't he know I'm her best friend?

Everything seems to be happening in slow motion. Erin runs her hands over the dog, checking him as Skid holds him, whispering and trying to calm him. I have a fuzzy sound in my ears, and I feel queasy.

"I'm sorry. I didn't even see it."

Matt's friend just stands there in a pair of cargo shorts and no shirt looking like he is about to throw up. The *yawp, yawp, yawp* of the dog is ear piercing and constant. Several children cry out loud or silently wipe at tears that wash lines down their dirt-stained faces.

"For fuck's sake, put the thing out of its misery," Jake says, unclipping a folding knife from his shorts and opening the blade.

"I think his back legs are broken, but he will be fine," Erin says to Jake. "If you can't tolerate it, go home."

The girl in the blue dress finally appears, holding Doc's hand and trying to pull him up the street faster than he can manage at his age. I avoid Doc. Seeing him makes me remember waking up in the hospital without Amber. My chest feels hollow, as if there is nothing in it but my heartbeat pounding faster and faster. As Doc steps past, I catch a whiff of his heavy cologne, and it makes me feel nauseous.

"Isn't there a vet in town?" I ask Brian.

"No. Doc takes care of the animals when he can. That's why he's helping Erin through school. When she's done, she will be the town's vet."

Doc has a small black doctor's bag in one hand. He pulls a handkerchief from his back pocket and wipes the sweat from his forehead before setting his bag on the street.

Doc looks to Jake. "I didn't know you were back."

"We just got in. I'll be home for dinner," Jake says.

"Hope you're cooking something."

"Erin will feed us."

She gives Jake a dirty look but nods. "Yeah, I'll feed you."

According to Erin, ever since Jake's mother died, he and Doc only eat microwave dinners or canned soup.

Doc opens his bag and takes out a small medicine vial and a syringe. He twists off the cap, sticks the needle into the bottle, tips it upside down, and draws in some medicine. "Hold him still," Doc says.

Erin loops her arm under the dog's neck, holding him to her with one hand and stabilizing his front leg with the other. Doc squirts some rubbing alcohol onto the leg before sliding the needle into a vein. In less than a minute, the poor dog goes silent and limp.

"Thank God!" Jake says, popping open another beer. The *pshttt* sound is loud and completely disrespectful.

I cannot believe Doc did that right in front of all the children. I cannot believe Erin and Brian let him. Doc scoops the motionless dog up into his arms. It is pressed against his big barrel chest as he and Erin walk off with the children trailing behind them.

Matt and his friend look like they are about to pass out.

"Why don't you pull your truck out of the street then come have a beer with us," Brian says.

Matt hops into his truck, turns over the engine, and rolls it to the side of the road as the crowd breaks up and everyone starts wandering away.

With my heart beating fast and nausea coming up, I move close to Brian. "I can't believe Doc did that right in front of all the children."

"Did what in front of all the children?"

"Killed the dog."

"He didn't kill it. He sedated it, and he's taking it to the hospital. Why would you think that?"

"I don't know…there was just so much going on. I just…"

Brian puts his arm around me, and I feel the warmth of his breath on my scalp. "You need to learn to trust people."

CHAPTER TWENTY-TWO

HIM

I TAP OUT A CAMEL, LIGHT IT, AND SET IT IN THE ASHTRAY. Amber's hair, bound in copper, sits in my open tackle box. I pull out a single strand and run the soft silkiness of it across my face. It catches and slides through my beard stubble. I click on the light and clamp a size twelve nymph hook in the jaw of my vice. A Pheasant Tail Nymph will be the perfect fly for Amber.

It's been nine months, and they still have not found her.

The brown thread slips through the tube of my bobbin, then I cut two inches of copper wire and lay it across the hook shank. Taking smooth and even thread wraps, I bind it down, my hands winding like the river.

I snip about eight fibers from a pheasant tail, place them over the curved end of the hook, and give them a good twelve wraps. Nobody will ever find her, and I will never tell. She is mine.

Laying the end of Amber's hair across the hook, I secure the strand to the shank then wrap the pheasant herl down, creating the body of my fly.

Amber didn't know Shawna, but they are sisters in death. Shawna with jet-black hair. The single strand of amber hair hangs thin and much more delicate than Shawna's. My cheeks tingle, and I can hear my breath as I run it between my thumb and index finger until I'm at the tip. I pinch it and slowly wind it around and around with evenly spaced wraps.

Amber's thighs were so soft, and I could do anything I wanted to her. She let out tiny, breathy moans. The blood begins to pulsate and surge through my veins. I get to the end of the shank and bind the strand right behind the eye. It is time to take another girl. Or two.

I spiral the copper wire around the body, over the pheasant herl and Amber hair, giving it some weight, segmentation, and flash. Trout love things that flash and shimmer beneath the surface.

I bind down more pheasant tail fibers and pull my bobbin down, opening up two inches of thread. I choose an emerald green prism dubbing, the same color as Amber's eyes, for more shine and sparkle. I lick my fingers and wind it around the thread for a nice plump thorax.

Emmy is the one I released. She is a living reminder of my generosity, and she better appreciate it. If she starts remembering any more, I will bind her to me in death, and she will be mine forever, a water nymph just like Amber.

My hands quiver as I tie the fibers down, winding and winding until my thread snaps. *Shit!* This fly had been perfect, and thoughts of Emmy ruined it. I should not have let her live. I hold the thread down with the tip of my scissors and drip two beads of head cement to hold it in place.

My insides churn, and it feels as if I have a bubble of air caught in my throat. My blood rises. Why did I let Emmy do this to me? I inhale and breathe out slow, emptying my lungs.

Emmy better stay silent. She does not want to witness the raging and thunder in my nature. She must respect me and beware of my strength, for I cannot control my own power.

I turn the knob on my vice and let the fly drop into the palm of my hand. An Amber-Haired Nymph. I open my fly box and hook it next to all the Amber-Haired Caddisflies, the jet-black Woolly Buggers, and Adam's dry flies. The ash of the Camel is long, like a snake shedding and scorching away its skin. The pressure drops, and I calm.

I lay out my hair color charts and run my hand over the photos. Over the shiny ash brown, ginger, burgundy, tan, auburn, copper, bronze, golden blonde, honey blonde, ginger, and platinum strands. My fingertips run over the indentation of the Xs over the amber and jet-black color samples.

Two new girls have come to town. One looks strawberry blonde and, if I had to guess, an espresso brown—but I cannot be certain yet. I will find out tonight.

CHAPTER TWENTY-THREE

A SUMMER THUNDERSTORM TURNS THE RIVER A DEEP GRAY-BLUE and darkens the sky behind Buckskin Mary's. We have not had a drop of rain yet, but the dampness brings out the scent of the earth. Live music blares out of the Buckskin for the first time this season. Brian and I came over during the winter, but it is different with no rafters. When it is not crowded, the patched and repaired cracks and fist-sized holes in the walls stand out, and the floor is stained with grime-filled gouges in the linoleum.

With the music and the line of people waiting for Darryl to check their IDs, I cannot stop thinking about Amber. Just last Summer, we stood here worried he would confiscate our fake IDs. Brian takes my hand as we head to the back of the line.

"Your hands are ice cold," he says and pulls me close to him.

A bolt of lightning streaks across the dark clouds, followed by a deep and rumbling thunder that causes several girls to shriek.

Darryl sits behind the podium in a black shirt and backward baseball cap. His puffy red chin beard is longer than last year and hangs down, almost to the collar of his shirt. He checks the IDs of the guy and girl in front of us by holding them up and comparing them to the couple. I try not to look at the tattoo on his arm. The skull is nothing but bone and shadow with raging water in shades of blue and white crashing up from behind it.

At our turn, Brian nods at Darryl and pulls me forward. We don't need to show our IDs. Everyone in town knows us—Brian and the girl who never left.

"Whoa there," Darryl says, "No minors in the bar."

When his blue-white eyes move from Brian to me, they shift into a glare that makes my skin crawl.

"You're kidding me," Brian says. "She's been coming here all winter."

"It ain't winter anymore, and the bar is packed. Nobody can monitor if she is drinking or not."

"I will monitor her."

"Just doing my job."

"Dude, can you step aside?" A guy, holding the hand of a very irritated-looking blonde girl, says. "We would like to get in."

Brian and I move out of their way.

"Wait here," Brian says to me. He goes in and disappears into the crowd of people as the band starts playing *Hit Me With Your Best Shot*.

Everyone in line stares at me like I am a complete idiot. The blonde girl gives me a snotty smirk as she walks past me and into the bar. If I cannot come to the Buckskin, what will that do to my relationship with Brian? Darryl sits behind the podium, checking the IDs as a crack of lightning flashes in the open doorway, setting off a line of shrieks from the girls in line. The people inside are so oblivious they don't even notice the coming storm.

Brian finally returns with Rose Unger beside him. She's not smiling, but she doesn't look upset either. If not for the hard-ass expression always on her face, Rose might be pretty. She is tall and thin with suspiciously big boobs compared to the rest of her body. Her hair is dyed blonde, and it is thin and always pulled back into a ponytail. I bet she was gorgeous when she was young, but she is skeletal-thin for a woman in her fifties with deep-set eyes and high cheekbones. I see where Skid gets his looks, but I cannot tell if she has a man face or Skid has a woman face.

When she walks up behind Darryl, Brian grabs my hand and leads me inside. The bar is hopping, just like last summer, with girls in short shorts and skimpy tops and guys slamming down shots and playing beer pong at the back table.

Erin sits alone at our usual half-circle booth.

"Where's Jake and Skid?" Brian asks.

"Moving some furniture at the Whitehorse. It has something to do with a leak in the roof that had been repaired, and they need to get the furniture back in it."

As soon as we sit down, Rose Unger motions to Brian on her way back to the bar. He gets up and goes to her. Brian's head is down as Rose talks into his ear. He shrugs his shoulders and says something to her. She pauses a moment, then nods back. Whatever it is, Brian looks reluctant. Behind him, three girls flash their boobs at Doug, and he lines up their free shots.

A group of guides from Wild River Rafting climb into the booth next to ours. One of them has a man bun, and none of them are locals. They only come for the summer season and live in the guide shack at their outfitters. One of them is Matt, the guy who hit the dog…and the one who was flirting with Amber that night.

"Hey Chad," Matt says, "saw how you took Wapinitia today."

He looks over to the other guides. "He rammed the rocks with the bow and turned a hundred eighty degrees, taking the rapids backward."

"The dumb-ass girls in my raft today couldn't paddle worth shit," Chad says. "They wouldn't listen to my paddle commands at all. And when they did, they were just lily dipping."

"At least they were hot as hell," another one says.

"Yeah, I'm waiting for them to come in tonight. Maybe they have other talents."

"I'll have to let them know that a good guide would have taken them through the rapids bow first."

They all laugh except for Chad, whose only answer is, "Fuck you."

Brian returns with his hands in his pockets. "I need to go help Jake and Skid move some shit at the Whitehorse."

"Tonight? Can't it wait?"

"No. The room is rented out for tomorrow by three o'clock, but we will be on the river." Brian looks frustrated and gives me an apologetic half-smile before he turns to leave.

"Doc and Jake have no idea how to run that place," Erin says. "They need to hire a manager. Jake's mom took care of everything, and now, those two are a mess."

I do not trust Jake, and I know he does not approve of me. The whole thing about a leak could be bullshit and them just trying to get Brian away from me. Maybe so they can hook up with those two girls they had been talking about. Except for Rose. I don't know how they would get her to go along with it.

A guide in the booth next to ours gets up and approaches two girls dancing together at the edge of the dance floor. He asks one of them to dance and leads her away from her friend, who then stands there alone just like Brian and I had done to Amber. When Amber had taken hold of my beer and Brian had hold of my hand, for one moment, I was connected to both of them at the same time—until I let go and left Amber all by herself.

"You okay?" Erin asks. "You look a bit pale and pasty there."

"I was just thinking about Amber."

Erin puts her arm around me, and I appreciate it. Erin's arm is strong and hard, nothing like Amber's soft touch.

"Evening, girls."

I look up to see Rose Unger standing at our booth holding a beer and Pepsi.

She sets the drinks down in front of us. "On the house."

Erin's eyebrows pinch together. "Uh…thanks, Rose."

She gives a single nod then turns her head toward me. "You planning on staying in this town?"

My throat instantly closes off, and I don't know how to answer her. She is so intimidating and direct. Brian had told me that Rose is practically his mother because she took him in when his mother died. She raised him from the time he was eight years old.

I manage to squeeze out, "I hope so."

"If you want to be a part of this town and part of Brian's life, you will need to pull your weight."

My head spins. Do people in town think I am using Brian? Does he believe that? Brian never said anything to me…

"Mary needs help cleaning the Whitehorse. You start tomorrow. Be there at nine o'clock." Without waiting for me to answer, she turns and heads back to the bar.

"Well then," Erin says. "I guess you got a job."

"She's scary as shit."

"Tell me about it. Rose and Joyce used to run this town. Most people think Russ and Doc are in charge, but hell no. Russ and Doc can't run shit. And ever since Joyce died, it's only Rose."

The band stops playing.

"We're going to take a short break," the lead singer says into the microphone just before someone turns on the jukebox.

As the crowd on the dance floor thins out, I see the two girls Jake and Skid had mentioned earlier. It's a relief to know the girls are not at the Whitehorse, and maybe they really did need help moving furniture. The girls start making out and running their hands all over one another.

The guys around them hoot and cheer them on. They ignore the girls they had been dancing with and move closer. The brunette wears a skimpy white dress that looks more like a nightie, a black cowgirl hat with silver studs around the brim, and black boots. The blonde is wearing jean short-shorts, a skin-tight halter top, and a pair of turquoise tennis shoes with rhinestones on them.

The blonde runs her hands up the bare legs of the brunette, lifting her dress so high I can see a red thong wedged in her skinny bare ass and stretching across her hip bones. The circle of guys close in and block my view.

"How do you stand it?" I ask Erin.

"Stand what?"

"Having a boyfriend around all these skanky girls."

Erin lifts her beer in the air. "By drinking. And if Jake acts like an ass around any of them, I flick the same shit back at him. Look at all these hot guys." She tips the bottle to her lips and takes a big swig.

Brian finally comes back without Jake or Skid. He sits beside me with a sullen expression and takes a long drink of the beer Rose had brought for Erin. After a minute, he puts his arm around me and kisses the side of my head. "Sorry about that."

"Where's Jake and Skid?"

"They had some other shit to do."

Without a word, Erin scoots out of the booth, grabs the hand of some random guy by the bar, and drags him to the dance floor. He has blonde hair, cut short in a military-looking crew cut and huge biceps. At least she chose someone bigger than Jake who can hold his own if it comes down to blows.

On the dance floor, Erin slowly turns around and backs up

to the guy. Brian shakes his head and takes another long drink. The guy puts his hands on Erin's hips, and she starts grinding her ass against his crotch. They stay on the dance floor for two songs with Erin hanging all over him. I can tell that Brian disapproves. He sits there with every muscle tense, and his jaw clamped shut.

"Where's Erin?"

I about jump out of my skin at Jake's voice. He stands at the table with two beers in his hand. Brian shrugs and does not say a word.

Just as Jake looks toward the dance floor, Erin reaches her hands back and slides them into the guy's pockets, guiding him in rhythm with her ass.

Jake clunks the beers onto the table and heads straight for Erin. He never has a problem yelling at her in public. We are all used to it—but the tourists are not, and they are causing a scene. Brian gets out of the booth, walks up behind Jake, and puts his hand on his arm. Jake jerks his head around, looking ready to throw some punches. Brian says something. Jake closes his eyes and stands there, taking huge breaths. He glares at Erin without saying a word for a good ten seconds. When he does say something, it looks barely under control, and the two separate.

The poor guy Erin was dancing with stands there looking confused.

Brian comes back to the booth. "Sorry about that. I'll be back. I have some damage control to take care of." He goes straight over to Jake and leads him to the pool table.

Erin comes back looking satisfied with herself. She picks up the beer Jake had left for her and raises it in the air toward me.

"To getting even," she says. "Watch and learn."

We click bottles and put them to our lips.

"Oh my God, look who's here," Erin says.

I turn to see Becky Stewart at the bar talking with Big Doug.

"Stay clear of her," Erin's words start to slur. "She has a thing for Brian."

"Becky? The llama girl?"

Erin lets out a snort of laughter. "Llama? Oh my God, she does look like a llama."

"I can not imagine Becky and Brian together." The *Becky Sucks Dick* graffiti in the tunnel pops into my head and makes me feel sick.

"Yeah, neither can Brian." Erin gets really close to my face. "If Becky is ever nice to you, then you better look out."

Skid appears in the entrance, looking as scraggly as one of the town dogs. He glances around until his eyes lock on Jake and Brian. "I feel sorry for Skid."

"You and everyone else in town, even his own brother and sisters."

"He has a brother and sisters? Where are they?"

"They moved away from Lodell—and especially away from their mother—the moment they turned eighteen. They are all doing well, and then there is Skid, guiding and laying around on his ass in the off-season—a true TLR."

"TLR?"

"Typical Lodell Resident. He'll be here his whole life and probably take over Buckskin Mary's when his mom passes on."

Brian is bent over the pool table, taking a shot. All last winter, we barely got out of bed or off the couch to cook or take walks between our lovemaking.

"Is Brian a TLR?"

Erin's eyes widen. "I…I didn't mean Brian. Skid is an Unger and has a family who will pay for him to go to college or trade school. Jake is getting his degree, he owns Rimrock Outfitters, and several houses he rents out."

I want to say, *like Brian's house?*…but she is backpedaling, and I sort of feel sorry for her. Sort of.

She brings the subject back to Skid. "Did you know that Skid is not his real name?"

"I never really thought about it, but it sounds like a nickname."

"It is." Erin smiles. "His name is Dylan."

"Dylan? He doesn't look like a Dylan. I picture Dylans as country boys with flannel shirts and a bit more...how do I say it nicely? Testosterone."

"Exactly!" She lets out a laugh. "When we were little, *Dylan* always ran around in his tighty-whities. And...how should I say it...he wasn't real good about wiping himself."

I had just taken a sip of my Pepsi and about spit it out across the table. I manage to keep it in, but it burns my sinuses. "He was named after a skid mark?"

We both laugh out loud, but then I look over at Brian. My heart aches, and I feel a bit nauseous. He lost his mother, but he still has this whole town filled with people who have known him his entire life. He may be a TLR, but he is lucky, and I love him.

Erin's laugh starts to fade, and her words string out, "...his brother Emmett...is...he is...."

"Are you okay?"

Erin shudders and is so drunk she knocks over her beer. It glugs from the bottle into a puddle on the table.

"Brian..." I put my arm around Erin and yell, "Erin, what's wrong? Brian..."

The next thing I know, Brian is beside the table with Jake right behind him. I scoot out so they can help her and feel someone watching me—not Erin or the guys. I turn around to see Becky's face staring straight at me from behind the bar.

"What's wrong with her?" I ask.

"Nothing," Jake answers me instead of Brian. "She's just drunk."

"She's only had two beers," I say.

"Maybe two here, but she's been drinking ever since we got back to town today."

As Jake and Brian guide Erin to the door, her head bobs on her bent neck. Outside, the storm completely surrounds us. With each crack of lightning, the sky lights up the black thunderclouds, the rimrock cliffs, and the shapes of Brian and Jake keeping Erin on her feet.

CHAPTER TWENTY-FOUR

The string of red plastic porch lights on the front of Jake and Erin's house swings in the wind. Their house is white clapboard with a tin roof and two plastic lawn chairs on the porch. Jake pushes open the unlocked door, and they take her inside just in time for her to vomit all over the floor.

"Damn it," Jake says, "That's disgusting."

Their house is a nice two-bedroom, but it is littered with beer cans, textbooks, and dead potted plants.

"Grab the blanket off our bed and put it on the kitchen floor," Jake says to me. "I'll be damned if she's barfing in our bed all night."

Their bedroom is dim and smells like beer and unwashed bedsheets. I grab the blanket without switching on the light, and it makes me feel dirty to touch their bedding. I spread it on the floor, and they lower Erin onto it. For a second, she looks up at me, and I cannot breathe. Something about her eyes reminds me of Amber, and I feel like I should not leave her lying there.

"Emmy," Brian says. "You okay?"

The entire house reeks of her vomit.

"Can you clean that shit up?" Jake asks me in a way that does not seem like a question.

"No." Brian takes my arm and leads me to the door. "You need to take care of your own shit."

Jake's entire body tenses, and it seems as if he will throw a punch at Brian. Instead, he grabs the blanket and drags Erin toward the bathroom until only her head and shoulders are through the door, but the rest of her is still in the living room.

Outside, the thunderclouds cover the town with only a slight glow of moonlight on the far rim of the canyon. Lightening cracks and lights up the underbelly of the clouds.

"Why were you so harsh?" I ask as soon as we are away from their house.

Brian does not answer me.

"Something strange is going on."

He stops and faces me. "What do you mean?" That deep pool of sadness comes to his eyes again. When he looks at me like that, it makes me want to apologize—to stop whatever pain I am causing him.

"Erin only had a couple of beers." Fat drops of warm rain splatter on my bare shoulders. "She cannot be that wasted. It's like she was drugged or something."

The smell of damp earth and sage saturate the air.

"She was probably half-plastered before she even came to the Buckskin tonight." Brian takes my hand, and we start walking. "That's what Erin does."

The moment we get home, Brian puts his hands on my cheeks and pulls me toward him for a kiss.

"I'm starting to remember," I say just before our lips touch. "I've been getting flashes about that night."

Brian backs away from me and stares deep into my eyes. "What do you remember?"

"Not much. I've just been getting flashes, almost like déjà vu. I'm not even sure they are real."

"Whatever you do," Brian's intense glare scares me, "do not say a word to anyone but me."

I try to nod, but he holds my face so tight in his hands that I cannot move it.

"Promise me, Emmy."

My eyes fill with tears. "I promise."

Brian puts his mouth to mine and presses hard, kissing me. His hands reach up the back of my shirt, expertly unhooking my bra.

Lightning cracks outside and lights up the window. It was just a flash, but I can swear that I saw the figure of a man outside.

"Someone's out there," I say.

Brian looks toward the dark window. "It's just the tree."

Still locked together, we move to the bedroom and drop down onto the bed. We make love just like we did when we first met—as if we still cannot get enough. We wrap our bodies, skin to skin, sweating with the warm thunderstorm raging outside. We kiss so hard that it feels as if I cannot breathe except through Brian.

Afterward, Brian collapses on top of me. I love the feel of his weight. The solidness of his body makes me feel safe. He slides off and rolls onto his back with his arms stretched out.

"Uhhhh," Brian says. "We need to get an air conditioner."

Brian turns onto his side and stares at me. He reaches out and pushes the damp hair off my forehead. He has such a loving but sad look on his face. My breath catches in my throat, and my heart starts racing. What will I do when he is tired of me? Nothing in my life has ever lasted.

"I'm glad I met you."

I let out a laugh.

"That's funny?"

"Relief." My throat feels thick. "I thought you were going to ask me to leave. You look so sad."

He pulls me to him, joining our damp bodies, and I lay my head on his shoulder.

"I was thinking that I do not deserve you," he says.

I raise my head and look up at him. I can tell he wants to tell me something. Something terrible that he is struggling with.

The screen door squeals on its hinges, followed by three pounding knocks.

"You've got to be shitting me," Brian says.

"What were you going to tell me?"

Brian stares at me for a moment, then shakes his head. "Later."

Someone knocks again.

"Hang on," Brian yells before kissing my forehead, sitting up on the side of the bed, and pulling his shorts on. I slide my feet beneath the sheets, then lift them until my breasts are covered. Brian pulls the bedroom door partially shut, but I can still see through to the living room. He opens the door.

Jake stands in the doorway, acting odd. He seems excited and anxious and says something to Brian that sounds like, *Come on*, but I am not sure. Is something wrong with Erin?

"Sorry, dude," Brian says.

Thoughts start swirling in my head. Jake does not like me. Is he trying to get Brian to go out and party with him and Skid? I do not trust Jake one bit.

Brian comes back into the bedroom, leans over, and kisses me. "I'll be right back."

I can tell he does not want to do whatever he is going to do.

"What's wrong?" I ask. "Is Erin okay?"

"She's fine. I'll be right back."

This happened several times last year too. There were nights when Jake or Skid would come for Brian in the middle of the night, and each time, he refused to go. Why is he going now? Now that the newness of our relationship is gone, maybe he will start going off with his friends and leaving me alone.

Brian steps outside into the darkness and the storm. Damn Jake. My heart starts racing so fast it makes my head spin, and I want to scream. I picture Jake taking Brian back to the Buckskin because he needs a better wingman than Skid.

I get out of bed and search around in the dark for my clothes. I lift the edge of the bedsheets that hang all the way to the ground and swipe my hand beneath the bed before I remember that Brian had dropped them on the living room floor. Dammit! I don't want to be that sort of a girlfriend—the sort who doesn't trust and always has to check up on her man.

"Sorry, dude." Brian's voice comes from outside.

He is still here and on the side of the house.

"Skid said she's been a stage-five clinger all winter." Jake's loud drunken voice yells out, "Fuck her!"

"Come on," Brian says. "Keep it down."

I go to the open window, stand with my back against the wall, and listen.

"I don't need to keep it down. This is my town. I own this damn town."

"Go home to Erin."

"Hell no. She's passed out on the floor puking," Jake says. "Come with me."

"I can't," Brian says.

"You don't know what you're missing."

"It's not right."

"You need to dump her. She's turning you into a little bitch."

"No," Brian says. "It's just wrong."

"Gods do what they want," Jake slurs. "Gods don't have the same rules."

"Go home to Erin."

"Bro, you're no better than us, and you know it." Jake's voice fades as if he is walking away. "She's got you pussy-whipped, but you'll get tired of it and come crawling back."

I jump back into bed and slide beneath the sheet. The front

door closes, and I hear Brian's footsteps coming toward the bedroom. His side of the bed sinks as he lowers himself down, not taking his clothes off or getting beneath the sheet. I breathe in, smelling the scent of our lovemaking still on him, mixed with the smell of beer and the sweet earthy damp of the thunderstorm.

"Are you asleep?" Brian whispers into the darkness.

"No."

Is he waiting for me to fall asleep so he can slip out? I think about all the times he has gone for *walks* by the river, and now I wonder if that is what he really does.

As those thoughts swirl around, I feel Brian get back out of bed. My throat tightens as his silhouette steps before the moonlit window. He pulls his shirt off and drapes it over Otis before kissing his fingers and putting them on the box of his mother's ashes. "Goodnight, Mom," Brian says before sliding his cargo shorts down and stepping out of them. He doesn't know who his father is, other than he was a fly fisherman named Bob who had come to town one weekend.

My love for Brian makes my heart ache. It feels as if we are on the verge of something crumbling away. He will get tired of choosing me over his friends. It's bound to happen—it always does.

The loud rumbling of a motorcycle comes from outside, growing louder and louder until it passes by our house and fades off. Everyone in town knows the sound of Don Stewart's Harley. He frequently leaves town in the middle of the night, not returning until dawn. He doesn't even try to hide it. I don't blame Don for needing an escape from his llama wife and six kids, but why is that always acceptable for a man to leave and have his space while a woman has to stay in the house and wait for him?

Brian climbs back in bed with me, laying on top of the covers as the sound of Don's motorcycle fades away, all the way out of Lodell, even during a thunderstorm. Jake's words, *Stage-five clinger* plays on a loop in my head. I thought Skid liked me. Why did he say that? Have I been too clingy? When I lost Amber, I lost everything. I have nobody but Brian. Damn them! They can ruin everything for Brian and me. I know Brian will never choose me over his life-long friends.

I turn on my side, away from Brian, and he curls around me. He runs his hand up my belly and cups my breast as I drift off to sleep with the beat of his heart against my back.

Something wakes me. The bed moves as Brian slides out. I watch, hoping he is only going to take a leak. His silhouette moves before the window again, and he pulls his shirt back on.

"Are you leaving?"

"Just for a bit. I can't sleep."

"In the thunderstorm? Come back to bed. I'll hold you."

"I think the storm has passed. I need to get my head straight."

I suddenly feel heavy, like my body has been filled with rocks sinking me into the bed. My face stings, and tears rise in my eyes. Breathe. Hold it together.

"I love you, Brian."

"I love you too," he says before he bends down and kisses me. He wipes my tears away and kisses me again. "It's okay. I won't be gone long."

Whenever Brian goes out, he barely makes it back before dawn. He comes in and crawls onto the bed, too exhausted to take his clothes off or get beneath the sheets. I always lay there unable to sleep, feeling the coolness of the night on his body and wondering where he has been.

CHAPTER TWENTY-FIVE

HIM

Kate's hair cascades over the side of the bed. It could be either espresso or dark chocolate. I kneel beside her and inhale her shallow breaths, taking a break so I can make love to her again.

Behind me, in the bed across the room, I hear him finish with her friend. *Shit*. I want to take Kate again.

"Time to go," he says.

I find my shorts on the floor and slide a leg into them.

"Damn! Look at your girl's tits. You should have shared some of that."

I hurry and pull my shorts on. I don't want him touching my Kate. He wanted Mandy, and he had her. Mandy is sprawled on the other bed with her hair in a tangle across her face and pillow. He left her legs spread open and unnatural, bent at the knees like a frog. He has no respect.

I slip my feet into my sandals and grab Kate's black boots. "I need a shoelace."

"Well, hurry the hell up. We need to get out of here."

Her suitcase is open on an aluminum luggage rack with a pair of Nikes beneath it. It is all tidy with the clothes folded. I pull a lace from one of her Nikes, loop it through the pull straps of her boots, and make a tight knot. When I look up, he is bent over Kate, running his lips and tongue over her nipple. It makes my anger rise, and I want to smash him in the head with Kate's boot.

"Come on," I say.

"Ohhh...someone doesn't like me touching his girl." He stands there mocking me with Mandy's sparkly turquoise shoes knotted together and dangling from his fist. He lifts Kate's red thong from the floor.

He does not know my power. He does not know my rage. One of these days, he will regret all he has done to me.

He hangs Kate's thong from the doorknob before turning off the light. Without a word, we step out, onto the patio, with both girls' shoes.

The glow of the moon washes the shoe tree in silver and shadow, leaving the shoes with no color and hard to distinguish. Many of them are from the girls I have taken. But in the dark, they hang in clumps, and I cannot pick them out.

He holds one of Mandy's shoes and twirls the other until he releases both, sending them high into the tree. I cannot do that with Kate's boots since they are big, and I'm afraid the laces won't hold. I pitch them underhand, and they catch on a low branch just as a coyote starts calling a long and pitiful cry.

"I think we gave them a bit too much," I say.

"Yep, it was like humping a dead fish. Next time, we'll reduce it by a few milligrams."

We slip silently through town, beneath the dark underbelly of the clouds. At the corner of his street, he holds a pack of smokes out toward me.

"Naw, I'm good." He knows I don't smoke cigarettes. If he offered me a joint, that would be a different story.

He flicks his lighter and holds the flame to the cigarette until an ember glows at the tip. He stands there taking long draws, blowing the smoke out in rings, and staring up just as a flash of lightning illuminates the cliffs and the clouds. I am done with him. I will do it alone next time.

He finally finishes and turns to walk down his street. As soon as he is out of sight, I turn back toward the hotel. I think Kate's hair is espresso, and Mandy's is strawberry blonde. I need to get some to be sure.

The hum of all the air conditioners along the back patio drowns out the sound of my footsteps. I slide my master key into the lock and turn it. Slipping into the darkness of the room, I close the door and listen. Girls are quiet sleepers. I need to get close and feel the warmth of their breaths on my face. I don't turn on the light. I am the river, and I flow into their room.

I drift over to Mandy's bed and run my hands over her. She is still splayed out and disheveled. I align her and sweep her hair smooth. He had no respect to leave her like he did. I transform her from a frog to a water nymph. My fingertips sweep across her skin and her curves. I become hard and ready as I play with her tits. I slide out of my shorts. I am hard as a rock, and I take her.

Before I crest, I pull out and return to Kate. Beautiful Kate. My Kate. I finish with her. My body rages and plunges, rising and peaking until I collapse on top of her, wet and slippery in the hot room.

Once I am able, I kneel beside her bed, lean forward with my open mouth to her lips, and take her breath into me. I rise and turn on the light. Both girls float perfectly on their beds with their arms slightly out, their legs spread, and their hair fanned out over their pillows. They are perfect. I will take their final breaths, and they will forever be mine.

I reach out and run my hand over Kate's hair. I cannot wait to take it home. I think it is espresso brown. I wind my finger in the strands, tighter and tighter until I lose feeling in the tip, then

I yank, pulling it from her head. She lets out a single high-pitched moan.

I scoop Kate up and slip back out into the night and to the edge of the river. I take her in and hold her beneath the surface with my mouth to hers, taking in her last breath. I rise up, leaving her beneath the surface, and let her inhale my water into her lungs. I hold her tight until she stops thrashing and is fully one with me.

When she is still, I reach out and feel her hair streaming out and flowing in my current, it too becoming part of the river, part of me. I lift her up and carry her back to the bank, over to someone's raft tied to a tree and half-hidden in the brush. I lay her down inside it. When I return to the room for Mandy, I take her hair and carry her to the river.

I complete my ritual with Mandy, take her to the raft, and lay her beside Kate. They are so beautiful it makes me ache. They will never know how much they are loved. I untie the rope and guide the raft into the water. I wade deep enough for them to catch the current and float away. The river and I are one. It is the fluid, and I am the flesh.

CHAPTER TWENTY-SIX

The Whitehorse Inn sits right in front of me, big and yellow, with its front doors gaping wide open. I have not stepped foot inside since the morning after Amber went missing. My heart pounds, and I feel as if I might get sick. All I want to do is go back to Brian's house and crawl into his bed.

In the lobby, all the animal heads stare at me with their glassy black eyes. I'm not sure where to go. Nobody is working behind the desk, but two men sit on the lobby couches drinking the free coffee. I can only see the back of their heads, but it looks like Henry Dixon, the fly shop owner, and his son, Jeremy. I have never seen Henry outside of the glass booth in the fly shop where customers gather to watch him tie flies.

"Good morning," I say, coming up behind them.

Both men turn, looking tired and surprised to see me.

"Oh, hi Emmy," Jeremy says.

They both have kind faces and goofy grins.

"I hear you're getting to be a pretty good fly fisherman...I mean fisherwoman." Henry takes a sip of his coffee from his paper cup.

"Brian's teaching me," I say. "I need to work on my cast and setting the hook. I lose more than I catch."

"Come by the shop, and I'll let you pick out a few flies," Henry says.

I don't know if he means for free or if he's trying to sell me something.

"No charge," he says as if he read my mind. "I'm always willing to help new fishermen…especially if they're girls. We need more girls with fly rods in their hands."

Even though he sits there smiling and looking harmless, something about him makes my creeper senses start tingling, and I take a step back.

"Girls in waders…" he nods his head. "Ummm hmmm. It's nice to have something pretty to look at."

"Is anyone working the desk?"

"She's probably in the back playing on the computer," Jeremy says. "You can ring the bell."

"Thanks." I feel their eyes on me as I go to the desk. Please don't let it be Becky. I raise my hand over the bell when I see Amber's red and white missing poster with her beautiful face smiling up from beneath the glass on the counter.

They are all around town, and whenever I see one, it feels as if the hole inside me expands like a balloon. A thick black balloon. Amber's poster has replaced Shawna's, whose body they found in the river a year after she disappeared.

Becky steps from the office.

"You're late." She says with her eyebrows raised. They are still a good inch from her bangs, even with them raised. "You were supposed to be here at 8:30."

I open my mouth to tell her that Rose told me 9:00, but no words come out. Amber's poster has knocked the air from my lungs.

"Mary has already started. Since you don't know what you're doing, you'll need to work with her for a few days."

"Which room is she in?"

Becky gives me one of those *you're an idiot* glares. "The one with a housekeeping cart outside it."

As I turn to leave, she says, "She starts upstairs. You'll need a uniform. Stop by the desk before you leave, and I'll have one ready."

Jeremy and Henry are gone, and the lobby is empty, except for the animal heads all staring down at me. The stairwell is one of those creaky wooden ones with no carpeting. The second floor looks like the first, with yellow walls, white trim, and red carpeting. A cart loaded down with cleaning supplies and towels is outside room 209.

"Hello," I call into the open door before stepping in. It looks like a bomb went off inside. How do people expect their room to be cleaned with their personal shit thrown all over the place?

A woman steps out of the bathroom with an armful of wet towels. She looks in her forties with long black hair parted down the middle. She has a harsh and leathery face with strong cheekbones and nose—until she smiles and her eyes squint into friendly crescent moons.

"Hello, Emmy."

I almost ask how she knows my name, but everyone in town knows me. *The girl who Brian saved. The girl who will not leave.*

"My name is Mary." She drops the towels into a bag on the side of the cleaning cart.

She turns, and I get a full view of the uniform. I cannot tell what fabric the thing is made of, but it looks like the type they use for those old lady pantsuits. The thing is past her knees and dark blue with a white collar, cuffs, and apron—and of course, a name tag. It is almost as ugly as the pioneer dress my eighth-grade mom bought me at Goodwill.

"You can start by picking up the trash and making the beds."

I stare at the chaos, paralyzed. There is just so much disorder. If not for the men-sized shoes, I would think this was where a pack of ten-year-olds had a sleepover. Clothes, soda and beer cans, Pop-tart boxes, candy wrappers, shoes, and towels are scattered on every surface, including the floor, beds, and end tables. If there was a hoarder show for teens, this is what it would look like.

"Don't just stand there," Mary says, grabbing a toilet brush off the cart.

"I don't know where to start."

She lets out a sigh. "Throw all the trash away, then clear off one bed and make it. After you do that, start neatly laying the clothes in piles on top of it. Then make the other bed and…"

I hold up my hands. "All right. I get it." I grab the empty wastebasket and start collecting the trash.

A used condom lays partially under one of the beds. It is disgusting, and I am not touching it. I go to the bathroom door and stand there waiting for Mary to notice me. Her skinny arm is like a windshield wiper blade moving across the mirror in big swishing motions as she hums to herself without any earbuds. There is an odd beauty to it, and I hate to throw off her rhythm.

"Uh, what do I use to pick up a used condom?" I finally say.

Without pausing or looking my way, she says, "There are latex gloves in a box on the cart."

I take a glove and try to snap it on like you see on television, but it doesn't work out so well. I end up having to twist and yank the rubber fingers onto mine. I look down at the slimy film of rubber laying there on the wooden floor. I use a beer can to scoot it into a paper cup—the same type Henry and Jeremy were drinking their coffee from.

Here I am, stripping beds where strangers sweated, drooled, or had sex. Imagine all the dead skin cells and hair strands on the sheets and pillows, in the sink, and in the shower drain. The piss splattered all over the toilet and on the floor. While Brian is out having fun, taking girls in bikinis down the rapids, instigating water fights, and posing for pictures, I'm dealing with their filth.

"Did you live through it?"

My heart jumps up to my throat, and I let out a squeal. Mary is standing right behind me.

"What?"

"The condom." She laughs. "Did it bite you?"

After getting the room straightened and cleaned, Mary grabs a clipboard with a checklist and starts marking it off. We have thirteen more rooms upstairs and fifteen down. *Holy shit.*

"Are we the only housekeepers?"

"You tired already?" She looks down at her clipboard. "Yesterday I cleaned most of them myself. Joan went into labor before lunch."

"Labor? As in having a baby? When will she be back?"

"You want to quit already?" She smiles one of those amused smiles that only middle-aged women can pull off.

Thank God there are no condoms or disgusting body fluids in the other upstairs rooms. We finish them just before lunch. Since there is no elevator in the Whitehorse, we roll the cart into a storage closet, restock it, and leave it there.

I have thirty minutes to run home and eat before we start in on the bottom rooms. The town is drained of tourists with everyone on the river. The dogs lie around in the shade, sleeping, biting at fleas, or wandering around and pissing everywhere. One of them, which looks like some sort of terrier and poodle mix, starts following me.

The house is stuffy and empty without Brian. It is a one-bedroom box with hand-me-down furniture and no screens on the windows. It is in worse condition than any foster home I have ever lived in, but I have never felt so loved and wanted in my life.

I make myself a peanut butter sandwich and grab a handful of Fritos. Amber used to put Fritos into her sandwich because she liked the crunch. I lift the top slice and start lining them up. The back of my throat stings, and the tears come. Thank God for Brian. Without him, my life would be a complete shit hole.

As I step out the front door, Dustin sits on our porch in stretchy green shorts and a striped T-shirt. He looks up at me with the biggest pout I've ever seen.

"I wish Brian was home." He lets out a big sigh and hangs his head down in an exaggerated movement.

"You look like you're having a bad day. Is there anything I can help you with?"

"We have a fort down by the river, and the boys won't let me in."

"Why won't they?"

"I don't know. Sometimes they're just mean."

"I have an idea," I say. "I was just about to go to the mercantile. How about if I buy you a bunch of Otter Pops? I bet if you show up at the fort with those, they will let you in."

Dustin looks up at me with a huge grin that's missing one front tooth and has another half grown in.

Bright-colored boxed and bagged foods fill the shelves in the mercantile. Several refrigerators are lit up and stocked with drinks. Dustin grabs a red handbasket and, like a little gentleman, carries it for me. We load it up with Otter Pops for him and a Pepsi for me.

"Morning Emmy," Mrs. Kaufmann says. "Looks like you got a helper today."

"Yep. Dustin's my new friend. We're helping each other out," I say.

Dustin sets the basket on the counter right next to the cash register with Amber's red and white poster still taped to the side. I try to swallow, but a lump has formed in my throat.

Mrs. Kaufmann starts tapping buttons on the register. Both her and Dustin do not seem to notice Amber's bright eyes and beautiful smile—it is like her missing poster has blended in with all the other bright-colored packaging in the store.

"Can you put it on Brian's account?"

Mrs. Kaufmann is taking her time looking through her account book. I can tell that Dustin is eager to get going with his Otter Pops.

"You can go ahead," I say to him.

Dustin grabs the little brown sack and sprints out the door. "Thank you, Emmy," he calls back to me.

Back at the Whitehorse, the downstairs closet has an identical cart with all the same supplies. I follow behind Mary and the cart all the way to room 114—the room Amber and I stayed in. My heart beats fast as she slides her master key into the lock. The door swings open, and the first thing I see is a twin bed against the left wall. It is the bed that Amber slept in.

My chest tightens, and my stomach churns. The damned taste of peanut butter and Fritos still in my mouth is making me sick.

"You okay?" Mary asks.

I step inside. The room is neat and tidy. The beds are made, but all crumpled like they slept on top of the covers. An eerie feeling sweeps over me, and I want to run. Breathe. I take a deep breath through my nose and slowly blow it out. The suitcases are open, with one on the floor and another sitting on top of a folding rack. A black cowboy hat is tipped upside down on the floor next to a white dress.

This is the room of those two girls, and something seems wrong.

"Do you feel it, Emmy?" Mary is talking. "This room has a bad spirit."

The other girl's shorts and turquoise halter top are also on the floor at the end of the bed. "Something is wrong."

"You feel it, don't you?"

A red thong hangs from the doorknob to the back patio. The

room starts pitching back and forth. I feel as if I'm going to vomit. Mary grabs hold of my arm, and the next thing I know, I am on the floor. Beneath the suitcase rack is a pair of Nikes with the shoelaces missing from one shoe.

"Emmy?"

Mary's voice trails off…further and further. It is as if I am in a dream. I am on the bed. Someone is over me, holding me down. I feel pain and warm breath on my face, and I turn my head away from it. I open my eyes and see Amber on the bed against the other wall. Amber…I try to reach out, but my arms are pinned to the bed. I am cold and naked. I turn back to see who is breathing in my face and see Doc Unger all sweaty and breathing hard. Someone is gasping in air.

"Emmy?" Mary's voice comes as if she is talking through a tunnel. "Are you okay?"

The room slowly lights as if someone is using a dimmer switch. I am still on the floor—not the bed, and the breathing is coming from me. "Doc Unger?"

"You want me to get Doc?" Mary asks.

"No—he's not here?"

"Nobody's here but us."

I try to push myself up and feel Mary helping me to my feet.

"You're all sweaty," she says.

"I'll be okay."

"Let's get you some fresh air." She steers me out the patio door and onto the back porch. I do not want to be here.

"What did you see?" Mary asks.

The air is hot and smells of sage. A crunching sound comes from the brush behind the blackberries, and Dustin stands there in his bright green shorts.

"What did the spirit show you?" Mary asks.

"Nothing," I tell her, but I can see that she doesn't believe me. "Were you working here the day my friend went missing? Did you clean room 114?"

"Yes."

"Were the beds slept in? Do you know if they brought me here after Brian pulled me from the river? Were the beds wet?" I cannot stop seeing the image of Amber across from me in the other bed.

The boys' fort is well camouflaged. Without Dustin standing there in his bright shorts, I would not have noticed it. There's more cracking and snapping as his shape kneels down and crawls in.

Mary looks toward the children but past them at the river. It seems as if she is waiting for the memory to float to the surface. "Your luggage was in the room. The bedspreads were wrinkled but still made. They were not wet. Becky told me that you were in the hospital, and I should pack up your luggage, put it in the hallway, and someone would bring it all to you."

Mary glances back toward the door. "That is a bad room. Bad things happen to people in that room. You felt it, didn't you?"

I nod but do not tell her what I saw.

"Ever since that girl, Shawna, went missing, there is an evil spirit. And then your friend disappeared from the same room."

The same room? My ears start buzzing, and I feel like I'm going to pass out.

"What did the spirit show you?"

"Nothing." A cold chill washes over me, like one of those intuitive feelings—some deep down warning system telling me to keep my mouth shut.

"I do remember something else the day your friend disappeared," Mary says. "There was a knife on the floor, partially beneath one of the beds. A fillet knife in a leather sheath."

A knife? "What did you do with it?"

"I put it inside your luggage just like I did with everything else."

There was no knife in my suitcase, but I have never looked

through Amber's duffle bag. If there was a knife, someone was in our room, and Amber did not drown. There could be DNA on it. "Are you sure about the knife?"

"Yes. I thought it was strange that two girls would have a fillet knife without any fishing gear."

The haunting coo of a mourning dove calls from the side of the hotel and draws me toward the shoe tree. I take the three steps down to the dirt.

A big gray dove flaps its wings, startled, and flutters out. Hanging from the branch it had been sitting on, a pair of black cowgirl boots sway back and forth, dangling from a white shoelace. The buzzing in my ears becomes high and piercing. Further up in the tree is a pair of turquoise tennis shoes with rhinestones blinking in the sun. I cannot breathe. It feels as someone has put their mouth over mine and is sucking the air from my lungs. I start running.

CHAPTER TWENTY-SEVEN

My entire car is covered with a coat of dust. It hasn't been moved since Brian drove it from the Whitehorse parking lot to his driveway. I lift the handle, but it is locked. Where did he put my keys?

I run into the house and pull open the junk drawer. The thing is crammed with matches, a glue stick, dice, at least a hundred rubber bands, pens and bright yellow highlighters, a plastic whistle on a string, an old pair of scissors, and a brown and yellow pack of Camel cigarettes. The pack is half-empty. Brian does not smoke, and I have never seen his friends smoke anything but pot.

I find my keys attached to the remote and a thin silver rape whistle I bought. I still have Jill's house key, which probably made her change her locks when I disappeared. That was shitty of me to do that.

I pop the trunk, and there is Amber's purple duffle bag, sitting untouched. My chest tightens. I unzip it. As soon as I stick my hand in, I catch the scent of Amber, and it feels as if a giant hand is squeezing the breath from me. I dig through it. My fingers sink into the softness of Amber's clothes. Her t-shirts and sports bra. Her jean shorts and pants. I want to stick my head into the bag and breathe it all in. I feel her makeup bag and hair straightener, but no knife. I turn the bag upside down and shake everything into the bottom of my trunk. Did someone go through our things and take their knife back? Or was it never there? Mary could be a liar.

All of Amber's things are spilled into my trunk, lying on top of the grease, bits of pine needles, and a giant brown stain coming from the corner. My forehead and armpits start to sweat, and it feels like I'm going to get sick as I pick up each piece of Amber's clothes, fold them, and place them in piles into her duffle bag.

I turn, and a whole pack of dogs are sitting in the street watching me, their mouths open and panting. Staring at me. What is it with the dogs of this town? They are everywhere, always watching. I know they saw what happened to Amber, and I want to strangle the truth from their mouths.

"Shoo," I yell, but they do not move. I wave my arms and step toward them. "Go away."

They do not budge, so I put the rape whistle in my mouth and blow. Nothing but a high-pitched hiss that wouldn't do shit to save anyone comes out. The dogs cock their heads, and two of them get to their feet. What a piece of shit whistle. Engraved along tube it says, *Good Boy* and in tiny letters below it, *Dog Whistle*. Shit!

We were so damned stupid. We ran away, completely unaware, thinking we were safe with our car and the goddamned rape whistle. I had Amber's life in my hands, and I let her fall through.

A big cloud of dust rises over old Lodell. It is too early for all the buses and trucks to be coming off the river. The entire pack of dogs stir and turn toward whatever is coming into town. They are antsy and on alert.

Between the houses, I see flashes of sheriff trucks dragging trailers with rafts and a white equipment trailer. I slam my trunk shut and run behind the dogs, straight toward the boat launch. As I get to the end of the street and turn toward the river, my feet stop, but my heart keeps going. Painted on the side of the trailer is a giant golden star and *Canyon County Sheriff Incident Command*. The same truck as the day Amber went missing. I cannot breathe.

People start crowding toward me, and I hear a jumble of voices mumbling. *This is not good. Not again. Does anyone know what happened?* And then, one voice calls out, piercing through my head. *They found a body in the river.*

CHAPTER TWENTY-EIGHT

THE NEXT THING I KNOW, I AM PACING BACK AND FORTH BEFORE Amber's cross, unable to stop my muscles from twitching beneath my skin. My brain replays that dreadful morning, over and over, like a video loop. The hospital, the helicopter, *Keep your hands off my jugs*, the incident command trailer, men in orange, yellow, and red. The river. Doc. Running with my IV bag and ripping the needle from my hand. The shoe tree with our lime green converse hanging and twisting in the branches. It's happening all over again. Our shoes still hang there, losing their color and turning as gray as the tree. And now there are the black cowboy boots and turquoise tennis shoes, clean and fresh and hanging by the laces.

"Emmy!"

I look up to see Brian standing there, bare-chested, still in his life jacket and water shoes.

"Oh, my god, I was so worried about you." His voice changes with each step toward me, like he is talking to a spooked horse. "Are you all right? You weren't at work, and then Mary said… and you weren't at home."

He kneels down beside me, and his touch sends an electrical current through every nerve in my body.

"Don't." I pull away from him.

He leans back and raises his palms between us. "Whoa…"

Every crease in his palms is dark, outlined with river dirt—his lifeline, his heart line, and his fate.

"It's not Amber." His voice is soft, just a whisper. His hands are still between us, and all I see are the lines. The black lines. "It's okay. It's not Amber."

He lowers his hands to my shoulders, and he pulls me into his chest. His life jacket is rough on my cheek, but the tip of my nose is touching his skin. His reddish-brown skin is the same color and smell as the dirt of Lodell. It is as if he had been born of the cliffs and the sage. I unclip his life jacket, and he lets it slip off his shoulders and into the dust. I bury my face in his chest, inhaling his scent as he wraps his arms around me where nobody can get me.

"How do you know?"

"We floated by her body. The current has her pinned against a rock."

"You saw? Oh my God. Who is it?"

"I don't know. All I saw was her hair. She has very long and brown hair." His breath is warm on the top of my head.

We sit there silent, and all I can hear is the beating of Brian's heart and the coo of the dove in the tree. "It's the girl in the black cowgirl boots," I say.

He puts his hand under my chin and lifts my head until we are eye-to-eye. He has a strange expression on his face. "What makes you think that?"

"Were they on the river?"

He takes a moment to answer as if he is trying to remember. "I didn't see them. Maybe they left town."

"They didn't. All their things are in the room." I pull my chin from his hand and look up to the shoe tree where her black boots hang like the corpses of two dead crows. "The same room Amber and I slept in."

Brian does not answer. He stares at the boots with his eyes twitching back and forth as if trying to read or calculate something. He starts breathing hard.

"How do girls' shoes get into the tree?"

He does not answer.

"Amber and I would never have tossed our own shoes away. And there is no way we could have thrown them that high. I doubt those girls would have done that either."

Brian closes his eyes and takes a deep breath. "It's a tradition."

He does not look at me as he speaks.

"When a guy scores with a girl, he takes her shoes and throws them into the tree."

My heart starts beating so fast that I cannot breathe. There are hundreds of shoes. Some of the dead branches are so heavy with them they clump together with their laces tangled and twisted together.

"Not all of them are from that…flatlanders think the tree is cool and want to be a part of it."

"And you?" I push him away and stand up. "Have you?"

"Emmy, please."

"Did you throw mine up there?"

He slowly shakes his head and gets to his feet.

"Other girls?" I shove him, but he is solid and does not move. "Have you thrown other girls' shoes up there?"

He does not respond. He only looks at me with hurt in his eyes.

"Which ones?" I step beneath the tree and point up to a pair of pink and gray sketchers. "This pair? Did you screw her?"

Brian does not answer me.

I point to a pair of white Adidas. "What about this pair?"

And a pair of black Nikes with a silver swoosh. "Or these?"

Brian does not move. He does not say a word. He just stands there taking it until I feel like an idiot raging on and on. It feels like he slammed a hammer into my chest. I'm going to get sick, so I run for the bushes along the river.

There is something in my vision. Something in the corner of my brain. It is lurking there, hiding, waiting for me to see it. I kneel down in the bushes, and my stomach heaves, but nothing comes up. My body is shaking and cold with sweat. I press my fingers to my closed eyes. A dark shape swims across my eyelids, sinking into the other corner. I feel Brian's hand on my back.

"Get away from me!" I scream. "Who is doing this? Amber and I did not go into the river on our own. Girls are not drowning themselves."

"I don't know," he says. Brian wraps his arms around me and holds me so tight that I cannot get away, and I cannot breathe.

CHAPTER TWENTY-NINE

Brian and I sit on the couch, and it feels like the entire river is flowing between us. And it is widening. I have so much to say, but I am afraid of what will come out of my mouth. I want to scream at him and make him believe that something is happening to the girls. I want him to take away what he said about the shoes in the tree, but he sits there silent, breathing in deep with his chest rising and falling.

I would rather him yell at me than not speak. Silence is what happens when people are done with you. Silence is what happens when someone has given up. Silence is something that I cannot stand.

I want to scream and pound my fists into him, but Brian is the only person who would give one flying fuck if I got in my car and drove away. He is the only person in this world who cares about me, including my own father. Who is God knows where, dealing drugs or in jail and probably still hooking up with any woman who will give him a place to crash.

Every ounce of me only wants to grab hold of Brian and hang on. He is the only person keeping my head above water.

Sometimes I think I will die in Lodell because I can never imagine anything past the railroad trestle and tunnel. Every time I think of leaving, I visualize my car hitting the dirt road with my dust cloud growing bigger and bigger, enveloping me until my car is nothing but a shadow inside it. As I drive beneath the railroad trestle and into the mouth of the tunnel, my car and I fade into nothing and never come out the other side.

I cannot stand Brian's silence. I need to know what he is thinking. I need him to talk or scream or rage at me, so I know I am worth fighting for. Brian is either going to love me or throw me out. Not knowing which one is killing me.

"Did you take a knife from my suitcase or Amber's duffle bag?"

His eyebrows pinch together. "What?"

"Did you take a knife from my suitcase?"

He just stares at me, looking confused and like I'm some dumb girl he doesn't know.

"Did you?"

"Are you okay?" He stretches an arm out along the back of the couch. "Come here."

I do not move. "Answer me. Did you? Did you see a knife? It's a filler knife in a leather sheath."

"A *filler* knife? Don't you mean a *fillet* knife?"

"Seriously?" I'm not in the mood for him correcting me. "You know what I mean."

"You and Amber had a fillet knife?"

"No!" I scream. Brian is so controlled. I take a deep breath in and blow it out. "It was left in our room by whoever raped us—or by the person who has Amber. She may still be alive."

Brian tips his head to the side, staring at me like one of the damned dogs in this town.

"Mary said she found it in our room and put it in my suitcase or Amber's bag, but it is not there. It could have some DNA."

"I did not see a knife. And even if I did, I would not steal anything that belongs to you. I don't take shit that doesn't belong to me."

"Like you stole girls' shoes? You fucked them and stole their shoes."

Brian lowers his arm and closes his eyes. "You're right. That's a shitty thing to do. I'm sorry, Emmy."

"I'm starting to remember things. Today in the room, I remembered Doc's sweaty face over me, breathing hard."

Brian's eyes twitch again, just like earlier at the shoe tree.

"Doc took care of you. I brought you to him. That is what you remember."

"What if…"

"You need to stop, Emmy. Please do not say these things to anyone. Promise me. You are not sure, and that shit can ruin a man."

"Someone is killing girls. What about Shawna?"

"Who?"

"The girl in the missing poster. The one they found in the river. How can you not remember?"

Brian does not answer me.

"Then Amber disappeared, and now these two girls."

Brian's knee starts bouncing, and he runs his hands over his thighs. "You don't know the girl in the river is one them. Those girls could be in their room right now."

"They're not. I know it."

Brian gets up and starts pacing back and forth between the bedroom door and the kitchen, shaking his head, clenching and unclenching his fists.

He freezes when someone knocks on the door. We look at each other, and neither of us moves. They knock again. I'm not in the mood for Jake or Skid, especially Jake.

Brian comes close to me, bends down, and says, "Not a word. Please, Emmy. Only talk to me about this. Not Mary, not Erin. Nobody. Promise me."

I nod my head, and he goes to the door.

He opens it to the last person in the world I expect to see. Rose Unger stands there holding a white plastic grocery sack. "Is she here?"

"Who?"

"Who do you think? My new employee who feels she can just run off from work in the middle of the day."

Brian is not inviting her in. He blocks the doorway like a giant boulder. "She is in shock about the girl in the river. This brings back memories of her friend."

"According to Mary, she left before anyone knew there was a girl in the river."

Brian looks back toward me. I pull my knees to my chest and wrap my arms around them. He turns back to Rose. "She will be there tomorrow morning."

"Let me in."

He steps aside. I have never seen a smile on her face, and there isn't one now. She is like a skinny stick of a brick wall, and she is coming toward me. Skid may look like his mother, but he is the complete opposite, always slinking around with his tail between his legs—and she's probably the reason why.

Rose stops directly in front of me and glares down. My heart about drops out of my butt.

"Mary gave me some bullshit about a bad spirit scaring you."

My throat is tightening, and it feels like I have a rock lodged in it. "We were cleaning the room where Amber and I stayed…"

"Yeah. So what?"

"It upset me to see it."

"It upset you? Well, I'm sorry…" The sarcasm in her voice makes me feel like a stupid child. "You had a job to do, and I don't give a shit about your fragile little feelings. You do the job. And if you want to curl up into a ball feeling sorry for yourself once you get home, that's your business. When you do it at work, you make it my business.

"Rose," Brian's voice is soft and pleading. For a moment, I forgot that she raised him since he was eight years old. She is practically his mother. "Emmy is really upset right now with the drowned girl and all the recovery…" Rose narrows her eyes at me then back over to Brian. "Letting her sit around stewing in her own pity is not going to help her. The girl postage-stamped to that rock is not her friend."

"Rose…"

"Those rooms are not going to clean themselves. Here's your uniform and name tag." She pulls one of the ugly uniforms from the bag and sets it on the couch next to me.

The name tag pinned to the blue polyester says ROY in all white capital letters.

"Roy?"

"Once I know you're gonna stick, I will order one with your name."

"You have a housekeeper named Roy?"

"He was our night manager, but the son of a bitch wouldn't leave the girls alone. Joyce fired him the summer before last."

I remember Joyce's office, the string of paper cranes, all the photos of Jake on the wall, and the mustard yellow couch. Wait, she said the summer before last. The summer that Shawna went missing.

"How is the recovery going?" Brian asks.

"She's still pinned to the rock, and one of the rescue workers nearly drowned trying to peel her off of it. They're calling it a day and will try again tomorrow."

"Shit. Do you know who it is?"

"They're not sure. Nobody has reported anyone missing, but

we have two girls who were supposed to check out today and haven't been back to their room."

"The ones in room 114?" I ask.

Both of them look at me for a long moment before Rose says, "Yes."

CHAPTER THIRTY

Brian slides out of bed, and I hear him bumping around in the dark. The room is pitch-black without even a hint of moonlight seeping in.

"Where are you going?" I whisper into the room.

"I can't sleep."

"Please come back to bed."

"Not tonight."

"You're leaving me alone?" With all the memories of Amber stirred up, I need him here with me.

"I'm sorry. Just go back to sleep, and before you know it, I'll be back."

Brian has been strange all night.

"Please, Brian, not tonight."

He walks out, leaving an empty hole in our bedroom where his warm body had just stood. I try to swallow down the pain in the back of my throat. I shouldn't have been so selfish, thinking only about myself. I did not think to ask how he was doing. I did not think of what he must have gone through, being there on the river. Seeing the girl's hair in the current.

He would rather be out moving through the night with the raccoons and deer than in bed with me. Of course, he needs to get away from me and all my emotional crap. I better get my shit together, or I will lose him forever.

CHAPTER THIRTY-ONE

HIM

They cannot pry Kate from my grasp. I have her pinned to a rock, taunting them and letting them see her, but they can do nothing. She is mine. They come with all their men and equipment, but they are powerless. I almost took the life of one man, but I let him go.

In honor of my two new girls, I will create a Caddisfly pattern for Kate and a nymph for Mandy—who is dredging the bottom like the deep little nymph she is.

I dump the old butt from the ashtray, light a new cigarette, and set it on the rim. The lid of my tackle box squeaks as I lift it, and the trays rise up, filled with hooks, spools of thread, yarn, wire, beads, and head cement. The strands of Shawna's jet-black hair, Amber's amber, Kate's espresso brown, and Mandy's strawberry blonde all lay in their compartments, each wrapped in copper wire.

Something small and dark is tucked in the back corner of my tackle box, hiding there like a spider. I scoot it forward with the tip of my scissors. An old and tattered nymph comes forward, scuffing along the bottom like the mangy mutt it came from. It is an old fly that I tied with dog hair back when I experimented with different materials. Now, I only use the soft underfur for dubbing. I blow off all the dust and set it aside. Later, I will put it in my canine fly box.

I pull out a single strand of Kate's espresso hair and hold it between my lips. I clamp an extra-fine size twelve hook into my vice and set out some brown thread, red copper wire, dark deer hair, and brown dubbing and hackle. My pulse quickens, and my blood surges. I slip the end of a thread through my bobbin and wrap the shank of the hook. Kate's thighs were smooth and firm.

I lay a length of fine red wire over the shank and secure it with thread. Her hair cascaded over the side of the bed, with the ends almost touching the floor. I twist the dubbing around my thread and wrap the shank, making a nice plump body.

The strand of Kate's hair tickles my lips as I pull it through, stimulating every nerve. I tie it down behind the hook eye and spiral it back over the body before attaching a hackle feather and winding it with evenly spaced wraps.

I bind it all down with the red wire, winding it around like the strings of Kate's thong. My blood surges and pulsates as I think of her white dress and red thong stretching over her hips and cunt.

I stack a trim little clump of deer hair and lay it along the shank. It flares out as I cinch it down with my thread. I give it a whip finish and a drop of head cement before releasing it from my vice and into my hand.

Trout love Caddisflies. They float high and long on the surface, just like Kate's hair in the current.

After I tie two Katie Caddis' and two Strawberry Blonde Nymphs from Mandy, I drop them into my fly box and lay out my hair color charts. My fingertips run over the indentations of the Xs over the jet-black, amber, espresso brown, and strawberry blonde color samples. There are so many more colors to go.

CHAPTER THIRTY-TWO

MORNING LIGHTS THE ROOM, THE DOVE COOS OUTSIDE, AND I AM alone. Brian never came home last night. My chest tightens, and the back of my throat stings. I went too far. I have to pee so bad my stomach cramps. I kick off the covers, sit up, and lift one of Brian's t-shirts from the floor. It's one of the gray shirts they sell at the outfitters with the silhouette of a raft filled with people and paddles. It says, *Need a Good Paddling? Rimrock Outfitters.* I pull it on without bothering to find my panties and head toward the bathroom.

I open the bedroom door, and there he is. Brian is asleep on the couch, uncovered and bare-ass naked with his mouth open and hair a mess. It is the most beautiful sight ever. My entire body feels light, and all I want to do is jump on top of him... after I pee.

I don't flush the toilet because I want to wake him myself. I put my lips to his cheek and climb on top of him. "Good morning."

He blinks and squints up at me. "What time is it?"

"I don't know." I feel tears coming to my eyes, so I lay my head on his chest.

"You can't be late to work," His voice is thick with half-sleep, "Or Rose will come for you."

"I'm sorry I was such a mental case yesterday. I didn't think about all you went through."

He kisses the top of my head. "I'll be all right. What time do you need to be at work?"

"I can't go there."

He doesn't say anything, but I feel his muscles tighten beneath me.

"There's a killer at that hotel."

Brian lifts me up by the shoulders, forcing me to look into his face. "Why do you jump to the worst conclusions?"

"I...I don't know."

"You're going to drive yourself insane doing that." Brian frowns, looking concerned. "What time do you need to be there?"

My tears start, and I cannot stop them. Dammit. Pull it together. I swallow, but my voice still sounds weak and pathetic. "Please don't make me go. All I will do is think of Amber and what happened."

Brian lowers me back down and puts his arms around me tight. "It won't be easy, but staying busy will help. Would you like me to come to work with you? All my trips are canceled until they recover the body," Brian whispers into the top of my head.

Body. The word is so impersonal. As if she is no longer human.

I feel his warm breath on my scalp. "With my help, it will go faster, and I will be right there if you need me."

"Okay," I manage to choke out.

He kisses the top of my head and rolls out from beneath me. "And you need to eat something."

After I get dressed in the terrible uniform with Roy's name tag, I come out to Brian in the kitchen, still naked and pouring some Cheerios into a bowl for us. He is so beautiful and tanned except for his ass and upper thighs. He kisses my cheek and runs his hand over my boobs as I pass by him. "You're still sexy, even in that old lady dress."

As we sit there eating Cheerios, I don't know what comes over me, but a lightness bubbles up, and I start to giggle.

"What?" Brian gives me his irresistible smile, the one that always has a hint of sadness to it.

"Just us sitting here with me in this butt ugly dress and you naked."

He nods and smiles bigger, then puts a huge spoon of Cheerios into his mouth.

Just as I start to feel better, the distant sound of a helicopter slices right through it. "Do you hear that?"

Still holding his spoon, Brian gets up and goes to the door. When he opens it, the sound is louder and pulsating. I can almost feel the tiny needles of dust piercing my face, arms, and bare shins like it did that horrible day. "What does that mean?"

"It means they're looking for another body."

CHAPTER THIRTY-THREE

Mary is not upstairs like she usually is in the morning, so Brian and I head back down. The cart is outside room 114—the room of the two girls. My and Amber's room. We walk in the open door. Becky is tossing their make-up bags and shoes into their suitcases, and Mary is stripping the beds.

"Don't touch anything," I say.

Becky and Mary look up at me, and Becky's face instantly melts into a smirk.

"This could be a crime scene."

They ignore me and keep working to clear and clean the room.

Brian puts his hand on my back. "Come on, we'll get started upstairs."

I swipe at his arm and step away. "Seriously! You need to wait for the police."

Becky still ignores me, but Mary comes toward us with a wad of sheets in her arms. "Chief Unger has been here and asked us to clear it out."

"Come on," Brian puts his hand around my waist, putting pressure and guiding me away.

"There could be DNA."

"You need to stop watching CSI," Brian says. "Your mind goes to the worst conclusions."

"Will you ask Becky their names?" I whisper to Brian.

"Hey, Beck," Brian says.

She looks up at him and gives a big llama-toothed smile.

"What are the girls' names?"

"That is confidential information," she says.

"Come on." His voice is thick and sweet. "It may already be all over the news."

"Not until they notify their families."

"Just their first names then."

Becky makes a point to ignore him.

I give Brian a pleading look.

"Come on, Beck," Brian says.

She pauses a moment, then gives a little shrug. "Kate and Mandy."

Mary, Brian, and I go upstairs and roll the cleaning cart out of the closet.

"Housekeeping," Mary says as she knocks on the door of Room 212.

No answer.

She knocks again, and we wait. Brian stands next to me with his hand wrapped around the vacuum handle. With all the trips canceled, some of the guests left early, but most are still around town, hanging out at the river and staying to watch the drama.

Mary slides the key into the lock and turns it.

"Hello, housekeeping."

The dim room smells sour and stale. I follow Mary in and almost run smack into the back of her when she comes to an abrupt stop. My eyes adjust, and I see a human-sized lump in the bed.

I back out of the room, but Mary doesn't move.

"What's wrong?" Brian asks.

"Someone's in there, asleep."

Mary still does not come out. "Hello, housekeeping…hello."

Brian peeks his head in, then enters.

I wait.

A moment later, I hear Brian yelling. "Call 911 and get Doc."

Mary comes out with panic smeared across her face. She runs into the corner of the cart and almost trips, then catches herself and runs for the stairs.

"Brian?" I step back into the room. "What's wrong?"

"Hit the lights," he says.

I flip the switch. A naked girl lies on the bed with the blankets thrown off and Brian rolling her onto her side.

"You're going to be all right," Brian says in a calm voice. "Hang in there with me."

Brian bends her legs and lifts her chin, positioning her on the bed.

Mary returns with Becky. "What's wrong?"

"I think she's overdosed," Brian says. "I'm not sure."

A different girl, still dressed for the nightclub, appears in the doorway. She is wearing a skin-tight mini dress with disheveled hair and holding her heels by the straps. "What's going on?"

Becky grabs hold of the door and swings it, blocking the view of the room. "We have a medical incident. Please clear out."

"This is my room," her voice is high and frightened. "Megan!"

She pushes into the room, almost knocking Becky down, runs straight for the bed, and drops her heels to the floor. "Megan! Nooooo! Is she alive?"

"Yes," Brian says, but she needs a doctor.

"Oh my God!" The girl wraps her arms around her naked friend. "Call 911."

"We already have."

The girl starts to violently shake her friend. "Wake up! Wake up! Don't you do this to me."

"Should we get her some coffee?" someone asks.

"What about a cold bath?"

"Is there a hospital here?"

"Noooo!" the girl screams. "Please, somebody do something."

"Stop," Brian says, pulling the girl away. "Emmy…"

"Megan! Nooooo!"

"Emmy…"

I just stand there, frozen and unable to move.

"Emmy, help me," Brian says.

I step forward.

"Hold her back."

I wrap my arms around the girl and pull her away from the bed. Her whole body shakes as she sobs and gasps for air. My own heartbeats hard against her back, and I cannot swallow. I remember running toward the river with my IV, screaming at the searchers, and running for our hotel room. This poor girl.

"She will be okay," is all that I can think to say.

The next thing I know, Brian's hands are on my arms, unwrapping me from the girl. Doc is in the room, leaning over the one on the bed. I cannot breathe.

"You did great," Brian says. "Mary, can you help?"

Two police officers, who are also the ambulance drivers, come into the room with a gurney. Doc leans over Megan with sweat shining on the back of his neck and the tips of his thick gray hair turning dark. The friend, now in the arms of Mary, stands in the bathroom, shaking with wide eyes looking barely able to stay on her feet.

I cannot breathe. A buzzing runs through my head, stretching ear-to-ear like an electrical wire.

"I need out," I say to Brian, but we are already headed to the door guarded by Becky. She swings it open, and we step into the hall, now packed with people.

"Excuse us," Brian says as we squeeze through the crowd and toward the stairwell.

Once downstairs, he guides me toward a couch in the lobby. The heads of all the dead animals with black eyes stare blankly across the room.

"No," I say, trying to pull away from Brian. "I need to go outside."

"You all right?"

I cannot breathe. I break free and run for the door.

CHAPTER THIRTY-FOUR

Brian wants to watch the recovery. We walk up the same dirt trail that Doc and Chief Unger drove me up when Amber was missing. I don't want to go, but I also do not want to be home alone.

As we stand there, all the feelings of that day come washing over me. Down below, the men work the river in red rafts and bright yellow gear. Further down and around a bend, someone is standing in the river casting a fly. "Who is that?"

"It looks like fucking Matt. What a dumbass."

I feel lightheaded and nauseous. "Can we go back?"

"We just got here."

"I know, it's just that…" I look to the ground. "This is where I watched them search for Amber."

I do not want to see them bring her up. The visions of Kate and Mandy on the dance floor play on a loop in my mind. I see them kissing and running their hands all over one another. I see Kate's bare ass and red thong. I hated them at that moment and wished they would disappear. And now they have. I know it's not rational, but I feel responsible. I cannot bear to see her body.

Brian puts his arm around my shoulders. "I want to see how they recover her."

"Why? Why would you want to see that?"

Brian looks at me, confused, then his eyes widen. "Oh, not for that reason. I work the river. I need to understand it. It will make me a better guide. I may be able to save someone's life because of what I learn."

I try to hold back my tears, but they are choking me. "I'm going to take a walk."

"All right, be careful and watch for snakes," he says, distracted and staring over the edge of the cliff.

I go down the trail that leads to Old Lodell, where the first settlers had lived. Some houses still stand, others have gaping holes in the roof or missing walls, and others are nothing but a stone fireplace and some wooden fencing. The cicadas buzz like electrical wires, and the sun is warming the juniper and sage, filling the air with their incense.

I head toward one old house that looks intact and sturdy. It has an old red wheelbarrow overturned in the front. The door creaks as I open it, and I smell the all too familiar stink of SpaghettiO's. Once my eyes adjust, I see a couch, a desk, and a rug. Someone lives here. Instantly, a shiver shoots through my body, giving me the most eery feeling I've ever had—like I have entered the den of something pure evil.

I turn so fast that I stumble, then trip, falling off the porch step and skidding across the dirt. I feel someone watching me from the house. I scramble to my feet and run straight toward Brian.

He stands bare-chested on top of the cliff with the wind rippling the bottom of his shorts.

"Brian, Brian," I yell, but the wind is so strong it pushes my words back down my throat.

I keep yelling, but he cannot hear. Finally, I am close enough, and my words reach him. He turns and hurries toward me. "What's wrong? Where did you go?"

My entire body is shivering, and my hands sting. Brian puts his arms around me, and I cannot stop shaking.

"What happened?"

I cannot catch my breath.

"It's all right. You're safe. What happened?"

I point down the trail. In between gasps, I say, "Someone is living…Evil."

Brian pulls me off of him and looks into my face. "You're bleeding. Did someone hurt you?"

I shake my head. "I…I just…I fell."

He takes my hands and turns them over. They are clotted with blood and dirt. "What the hell?" His voice sounds odd.

"I thought the house was abandoned." I gulp in a breath. "Someone lives there. It felt evil."

"Evil?" His tone is dismissive. "Which house?"

I point toward the house with the overturned wheelbarrow.

"That's Bobby Byrd's house. He's a bit off, but not evil."

"It was evil. I have never felt that before. Can we go?"

He glances toward the cliff, then back at me. "Sure. We need to clean that dirt off and get you a few bandaids."

At home, Brian pours hydrogen peroxide all over my scrapes. The liquid fizzes into rose-colored bubbles. He pours more, washing away the blood and dirt until the peroxide turns white. After he pats them dry and sticks bandaids on the worst areas, we head over to the guide shack.

My heartbeat throbs and pulses through the scrapes in my hands. I am still creeped out about that house. Maybe it is Bobby Byrd who is killing the girls. I'm afraid to say that to Brian because all he will tell me is that I jump to the worst conclusions.

It seems every guide in town is at the guide shack, gathering together. As Brian heads toward Jake and Skid, I sit down next to Erin. She bites her nails and spits them into the dirt.

"Which guide spotted her in the river?" I ask.

"Matt, the one who hit the dog."

"You're kidding me!"

"Nope."

Matt sits there with his elbows on his knees and his forehead in his palms. He looks horrible. Brian holds a beer out to him, but Matt just shakes his head. He was also the one hitting on Amber the night she went missing. A tingle rises up the back of my neck. And the one who walked us back to our room with Brian.

"Any news?" I ask. "Did they find the other girl?"

"I haven't heard if they found the other one," Erin says, "but they can't get this one's body off the rock. Two of the rescuers have been injured now."

"Are they all right?"

"They will be. One broke an arm, and the other has a concussion."

"Oh, my God! They won't leave her there, will they?" I ask.

"No. I heard Portland General Electric is going to close the gates of the dam and lower the force of the river."

My head starts buzzing, and everything goes foggy.

"I had no idea they could…" Erin's voice sounds like it is coming from a tunnel. "Are you all right?"

I imagine the river draining and dead bodies lying among the rocks and flopping fish. And Amber, my beautiful Amber Ward, nothing but bones and hair.

CHAPTER THIRTY-FIVE

The town is on hold. Like someone pressed the pause button.

A low buzzing keeps running through my head. I can't tell if it is the cicadas or something in me.

Two sheriff's trucks and the incident command trailer are still parked near the boat launch. They have a blue pop-up canopy where people stand behind food tables for the search and rescue team. This is the third day of the rescue, and everyone is silent, knowing that they will be pulling her from the river today.

The townspeople also brought food for the rescue workers. The casseroles, plates of cookies, and fried chicken sit on a separate table crawling with yellowjackets. With their wings folded back, they creep around the rim of dishes and disappear beneath napkins tucked around paper plates. One lands on the mouth of a straw sticking out of a Shasta Root Beer.

With the river lowered, the kids pick around the bottom. They overturn mossy rocks and rummage through the debris like little packs of scavengers. Erin walks over to the food, slowly waving away the yellow jackets and taking the napkin-covered plates to the trash.

"I hate these damn things," Erin says, carrying the soda, still with the yellowjacket on the straw. She drops it in the garbage.

Shivers brush across my shoulders, and I have the feeling of being watched. I glance around. Carl and Vickie stand by their cafe at Carl's Cabins, talking to Jed and Henry Dixon from the fly shop. Becky sits on one of the chairs on the porch of the Whitehorse Inn, and Rose Unger stands on the porch of Buckskin Mary's, talking with her bartender, Big Doug, and Jemmy, the female city police officer. Around them, the distraught families of the girls huddle together, crying on one another or pacing around aimlessly.

Erin follows my gaze toward the families. "I cannot imagine what they are going through."

I can, but I don't say that out loud. None of them are looking toward me, but I feel someone watching. A couple of the town kids sit under a tree petting Lieutenant Dan, the three-legged Jack Russell mix that Matt had run over. I don't know if he even had a name before the amputation.

A reporter stands talking to Officer Rubio, one of the three reserve officers in town, which I found out means that they do not get paid and work part-time. Chief Unger is the only one collecting any money, which must be nice for him.

Nobody is looking at me. I am getting paranoid…or going insane. Then, I see him. From this angle, I can see along the back porch of the Whitehorse to the far corner. Beneath the shoe tree, a man stands and stares directly at me. He is thin and sharp, with a possum-like face. I remember him from our first night in Lodell when Amber and I saw him squatting by the river. A bubble of air expands in my chest, and I cannot breathe.

"What's wrong?"

I turn back to see Erin looking at me.

"Who…" I let out the air and point toward the man. "Is that?"

Her eyes follow my finger. She shrugs and does not look concerned. "Just Bobby Byrd. He's a creep who's usually in and out of jail."

"Is he dangerous?"

Erin shrugs again. "I wouldn't go near him."

"Why haven't I seen him in town before?"

"I don't keep track of Bobby Byrd, so I don't know."

A cold chill prickles my scalp and cheeks. "I accidentally walked into his house the other day."

Erin lets out a laugh. "How did that go?"

"It freaked me out. It felt pure evil."

She shrugs. "He's creepy, but I don't think he would hurt anyone. You probably felt the spirit of his grandpa. He died in that house. Bobby had been in prison at the time, so the poor old man sat dead in his recliner for two weeks before anyone found him. Now, Bobby lives there. Why would you go in?"

"I thought it was vacant."

She puts her hand on my arm. All her nails are bitten clear down to the quick. "You need to stay away from Old Lodell. There are all sorts of abandoned houses there for druggies, teenagers, or anyone else, to do whatever they want." She waves a yellow jacket away from the mouth of her soda can. "…and where most of us lost our virginity."

I look over at Erin. "Did you? Sorry…that's none of my business."

She smiles as if it is something normal and inescapable. "Of course I did. At the Unger homestead, right in the squeaky old bed of Jake's grandparents. The Ungers want to restore Old Lodell. Doc and Russ are going to level their farmhouse and barn to build a nice home there for Jake and me once we graduate and get married."

Out of the corner of my eye, I see Bobby Byrd, still there by the shoe tree and still staring. The buzzing in my head is high-pitched and fuzzy. I had been inside his house. A shiver runs over me, and it feels as if every single nerve is vibrating.

A hand touches my shoulder. I gasp and turn to see Brian behind me. "You all right?"

"You startled me."

He laughs and puts one foot over the bench to sit down. "What were you spacing out about?"

I look back toward the shoe tree, but Bobby Byrd is not there. The shoes hang heavy and limp without a single gust of wind.

Just as I open my mouth to tell Brian about Bobby Byrd, an ambulance without lights or sirens comes down the road. It passes the cabins, makes a loop at the mouth of the boat launch, and starts backing toward the river.

A voice comes from the crowd. "They've got her!"

CHAPTER THIRTY-SIX

After the ambulance drives away with Kate's body, Brian takes me home, and I crawl into bed, still in my clothes. I am so exhausted I don't even remember falling asleep.

It is still daylight when I wake to voices in the house. At first, I think it is the television until I hear my name and the dull clink of a beer bottle on wood.

I listen.

The house is silent for a moment, and all I hear is the soft pillowy coo of the mourning dove. Otis, the stuffed bobcat, stares at me with his glassy eyes and pointy ears.

"Are you going to tell her?" It's Erin's voice.

"I don't have a choice. Everyone in town is talking about it."

"I don't think she will handle it well."

"For fuck sake," Jake says, "why are you with someone so high maintenance?"

I get out of bed and head toward the door.

"High maintenance?" Erin asks. "She's grieving. She lost her friend."

"She's homeless. Without Brian's pity, she would be on the street."

"Get the hell out of my house," Brian says.

"You know it's true." Jake's voice is filled with hate. "Without you, she would probably be fucking people for a place to sleep. Oh wait, that is exactly what she's doing."

Something crashes to the floor, like a chair tipping backward. The doorknob is cold in my hand, but I'm afraid to turn it.

"That's enough," Erin says. "We're leaving."

"We're not going anywhere. I own this house. Brian and his bitch can leave."

A loud scraping sound comes from the other room, like the legs of the kitchen table against the floor, comes from the other room. Then a crash, something breaking, grunts, and knuckles on flesh.

"Stop it!" Erin yells.

It sounds like they are breaking everything in the entire house. Things are crashing and scraping and breaking. I jump back as a body hits the other side of the wall with a grunt.

"Stop!" Erin says just as the sound of breaking glass explodes on the floor. I hope it isn't Brian's mother's vase—the one Brian keeps filled with dry desert flowers or juniper.

I turn the knob and creak the door open. Jake and Brian are on the floor like two wrestlers, winding their arms and legs around one another, trying to pin each other to the ground. Erin is circling them, screaming and trying to grab an arm to pull them apart.

Brian rolls out from beneath Jake and gets to his feet. His eyes catch mine for an instant just as Jake's fist slams into his jaw. I freeze. I want to scream at them and tell them I will leave, but I cannot move. The mass of their bodies is unbelievable.

Brian's knuckles crack into Jake's nose. He howls like an animal, and there is blood. A lot of blood. Instead of Jake pausing, it gives him power, and he rages at Brian like a bull. Brian steps to the side, and Jake crashes onto the coffee table, knocking the cups and Brian's tackle box to the floor.

Brian steps backward, staring at the box. It is still latched, and nothing spilled out. He puts his fingers to his nose and checks them for blood.

"Let's go," Erin says, helping Jake from the floor.

With one jerk of his arm, he shrugs her off, and she falls on her ass. Jake smears the blood across his face and wipes it on his shorts, leaving a red smear on the tan cargo pockets. His face is nothing but rage as he moves toward Brian.

"Stop it!" Erin gets up and grabs Jake's arm, trying to pull him back.

He is in a rage and doesn't even register that Erin is there. She doesn't even slow him down. Brian stands there, bracing himself and ready to throw more punches.

Jake is out of his mind. His arm cocks back, and just as it comes forward at Brian's face, Erin jumps between them. The blow lands on the side of her eye. She lets out a piercing screech that snaps Jake to his senses. There is a moment of silence.

"Oh my God. Why did you…? I didn't mean to…" Jake takes her face into his hands and turns it to see the damage.

Brian glances at me standing there, peeking through the crack in the door. He looks confused as if he is wondering if he should come to me or not. He turns away, moves toward the kitchen and yanks open a drawer. He pulls a baggie from the box and fills it with ice.

Jake is leading Erin to the couch.

"I'm all right. Let's just go home," she says.

Brian brings the bag of ice and holds it out to Jake, who takes it and puts it to Erin's eye. She flinches but lets him hold it there.

Jake and Erin then move toward the door, and Brian opens it for them. Once they are off the porch, he closes the door then plops down on the couch without even looking at me.

I step back into the bedroom. It is filled with the smells of juniper and sage and the sweat of our bodies on the sheets. As I slide the closet door open, it scrapes along the metal tracks.

I take my suitcase from the back corner, lift it onto the bed, and unzip it. The inside fabric is black with a silver designer bag pattern, but it's really nothing but a cheap knockoff and a fake.

"Emmy," Brian calls from the living room. "Come here."

I close my eyes and swallow, but it gets stuck in my throat.

"Emmy, please…"

Brian stands in the doorway bare-chested, in nothing but his shorts. His lip and eye are swelling, and he has blood on his knuckles and chest.

"I'll get you some ice."

"No." His voice is harsh, but then he softens it.

His eyes are so pained that it hurts my heart. This is all because of me. He doesn't speak for a moment, and I know what he will say is hard for him.

He sits on the edge of the bed. "Sit down."

I want to save him from it, so I open my mouth, and the words that were caught in my throat come out. "I'm already packing."

His eyebrows pinch together, and his eyes move back and forth, scanning my face. They land on my suitcase, but it still does not register. "What?"

"I'm already packing. I will leave."

"No…" he pats the edge of the bed for me to sit down. "That's just Jake. He'll feel like shit about it tomorrow."

Jake's blood is smeared across Brian's knuckles and drying on the strands of his chest hair.

I sit next to him. He puts his arm around me and kisses the top of my head.

"I love you, Emmy." His words feel warm on my scalp. "They found the other girl in the river."

The lump in my throat sinks down to my chest.

Brian's arm around my shoulder tightens, pulling me so hard against him it squeezes the breath from my lungs. "And a third body."

CHAPTER THIRTY-SEVEN

My legs quiver, and I barely make it to the boat launch. Most of the townspeople are already there. Brian holds my hand and lets me take him where I need to be. A white sheriff camper truck with *Coroner* painted on the window backs down the launch.

We go to the edge of the water, to the newly exposed shore. They started lowering the river eight hours ago, and the kids are still out there, laughing and exploring a part of their world that is usually out of reach. The moss on the rocks is drying into a sun-bleached felt.

Brian stands between the people who are staring and me. They want to console me. They want to say something to make me feel better, but no words can do that. My cheeks sting with tiny pinpricks of heat. I want to scream at them and tell them to go away because their concern makes this true.

Images of Amber laughing when we rode the Tilt a Whirl at the fair will not leave my mind—or the time she was afraid to walk across the railroad trestle, but I talked her into it. The entire way, she kept asking what we would do if a train came. I am great about planning for fun, but I never think things through. And that is why she is no longer here.

A boat comes whining up the river at full throttle, barely making headway against the current. Brian holds my hand and anchors me to this earth. His love is something that I do not deserve. I only have him because I lost her. I look for Amber sitting in the back wrapped in a silver space blanket with her wet hair plastered down her head. I watch for a big smile to come to her chattering teeth when she sees me. But all I see is the boat with three men and a black body bag, barely filled.

We have not moved, but the tips of my sneakers are wet. They must have opened the dam, and the river is rising. They are done. It is done. It feels like the river is swelling in me and filling me until the tears spill out.

CHAPTER THIRTY-EIGHT

HIM

No, no, no. They are taking my girls from me. They were never meant for the dirt. My girls are nymphs and will shrivel in the dryness of the earth.

It took three days and the best men they have. They could not take Kate from me without diminishing my strength and choking my power. When I replenish, I will not be the same. All those who think they know me will realize they do not. I will take a slightly new course that will take them by surprise. Even the best river guides will have new alertness and respect for my power.

I should not have let Emmy live. She has become a problem. I thought she was just a dumbass bitch who cared about nothing but partying and spreading her legs for a place to sleep. She is starting to remember, and she will not let it go. There is no way in hell I will let her ruin me. It is time to take her ash brown hair and breathe her in.

That old ratty canine fly sits on my desk, giving me an idea. I tied that with bitch hair, so why not give it to the bitch? Why not give a whole box of them to the bitch? I cannot take Emmy now, but I can toy with her. I can watch her fish with my flies until it is time.

I turn to the stack of boxes and crates against my back wall and lift off the red plastic milk crate where I keep all my old flies. I dig through them and find the black plastic fly box with my canine bitch flies. One by one, I take them out and make a pile of Canine Caddis', Yellow Dog Stones, Maddog Woolly Buggers, and Little Lassie Nymphs.

I run my hand over the cold metal of my tackle box that holds all I have left of my girls. My fingers tremble as I unclasp the lid and reveal the jet black, amber, espresso, and strawberry blonde strands—all bound and sitting in their own compartments. I can spare a dozen or so strands of amber hair for Emmy.

One by one, I clasp a canine bitch fly into my vice, tie in a strand of amber hair, and arrange them in the foam lining of the box. My heart beats faster. I am replenishing.

Once I am done, and the box is filled, I latch it closed. My energy is increasing. With my fillet knife, I scratch her name onto the surface. Tiny black shavings of plastic rise up, writhing and falling away from the tip of my knife as I form an E, M, M, and a Y.

Once I am done, I grab the bottom of my shirt and slide it up over my head, stripping off all of my clothes and letting them fall to the floor. I am free. I am me. I am the river.

I lift the remainder of amber's hair, along with the jet black, espresso, and strawberry blonde strands. I hold them together, winding their ends around my finger, wrapping them into one silky rope. I lay down on my bed and run the strands across my cheek, over my lips, down my neck and chest.

I am rising, and soon, I will rage. For, I am the river. It is the fluid, and I am the flesh.

CHAPTER THIRTY-NINE

The cold night air blows in the truck's windows and whips the ends of my hair across my face. We didn't even start out until after midnight and after we had all downed a case of beer. Jake is driving, Brian sits shotgun, and Skid sits between Erin and me in the tiny back seat. He leans forward with both elbows on the front seats, like he is sitting bitch in the front instead of the back.

"Holy shit, I think we got one, boys," Jake yells.

Erin and I lean forward. In the road, caught in the truck's high beams is what looks like a section of rubber hose. I didn't think we were really going rattlesnake hunting. I thought it was the same as going snipe hunting—just an excuse to act like dumb asses with no hope of catching anything.

The truck picks up speed, and Jake whoops and calls, "Hell ya!"

The snake is stretched out across the road, trying to warm itself in the cold night air as we barrel toward it with the engine racing. Jake seems instantly sober and focused, almost deranged. Brian sits calmly with his hand gripping the overhead handle, and Skid leans forward with his long neck stretched out so far that his head is in the front seat.

I try not to pee myself and pray that we do not roll the truck. With a tiny thwack, we run over the poor thing. The tires squeal, and I fling forward. The seatbelt tightens around me as we screech to a stop. Jake shifts into reverse and guns it backward. He turns his body and stares out the back window with his eyes lit in excitement. We run over it again, and he locks the wheels, flinging me back against the seat.

In the beam of the headlights, the thing is smooshed and bloody and in three separate pieces.

"That was cool as shit," Jake says.

"Let me out," Skid unhooks his seatbelt and rises off the seat.

We pull off into the gravel, and Jake swings the truck at an angle with the headlights spreading out over the carnage. The front doors swing open, and Jake and Brian hop out. They open the half-doors for us. I don't move, so Skid slides out after Erin. She seems unfazed by what happened and along for the fun.

"Come on." Brian puts his hand out for me to take.

"No thanks." I slide my fingers beneath my thighs and sit on them.

He gets that sad look and shrugs. "Alright."

He joins the others in the beam of the headlights. They ask him something, and he shrugs. Jake just shakes his head and turns away. Skid is already at the dead snake, and Erin glances back at me before catching up to Jake.

I should have gone, even if I did not want to see it. I could have stayed next to Brian and pretended it was okay—but I cannot shake the heaviness of death. I am in limbo, waiting for the coroner to identify the bodies. The third body had been in the river for a long time and is nothing but bones.

Chief Unger and B.J., one of our local policemen, interrogated me again. They made me relive that night, questioning me as if they were trying to understand how girls could be so stupid and not about how and why girls are being murdered. I wanted to tell them that the town has a serial killer, but Brian was sitting right next to me, and he made me promise to keep my theories to myself. I did because if Brian does not believe what I have to say, who would?

Brian is the only one not squatting down to examine the snake. Skid picks the back part up by the tail and swings it at Erin. She does not even flinch. If I had gone with them, that would have been me, and I would have freaked out. With the darkness of the night, and the four of them in the headlights, it seems like they are acting out some redneck play and nothing exists outside of their current scene.

I don't know how they can function with what happened. The body they think is Mandy's was found far down the river at Mullins Falls, a chute where the river narrows and cuts through the rock in a class VI rapid. She was caught in a flow that tumbled her around, like a commercial washing machine, leaving nothing but bones and shreds of hair and skin. Just the night before, she had danced at the Buckskin, all cute and sexy, putting on a show for the boys in her glittery turquoise shoes.

They come back to the truck with Skid carrying two sections of the snake. It is thick and brown and bloody. The snake's body makes a thwacking sound as he tosses it into the bed of the truck.

All the doors open. Skid wipes his hands on his jeans before he climbs in, forcing me to scoot into the center and bringing a new musky and bloody smell into the cab. Erin gets in the other door with Jake and Brian in front. They all surround me and wrap me so tight in their excitement that I cannot breathe.

CHAPTER FORTY

The bathroom is steamy and smells like Brian—of the earth and his shampoo. His cargo shorts and underwear lay in a pile on the small honeycomb tiles. The shower curtain pokes out as his elbow brushes it. I have been a shitty girlfriend, and I have no idea why he keeps me around. I strip off my clothes and reach for the edge of the curtain.

There is something bad growing between us, and I don't know if it is me, this town, or his friends. I have been pissy and distant and closing into myself instead of leaning on Brian. His knees are bent, and his head is back in the shower spray. I step over the rim of the tub and let the curtain close behind me.

Suds stream down past his closed eyes, his temples, and over his shoulders. He is beautiful and tan, except for the pale area his shorts cover and where the straps of his water shoes go over the top of his feet. I reach out to run my hand over his cock. He jumps when I touch it, breaking the nozzle off with his head. Water gushes out the bare end of the pipe as the showerhead bounces off the rim of the tub and drops to our feet.

"You scared the shit out of me."

Brian appears stunned for a moment, then looks me up and

down, noticing I am naked. He shuts the water off, pulls me to his wet body, and kisses me with slippery lips that taste like soap. I feel his erection between us as he runs his hands over my ass and picks me up. I wrap my legs around him, and he carries me to the bed.

"We'll get the bed wet," I say.

"That's the plan." He lays me down and kisses me hard before sliding down to my breasts, then between my legs.

Afterward, we lie there, damp and sticking to the sheets. Brian is on his side, pushing my hair off my face and running his fingertips over my cheek.

"Are you getting tired of me?" I ask.

His eyebrows pinch together. "What do you mean?"

"I've been bitchy and moody and not a good girlfriend." The look in his eyes makes me want to cry. "I'm sorry. If you want me to leave…."

Brian sits up, cross-legged on the bed.

I push myself up and face him. His hair is a mess and still full of shampoo. He takes my hands in his. "I love you. People are not disposable. You do not throw them away just because they are going through tough times."

I feel the tears rising, and I try to hold them back. I have always been disposable. My mother was disposable. I was too young to understand when she died. I thought my father had locked her away in a pumpkin shell, just like Peter, Peter. For years, I imagined it rotting away with her inside it.

"We will get through this together," Brian says.

I think of Erin and Jake and the shit she puts up with. She stays by him. Erin pushes back, but she does not leave him. I cannot hold the tears back, and they spill down my cheeks. I do not understand this sort of love.

"What about your friends and the town? They all hate me."

Brian cups my face and lifts until I look directly into his

eyes. "They do not hate you. They don't know you, and they want to make sure you will not hurt me. Give them time."

A shuffling noise comes from the porch. We both pause and look toward the door, waiting for a knock. It does not come, and the steps retreat.

"Do you think it was one of the dogs?" I ask.

Brian shakes his head. "That was a person."

We listen, and it is quiet except for the sound of a car going by and children playing in the street.

"I will try to not be such a downer with your friends. I want them to like me."

Brian gives me a gentle kiss on the mouth, then says, "Just relax around them and be yourself. And whatever you do, don't start kissing their asses. They don't respect that."

"Sorry I startled you in the shower," I say, changing the subject. "Now, you'll need to replace it."

Brian shrugs. "I'll give B.J. a call. He needs the work anyway."

"Do I know B.J.?"

"Yes." He puts his lips to mine and gives me a tender kiss. "Officer Green is a plumber by day and reserve officer by night."

There are more footsteps on the porch and two women talking, but they don't knock. Brian gets off the bed and pulls on a pair of shorts. I crawl off and go to the closet for a new shirt and pull it on.

As I open the drawer for a pair of underwear, the front door creeks open. I pull them on, then open another drawer to get some shorts. It is silent in the front room. When I step out of the bedroom, Brian is standing at the front door, frozen and staring.

I come up behind him and see that porch is filled with flowers, stuffed animals, cards, and casserole dishes.

"What day is it today?" Brian asks.

I do not know, so I go to the magnetic calendar on the

fridge. It was a freebie from Bud's garage with his logo at the top.

"August eighteenth," I say. There is something familiar about that date. It hits me. How could I have not known? It is the one-year anniversary of the day that Amber went missing.

CHAPTER FORTY-ONE

I sit on the couch as Brian brings everything in, setting the flowers, cards, and gifts on the coffee table and putting the casseroles in the kitchen. There are handpicked bouquets and florist arrangements with cards attached to plastic stakes. Some cards are written in crayons, with childish drawings. Other cards are in pink, green, purple, and white envelopes. There is a dingy stuffed bunny that looks well-loved and brand new beanie babies with the tags still on them. And there, mixed in with all the bright-colored gifts, is a black fly box with my name scratched into the top in deep, uneven letters.

Something inside me starts bubbling and wanting out. I try to stay still and hold it down, but it rises, and I sob. The next thing I know, Brian pushes things aside on the coffee table and sets two paper plates full of food in front of me. He sits down, puts his arm around me, and lets me cry into his chest until it is all out and I can breathe again.

"How could I have forgotten?"

"You didn't forget. You didn't know the date."

I put my hand out to all the gifts. "Why did they do this for me?"

"This town is full of good people," Brian says. "And they care about you."

He reaches forward, grabs my plate of food, and places it on my lap. There is a scoop of potato salad, pasta salad, layered bean dip, chips, and fried chicken. People spent their time making this for us.

I try to eat but have no appetite, so I set my plate on the coffee table and start opening the cards. There is one from Becky's family, the Stewarts, and one from Becky herself. It is sweet with a closeup of two little girls holding hands in a meadow of flowers. There are two cards from the Ungers, one from Rose and Russ and another from Doc.

"I bet Rose bought that for Doc," Brian says before taking a bite of chicken leg. "It's a bit mushy for him."

I have been dying to see who gave me the fly box. Hopefully, there are flies inside it. Maybe it is from one of the Dixons. I open the lid, and it is filled with flies. Eighteen flies.

"Nice!," Brian says and sticks a forkful of pasta salad into his mouth.

"There are eighteen," I say. "And it is August eighteenth. Do you think that is on purpose?"

"Maybe. It could be a coincidence."

Dry flies are hooked into the foam on one side and wet flies and nymphs on the other. I recognize some Caddisflies, Woolly Buggers, Stimulators, Stoneflies, and Nymphs.

"That is a lot of money in flies," Brian says. "Who sent it?"

There is no card or tag, so I shrug.

"Looks like you have a secret admirer," Brian says.

"Are you jealous?"

"Maybe..." he pulls me to him and kisses me. "Looks like I need to stay on my A-game."

We start going at it heavy when there is a knock at the door.

"To be continued..." Brian says.

He answers it and smiles. "Hey, thank you for all the..."

"Can we come in?"

His smile drops, and I can tell that something is wrong. He steps back and lets Rose, Chief Unger, and Doc into the house. I rarely ever see Rose and Russ together and never realized that she is taller than him. They all have long faces and sad eyes. Brian goes to the kitchen and grabs some chairs while they stand there looking down at all my gifts.

"Quite the haul there," Chief Unger says. He is not dressed in his uniform and looks like any ordinary man in a T-shirt and jeans.

"Everyone was very kind," I say.

Once they are all seated, Brian sits next to me and puts his hand on my leg. "What's up?"

"We have some news," Rose says, then looks to her husband to finish.

"We have the results back from the coroner. The third body is Amber."

A fuzzy ring starts in my ears and keeps getting louder. I see Brian's mouth moving, but I cannot hear any words. The four of them are taking turns talking, and I feel the vibration of Brian speaking next to me, but I cannot hear anything. Finally, they stand and walk out, leaving Brian and me alone on the couch.

CHAPTER FORTY-TWO

I've barely slept for the last five days. Every time I close my eyes, I see Amber sitting in the raft with blue lips and the silver space blanket wrapped around her, still alive and staring at me. When I do sleep, I dream of her bones on the bottom of the river—or of trout picking her clean then rising for my fly.

They found Amber and turned her over to the authorities. Even in death, she cannot escape being a ward of the state. Amber Ward. Ward of the state. Ward of Bones. I don't even know where she will be buried or if they will incinerate what is left and put her in a box.

Now, I sit on the front step of our porch and watch the children play hide-and-seek. It's curious how children hate rules, but that is the first thing they establish when playing a game. Even foster kids, who have nothing but rules, do it. The raccoons or dogs got into the garbage can of the rental across the street. It is tipped over, and the trash is strewn out all around it.

Rose told Brian that I could have a week off of work for bereavement, but then I had to get my ass back and get busy. I have two more days, and I still feel like my body is filled with cement.

It takes fifteen minutes for the kids to discuss the rules of where they can and cannot hide and how high the person who is the seeker needs to count. They make a special exception for one of the younger redheaded Stewart kids since she can only count to twenty. Dustin tries to explain that if she can count to twenty, all she needs to do is go to thirty and start over with thirty-one, but she is not having it.

The children run off with one boy staying behind. He covers his eyes and counts out loud, "One, two, three…"

When he gets to one hundred, he calls out, "Ready or not, here I come."

One girl, in dirty yellow shorts and two uneven pigtails, is immediately found behind a trash can because a small German Shepherd mix, stands there staring at her and wagging his tail. She joins the seeker and starts looking for the other kids.

It's late afternoon. The cicadas are buzzing like electrical wires, and soon the buses will start rolling back into town, stirring up the dust and bringing back the tired and sunburnt rafters.

The pack of kids comes out from between the two bungalows across the street. It looks like most of them are found.

"Who are we missing?" a girl asks.

"Only Dustin," a boy with dark wavy hair and overly large front teeth says.

Several of the children groan.

The first of the shuttle buses rattles and bumps past our street. It is cram-packed with rafters, and it drags a trailer piled high with four blue rubber rafts.

"They're back," a kid yells.

"Let's just leave Dustin," a girl with short-cropped hair and baggy pants says, and they all run off, following behind the shuttle.

The kids love to watch the guides. They are their heroes, and half the kids in town will probably do the same thing when they grow up.

Poor Dustin. I don't know what it is about certain kids, but no matter how much they try, the others never accept them. The mean boys wouldn't let him into their fort the other day either, so I slip on my flip-flops to go look for him. I cup my hands around my mouth and call, "Dustin…Dustin, you can come out now. Olly olly oxen free."

I turn down an unfamiliar street with a dead-end sign at the corner. If I were hiding and didn't want to be found, this is where I would go. The houses are run-down, and the yards are filled with trash and old beater cars.

Two men sit on the porch of a red house with a dirt yard. The railings are bare wood and look all dry and splintery. There is a rusted old barrel and a dead tree in the front. I smell pot. All my intuition tells me to turn around, but they saw me, and I don't want to be rude.

"Hey there, Emmy," one of them calls.

I raise my hand in a wave. The porch is so littered with boxes and stacks of firewood that the men are mostly hidden, and I cannot tell who it is.

"You looking for someone?"

I step closer. My feet freeze when I notice Darryl, the bouncer with the zombie-eyes, and Bobby Byrd. Darryl stands, leans one arm on the porch rail, and I see his tattoo of the skull with waves crashing around it. I cannot speak. What if he is the one killing the girls? He had offered to walk Amber and me to our room that night. He knows when the girls come and go from the Buckskin. He knows how drunk they are and if they are alone.

Darryl lets out a laugh. "Cat got your tongue?"

My entire body shivers. I take a breath and manage to say, "I'm looking for one of the children."

"Was that you calling for Dustin?"

I nod.

"What did he do? I'll whoop his ass."

Bobby Byrd has not said a word. He puts a joint to his mouth, inhales, and holds it in his lungs.

"You know him?"

Darryl lets out a harsh laugh. "He's my son."

"Is he there, in your house?"

"Maybe…"

Every nerve in my body starts to shiver, and I want to run.

Bobby exhales and chokes out, "Why don't you come on inside and see if you can find him."

I am stuck in this spot, and I cannot move one way or another.

"That's what you do, ain't it? You trespass into other people's houses without knocking or offering a *howdy-do*. I'd like to give you a howdy-do."

It feels as if someone has a foot on my chest and is pressing the air from my lungs. A faded red beater car turns down the street. I run away with the sound of the tires on the dirt road, and Darryl's gravely laugh behind me.

I head straight for Rimrock Outfitters. Please, God, let Brian be back. The guide truck, trailer, and bus are there, and the guides are wrapping it up with their customers. My breathing instantly slows, and I feel safe. A group of middle school girls in bikinis surround Brian. They're thanking him, and he's giving them high-fives as a van with *First United Methodist Church* stenciled along the side pulls into the yard. An exceptionally tall and thin man in baggy shorts with huge knobs for knees clambers out of the driver's seat. He opens the van doors, blows three short high-pitched whistles, and all the kids in the yard, soaking wet and hyper, pile in.

Brian notices me as he takes the other end of a raft that Chris is trying to lift off a trailer. A huge smile comes to his face, and he winks at me before disappearing into the boathouse.

I grab some life jackets and spread them out to dry, draping them over plastic chairs and the top of the chain-link fence. The orange and gray hammock strung between the trees next to the bunkhouse is sagging with someone inside it. Someone kid-sized. I try to peek in, but the top is wrapped over and held tight in a small fist.

"Dustin?"

"Shhhh…pretend I'm not here."

"The kids aren't playing anymore. They couldn't find you. You won."

The top opens, and he pokes his head up, looking like a gopher with his hair all shaved off. He swings his legs over, tips out of the hammock, and runs over to the guide truck. He looks nothing like his father, and I wonder why the kids tease him when Darryl could kick the asses of all of their fathers.

A Coke machine against the back wall of the shop hums and drops an ice-cold soda for a woman in a skirted swimsuit. There is laughter everywhere and children running around without a care. Maybe I just freaked myself out with Darryl and Bobby.

"Emmy!" Erin emerges from the boathouse. Her blonde braids dangle down beneath a lime green bandana tied around her head. "You're out! Great to see you."

She gives me a side hug that feels a bit awkward, but she has a huge smile.

"The shock is wearing off," I say. "But I still cannot believe that Amber is gone."

She has a sad face, and I can see that she is trying to think of what to say when Brian and Chris come out of the boathouse with Skid and Jake right behind them.

Brian comes over and kisses the top of my head. "It's good to see you out."

I force a smile.

"You all right?" he asks.

"Yes, I needed a change of scenery." I cannot tell Brian my fears about Darryl and Bobby Byrd. He will just tell me that I jump to all the worst conclusions. "Want to go fishing when you're done? I would like to try my new flies."

Brian has an odd but excited expression. "Of course. Why don't you go get all our gear together, and I'll meet you in our usual spot."

Everyone turns at the blasting sound of *Wild Angels* by Amy James. A white soccer mom car rolls up with five girls leaning out the open windows hooting to Brian and the other guides. "Hey, there, sexy!"

Jake and Chris raise their hands to wave at them. The girls break out into excited giggles before the car slowly rolls forward toward the Whitehorse Inn, and all four doors swing open.

CHAPTER FORTY-THREE

HIM

I SHOULD HAVE KNOWN THE KIDS WOULD MAKE A FORT OUT OF MY hideout. I leave it for a week, and empty Otter Pop wrappers are scattered on the ground. Orange, red, green, and my favorite, Louie Blue Raspberry, rivulets of liquid are pooled up in the creases. A book of matches and an empty pack of Marlboro cigarettes are stashed in the corner. The damned kids could catch the thing on fire.

I peek through a gap in the branches, directly at the Whitehorse back patio. I slow my breathing and listen to people on the river and the distant hum of the hotel air conditioners. I don't know how to keep the kids from my hideout. Maybe a dead dog with a knife in it and a warning note would work.

The wooden deck of the Whitehorse is only thirty feet away. I am invisible and hidden in the branches and blackberries. Tiny bikini tops and bottoms hang over the rail like a party banner. Two doors stand wide open, exposing the new girls who arrived in the white Lexus RX.

In the dark cavern of one of the rooms, a girl takes off her T-shirt, and I can see her dark nipples against the whiteness of her breasts and tan lines. She leans toward a girl sitting on the bed, and I wait for her to stick her tit into the girl's mouth, but she reaches past her and picks up a bra instead.

She turns toward me and becomes alert. She cocks her head like she knows I am here watching. She steps closer to the door with both of her white breasts glowing against the tan of her skin. Her hair is an ash blonde. She stares past the blackberries, momentarily frozen like a deer before she hooks her bra around her waist, twists it around, and slips her arms into the straps.

She is a goddess. She is the one, and I will do her alone. I don't need his bitch-ass barbarity. He only wants to satisfy one need, and he has no respect. All I need to do is get her away from her friends long enough to grab her. I don't need him for the ketamine anymore. I know where he keeps it.

Branches crack. I peek through the sticks of the doorway at a pack of kids, bickering like little brats and coming toward me.

"Go away," one of them yells.

"It's my fort. I found it."

"No, you didn't. We found it first. We just didn't tell you."

"Yeah, we didn't tell you because you're a whiny baby. Why don't you go home and suck on your mama's tit."

"I'm going to tell my dad."

"Oooh…he's going to tell his dad. Go ahead. He'll get in trouble if he touches us."

Kids are so damn mean. My temples throb, and I want to put my hands around their throats. I need to get rid of them. They will blab their dirty mouths about me hiding in the brush. The outline of a boy kneels in the doorway. I see his beady eyes as his hand reaches to move the sticks aside.

I growl a deep animal sound, and he falls backward onto his ass.

"Something's in there," he screams as he scrambles to his feet. "Run!"

They scatter into the brush with a great crunching and snapping of branches.

"What is that?" A female voice asks from the direction of the hotel.

"It's just a bunch of kids," my girl with the ash blonde hair says.

The kids are screaming and scared, but I know what it is to be a young boy. They will hide like predators and watch, waiting to discover what is in their fort. They will probably arm themselves with rocks and sticks, and I wouldn't be surprised if the damned heathens had their own knives.

I am trapped with the boys on one side and the girls watching to see what is going on. I turn my body toward the back corner and hope none of the kids have circled around.

I pry the sticks apart and slide between. Just like the river, I slip out. I know the land, and I know the river. I stay low until I get to the edge of the water and slide down into it. It clears my head and my nerves, snapping me awake and alert. I am back to full flow, strong again, and raging.

They took all my nymphs from me, and I need to restock.

Upriver, Emmy stands on the shore casting one of my flies. She throws without fully loading the rod, but it unrolls smooth and straight, dropping the fly onto the surface. I bet Emmy is using an Amber Haired Caddis. She is trying to dead drift her fly, but she is not throwing enough slack in her line.

My heartbeat quickens, and I want to take her now. I will fill her waders, slip her from them, and take her. I will breathe in her final breath, and all the tension will be gone. She will finally experience the perfect dead drift—below the surface like the slippery little nymph she is. I am the river. It is the fluid, and I am the flesh.

CHAPTER FORTY-FOUR

My Caddisfly floats over the riffle where I've seen both Brian and Skid catch trout, but nothing rises for it. I cannot read the river like them. I cannot think like a fish or know where to put my fly. It floats, all grayish-brown, on the blue-green river until it gets to the end of my line and sinks. I'm supposed to pop it off the surface and throw it back upstream, but I have not mastered that either. Instead of dead drifting, my line drags or floats across the current in an arc.

I should wade out, but I cannot. I still have not stepped into the river deeper than my ankles since the night Brian saved me from it.

I reel in my line and squat down to watch the river. I have a creepy feeling that someone is watching me, but there are no other fishermen out. Nobody is at the shoe tree or looking my way from the Whitehorse inn. The cicadas buzz their dry electrical hum, and the damned mourning dove calls its throaty cotton ball sound.

I turn to see if Brian is sneaking up on me, but all I see are the willows and two town dogs lying in the shade of a juniper.

They watch me. Maybe that is what I'm feeling. One is a Jack Russell and the other a Lab, both mixed with something else. They know what is happening in this town. They watch everyone and see everything.

Behind them, the sole tree drips heavy with shoes. Amber and my Converse are toward the top, fading to the point that I have trouble picking them out—just two more girls screwed and their shoes hanging in the tree like trophies.

I kneel down and look for the fish on the backsides of big rocks or in the shade lazily waiting for food to come floating by their mouths. A small pod of trout feed in the shade of the willows with their noses down, but there is no way for me to cast there from the shore.

I take out my new black fly box with my name gouged into the top. It looks like a child formed the letters with the E at a slant and the M's uneven, with one larger than the other. The flies are beautifully tied and little works of art made from feathers, fur, wire, and thread. The Woolly Buggers are fluffy, and their black down ripple in the breeze. Others, like the nymphs, are tight and thin, so they sink to the bottom.

I suspect Henry Dixon gave me the flies—since he ties them for the fly shop, and he said he wants to encourage girls to fish. I choose a tiny green and brown nymph and tie it on.

Something terrible is happening here. I know it, but nobody believes me. Maybe Mary. She senses it too, but she thinks it is an evil spirit. I will ask her about Darryl and Bobby Byrd.

Why would someone get a tattoo of a skull in the river? Bobby Byrd is creepy from head to toe and looks like he belongs in a mental hospital. While I'm at it, I will ask her about Big Doug. When he drove Amber and me back to town, he gave us the creeps, and then she went missing.

When Brian shows up, he is soaked from head to toe. All his clothes and even his baseball cap are dripping wet.

"What happened to you?"

"I was hot after unloading the gear, so I jumped in."

He stares at me with a slight but forced smile.

"Everything okay?" I ask.

"Of course. Thanks for bringing my gear." He steps out of his water shoes and into his waders, pulling them up and over his bare chest. "Anything biting?"

"No."

If I had not seen photos of Brian with his mother, I would believe that he physically sprung from the landscape. His hair and skin are as brownish-red as the steep canyon walls, and his eyes are the same deep greenish-blue and white as the churning river. Sometimes it feels as if one day he will lay down, sink back into it, and I will never see him again.

He slides his feet into his wading boots and ties them. An eruption of high-pitched laughter comes from the hotel. That new group of girls is screeching and laughing and acting stupid on the back patio.

Brian turns his head and stares at them, watching as they pass around a bottle of booze and dump it into their yellow Solo cups.

"Looks like they are pre-gaming," I say.

Brian slowly turns his head toward me. "What?"

"Pre-gaming. You know, starting the drinking early."

He shrugs, "Yeah, that happens a lot. They come here for fun, but they get so drunk they can't remember shit and feel like puking while rafting."

When the girls disappear around the corner of the hotel, Brian moves to the river, squats down, and studies the water.

"You need to wade out and toss it toward those willows."

He knows I'm afraid.

"It's okay. I'll help you."

I suddenly cannot breathe. Brian is right behind me, and I

feel his breath against my ear as he whispers, "It's okay. I'm right here."

My body shakes as his arm slides around my waist and leads me deeper. My ankles twist as I step across submerged rocks that are blurred and out of proportion beneath the rushing water. I picture my wading boot sinking into a dead girl's chest and breaking through her ribs. A cold wave of chills trickles up my spine.

We are deep, and the water is up to my hips, but Brian is here, holding me steady. I have a terrible feeling like the river bottom will crack open and swallow both of us.

"This should be good," Brian says, "Get your footing."

I adjust my feet on the rocks, and Brian slips his hand over my breast. His warm breath and lips on my neck send a shiver across my shoulders.

The river is cold and strong against my waders. I am trapped between it and Brian. Without him, the river would wash me downstream and pound and tumble me against the rocks.

"I wish I could take you right here." Brian's hand slides down my belly, and he pulls me tighter against him. I feel his hard-on against my back.

My boot slips off a rock and sends a shooting pain through my ankle.

"It's okay, I'm here. Get your footing."

I find a flat spot and wiggle my feet to make sure I am stable.

"You are sexy in your waders, but I want to see you butt ass naked in the river."

I cannot breathe. The river, willows, and cliffs melt into a red clay, green, and brown blur. I shiver with cold as if the river has flooded into my waders and is seeping through my skin, filling me up. Higher and higher, up my legs, over my belly, and filling my throat.

Brian backs away from me and leaves nothing but cool

water where his body had been. Nothing is solid. It is just me and the river.

"Go ahead. Throw your fly."

I cannot do anything. I am frozen and shaking. The water is rushing against me, wanting to take me. The next thing I know, Brian's arms are around me, and he is helping me to the shore. "It's okay. At least you did it. Next time will be easier."

CHAPTER FORTY-FIVE

The guys grab their beers and head straight to the pool table, leaving Erin and me alone in our booth. It's early enough that no panties or bras dangle from the antlers yet, but boobs are already flashing at big Doug, and he's lining up the shots.

"What's up with Jake?" I ask Erin. "He seems extra tense."

"He's still got a stick up his ass about that fight with Brian. And on top of that, his dad got all over him about his grades."

The five girls from the soccer mom car strut in wearing skanky dresses and stripper shoes. The neckline of the blonde girl's dress goes all the way down to the top of her belly button. She has no bra, and the tan from her bikini top makes a thin white line from breast to breast.

I glance over at Brian. He and the guys around the pool table have paused their game to drool over the girls. I can almost see the saliva dripping from their mouths.

"Is there any end to the pretty girls coming to this town?"

"Nope," Erin says and tips her beer up to her mouth.

"All they do is come here to get drunk and stumble around half-naked."

Erin raises her eyebrows and gives me a look. "I remember you all wasted in here last year."

My throat stings as I try to swallow the memory. "We were stupid and just didn't know any better."

"Yeah, neither do they," Erin says. "You need to stop worrying about other girls. It will drive you insane."

I try to hold them in, but the tears squeeze out anyway. She does not understand that nobody ever keeps me around. As soon as the newness wears off or a different girl shows up, it is *adios* and *hasta la vista. It's been nice, but it's time to move on.*

"Brian loves you. I've never seen him care about any girl the way he does about you."

Her eyes lock onto something and narrow. I turn and see Jake walking toward the group of girls.

"Jake, on the other hand, needs to be popped in the head." Erin scoots out of the booth, grabs one of the guides from another outfitter, and drags him to the dance floor.

I have an eerie feeling in my stomach, not so much about Brian or about Jake starting a fight, but like something bad is about to happen. Something terribly bad. I need to get ahold of myself...and I need to pee.

The bathroom is only one step up from a gas station bathroom with one of those old dispensers with a long strip of blue and white towel that rolls out. I step into a stall, pull down my shorts, and squat over the toilet without sitting on the disgusting thing. Just as I finish, the stall door flies open.

The prettiest of the girls, the one in the skimpy white halter dress, stands there with a desperate and panicked look on her face. I barely jump aside fast enough before she drops to her knees and vomits into the toilet bowl. I am trapped against the wall and pulling my shorts up as she hurls.

Her entire back is bare and thin, with the knobs of her spine poking up. She grips the sides of the toilet bowl with skinny arms and her elbows poking out. A black dandelion tattoo blowing in the wind is on the back of her shoulder. The dandelion seeds rise up and turn into birds that fly up the back of her neck.

"Oh, hey. Sorry about that."

I flinch and look up to see one of her friends in the doorway of the stall.

"She didn't even drink much." She grabs her friend's hips and rotates her so I can get by. "Maybe it's from the sun. She could be dehydrated."

The girl stands in red heels with legs that go on forever under her short dress. She holds her friend's hair back and pulls her skirt down to cover the strip of pink thong that was showing.

I remember Erin so sick when she didn't drink much. And that night with Amber and me. We hardly drank anything before the room began to spin, then there was nothing until I woke up in the hospital the next day.

I turn to leave, but something stops me. "Who touched her drinks?"

"What?" She seems confused as to why I am speaking to her.

"Did anyone buy her a drink?" My voice sounds high-pitched and panicked. I try to calm down. "You need to leave."

The girl at the toilet raises her head and sits down on the floor. She looks up at me with a glazed expression and wet mouth.

"Get in your car and leave town right now."

The standing girl gets a condescending smirk on her face, and she looks me up and down. "Right. We are not going to drive in the middle of nowhere in the dark when we have all been drinking."

She unrolls a bunch of toilet paper, pushes past me, and wets it in the sink. "You got a boyfriend here?"

I nod, and she gives me a tight-lipped smirk. The bathroom door opens, and two more of the girls come in. "How's Crystal?"

"Better." The red-heel girl wipes Crystal's mouth with the wet toilet paper.

"You all need to leave…"

The girls notice me and look back and forth between their friend and me.

"Ignore her. She's just a jealous-ass bitch trying to get rid of us."

"I'm trying to help you. My friend was killed last year."

"Then what the hell are you still doing here? Crazy bitch. Leave us alone."

"Really…she's the girl in the red and white missing poster. The one on the hotel counter and the cash register at the…"

"I didn't see any poster." She narrows her eyes.

Right…there are no more posters. Since Amber has been found, every trace of her is erased from this town.

"I need to lay down," Crystal mumbles. She tips sideways and starts lowering herself onto the bathroom floor.

"Uhhh, no…" her friends say in unison before helping her to her feet and guiding her out.

I follow them. As they walk past Darryl, he stands up from his stool and looms over them. From this distance, his tattoo looks like a black, blue, and red smear of color on his forearm. He reaches out like he is going to take Crystal from them.

No, no, no…I want to scream.

They almost let her go into his arms, but then one of them shakes her head and gives him an uneasy smile. Maybe she is thinking about what I said. They all walk out together. I follow them out then turn toward Brian's house, alone.

CHAPTER FORTY-SIX

HIM

I heard them call her Crystal. She is there on the bed, alone in the room with the bathroom light on, just where her shitty-ass friends left her. She is on her side, not even covered with a sheet. Her dress is bunched around her legs. One tit hangs out of her dress, and her ash blonde hair spreads out on the pillow and off the side of the bed.

The bed creaks, and she tips toward me as I sit beside her. She has a dandelion tattoo on her shoulder. It blows in the wind, with its seeds soaring and carrying all her hopes and dreams. As they rise, four of the seeds turn into birds flying up the back of her neck. As a child, I blew the fluff from the dandelions, letting my wishes float away in the wind. And now, here they are. Not wasted after all.

She moans as I roll her onto her back and spread her thighs. The insides are soft and tanned all the way up to her pink thong that stretches across her hips. I peel off the layer of bright pink and reveal deep pink folds and a shaved pussy waiting for my tongue.

I take her slow, tasting and touching before I finally enter her. I rage and crest. I keep it inside her as I pant and drip with the water coming from me, even on land. Her eyes flutter and peek open to their whites, and a smile comes to the corners of her mouth.

"You like that?" I let it slip out of her and crawl back down between her legs. I put my mouth to her lips and taste both of us on my tongue. She moans again, and I know I have hit her sweet spot.

Afterward, I kneel beside her on the bed and smooth her hair out. It is soft and ash blonde, just like dandelion fluff. I wind it around my fingers and pull. She lets out a soft whimper that rises and floats around the room on the electric hum of the air conditioner. I slip her hair into the pocket of my shorts before I pull them on.

I strap both of her sparkly gold heels together before I turn the bathroom light off so we can slip into the night without a trace. She is so light in my arms that I could carry her forever. It is time for the river and time to bind her to me forever.

Nobody is on the patio, so I take her to the far side, where the shoe tree glows in the moonlight. The first step creaks. I freeze in the darkness and listen but hear nothing but the air conditioners and the band playing in the distance. My heart pounds as I step down from the patio with Crystal in my arms. I position her in one of the Adirondack chairs, all naked and beautiful with her thin white ghost bikini over her tits, with her small pink nipples in the center.

The shoes hang there in clumps, like swarms of bees clinging to the lifeless branches. I fling her heels, and they spin like two conjoined dandelion seeds, rising higher and higher until they catch into a clump and hold the moonlight in their sparkles.

As I lift Crystal back into my arms, a low growl comes from beneath the hotel patio. They always watch me with their beady eyes, always slinking around town, rummaging in trash cans, and waiting for the kids to play with them. They know who I really am. And they sense my power, but there is nothing they can do.

The cool river rises up my ankles, calves, and thighs, seeping into the fabric of my shorts. As Crystal's toes and ass dip into the water, a shiver washes through her body and into my arms. Her eyes flutter, and they open. She sees me. They are steady, with the blue iris' and black pupils looking straight at me. Two lines appear between her eyebrows, and her mouth opens. "What?"

"It's okay," I say and pull her up from the water and against my chest.

She tries to turn her head, but I have her pressed tight. Her eyes look around at me, at the stars, and back to my face. "Where are we?"

We? Where are We?

"I found you here. In the river."

She is groggy. I should have given her more Ketamine. I cannot drown her when she is aware. When she can fight me and possibly get away.

"River? What river?"

"Shhh. You must have come here drunk, and you almost drown."

She starts hyperventilating, and her eyes widen. Her thin arm reaches out and clasps onto me, clinging to my body. "Oh my God, thank you."

She is a naked water nymph as I take her from the water to the shore. "It's okay. I got you. You're safe."

CHAPTER FORTY-SEVEN

The red letters of the alarm clock laser onto my eyeballs. It's two-thirty in the morning. Brian's side of the bed is empty. I slide out, bare ass naked. Even with the window open, it is hot as hell in the house. Please, let Brian be on the couch.

The moon shines into the window, throwing a dim glow across the living room. He is not there. I flip on the bathroom light to make sure, and it washes across an empty couch. It feels like someone is squeezing my insides, and I want to puke. Did Brian even come home to check on me when I disappeared from the Buckskin? Did he care?

What did I expect? I was stupid for leaving the bar without telling Brian. He is probably paying me back by...by what? By crashing on the couch at Skid's or Jake's? Or by crawling into bed with one of the girls from the bar? Damnit!

I sit down on the couch, and my stomach starts to churn, then it rises hot into my throat. I know when I've gone too far. I feel it in my gut when it is the end and when I will be asked to leave.

This is the smallest and trashiest house I have ever lived in, but I felt loved here. We cocooned together all winter, our naked bodies wrapped up in the blankets, and we made love every day—sometimes more than once a day. I know every bit of Brian's body, including the scar from an appendicitis attack that almost left him dead. My fly vest and waders hang from the coat tree, my flip flops are by the door, and my shampoo is in the shower. I am all over Brian's house.

Will he throw everything of mine into boxes until I am completely erased? I should not have left without him last night. I know better than to become a problem, but I have not been able to get myself together. Of course, Brian would want a good time, not always having a mental mess of a girlfriend. There are so many girls prettier than me, and they probably do not have as much emotional baggage.

The not knowing sucks. If he does not want me, I will leave. I cannot stay here and be tortured. I can live through rejection. I have done it my whole life, but losing Brian will be like having the breath sucked out of my lungs.

Please, God, let Brian still love me. Give me another chance, and I will put on a happy face. I will show him what a good person I really am.

What in the hell am I doing, sitting here like a child? If I want my man, I need to fight for him. As I change into my shorts and T-shirt, I smell the mustiness of our bedroom, of our lovemaking, and the sage and juniper coming in the open window. I run the brush through my hair and step out into the night.

There is nothing as dark as the desert with no moon. The night is lit with nothing but the stars and a few porch lights. The river slips by silent and dark, like a gash in the land separating Lodell from the reservation, or Rez. The town side of the river is filled with loud people, bright-colored rafts, trash, and fishermen pulling the trout, steelhead, and salmon from the water. The Rez is silent with nothing but the wind blowing through the trees and grass—or the occasional whinny of a horse.

A dim shape slinks around between a boulder and the blackberries. At first, I think it is a raccoon until the silhouette gimps by on three legs.

"Hey there, Lieutenant Dan. Come here, boy."

He hobbles over to me, wagging his nub of a tail.

"Sorry boy, I don't have a treat." I reach out to pet him, but his entire body turns rigid, and a line of hair stands up on his back. He stares just past me with a growl bubbling in his throat.

I turn to see the dark shape of a man against the brush. He is still, and I cannot tell if he is facing me or turned the other way taking a piss.

My mind tells me to run, but I cannot move. What if it is Bobby Byrd or Darryl? I wait for the whiff of pot to come toward me or a horrible scratchy voice saying, *I'd like to give you a howdy-do.*

My breathing comes so fast that I feel lightheaded. Lieutenant Dan inches in front of me with the growl still caught in his throat. I should run while he holds the man off.

"Emmy?"

It's Brian. Lieutenant Dan stops growling, and his entire body wiggles as he gimps over to Brian.

"What are you doing out here?" As he wraps his arms around me, the cold hem of his shorts touches my bare legs.

"Why are your shorts wet?" I pull away from him.

"Why are you out here?"

"Your shorts are wet," I say.

"I saw something floating in the river and waded in. It was just someone's empty cooler."

My heart feels like it is about to beat through my chest. Brian stands there, so close to me that I can feel the humidity of the water evaporating from his shorts.

"Why didn't you come home? Where have you been?" My

voice is rising in pitch, but I cannot stop it. "Did you even worry where I was? Did you check on me?"

"Calm down." Brian puts his hand on my shoulder, but I pull away.

"Don't tell me to calm down."

"Okay." He puts his hands up in surrender. "What are you doing out here?"

"I'm not allowed outside? I'm not allowed to leave the house?"

"Emmy…" His voice is soft. "What happened?"

"Why don't you just tell me that you don't love me anymore?"

"What? What are you talking about?"

"I see it in your eyes. You used to look at me differently. And you didn't even care that I left the Buckskin tonight."

His eyebrows pinch together like he has no idea what I am talking about, trying to make me feel stupid.

"Tell me." I shove him. "Tell me you don't love me."

"What happened?"

"I saw you looking at those girls, and then you didn't even come home."

"I…what? No…" He drops his head and runs his hands through his hair. "I came home, and you were in bed."

"No, you didn't." Did he? I may have felt the bed sink on his side. No, that could have been another night. He is always leaving. My chest tingles, and my mouth feels dry.

"Please, you have to trust me." His voice is so soothing, trying to trick me and make me believe.

"Trust you? How can I trust you? You are always leaving me alone…I don't know what you do."

"I come to the river. It calms me."

I cock my arm back and make a fist. Brian stands there, knowing I will not punch him, so I do. My fist grazes by his jaw, and he grabs my wrist.

"I've been coming out here my whole life." He squeezes my wrist so hard that my hand starts to swell. "The river is part of me, and it calms me."

"You're hurting me."

Brian twists my arm behind my back and kisses me so hard that my mouth bleeds. I know he can taste it, but he does not stop. We drop down onto the grass, right there by the river. We pull at one another's clothes until we are naked in the night with the stars and the sage and red rimrock cliffs.

We make love like we used to. Brian is part of the land, and I am becoming one with him. When we finally lay panting with the river rushing over our bare feet, I have a flash of memory. Not the one of Brian saving my life, but of being carried to the river and rolled onto the hard rubber boat tube.

CHAPTER FORTY-EIGHT

HER

"Rise and shine. The sun is in the sky. Get up, get up, drink sunshine from a cup."

What?... My head. I open my eyes, but I'm blind. I can't see anything. What the...Where am I? My mouth tastes like vomit, and I...How did I? What the...I need to get up, but I can't move my arms or legs. I am tied to a bed. Holy shit.

"Good morning, gorgeous." The side of the bed sinks.

"Help..." I scream as loud as I can. "Help..."

Something is shoved into my mouth, and I start to choke.

"Oops, I didn't mean to be so rough." He pulls the gag. I can breathe, but it is still there.

"Sometimes, I get carried away." His voice is so tender. "I saved your life. I pulled you from the river."

I shake my head. This is not saved. I cry out, but the words are stuffed down and only vibrate in my throat.

"If someone saves your life, you are theirs forever."

No, no, no...Pain shoots through my wrists and ankles. I'm tied down. I buck and kick. I need to make noise. Maybe someone from another room will come or call the front desk.

"It's no use. Nobody can hear you."

My chest starts heaving. I'm going to aspirate and choke to death.

"Go ahead." The gag is pulled from my mouth. "Scream all you want. Nobody comes to this part of town."

Now that I can, nothing comes out. I gasp and gasp, pulling in the air.

"There you go. I think you will come to love me. I will take better care of you than any man ever has. I will spoil you, and you will be my goddess."

I cannot get air. My lungs spasm. He is combing through my hair with his fingers.

"You will be mine in life or in death. It will be your choice."

He fans my hair out around me.

"Hmmm...let's see... Just as I thought. It is an extra light ash blonde. But it could be vanilla creme. No, it is ash."

I feel him rise off the bed. Footsteps on a wooden floor. Then silence, except for a cooing bird sound outside. Far away, a train whistle blows. Lodell. We came to raft. Before classes start. A door squeaks, and the footsteps come back.

"Let's see your kissy face now." He grabs my cheeks and squeezes.

My lips pop open, and something bitter drips into my mouth. I shake my head and spit, but it coats my tongue.

"There you go. You'll just be taking a little nappy now. I have saved you. For I am the river. It is the fluid, and I am the flesh." He runs his hand over my breasts and down my stomach. Then something warm comes over my breast. He is sucking it like a baby.

"No...Stop."

"Oh, come on, that feels nice. You need to say nice things, or the gag will go back in. Tell me how you like it." He bites on my nipple. "Is that good? Or harder?"

A cry starts up my throat, but I swallow it down. "Softer."

How did I?... We were at a bar. Where is Mia? And Lauren?

My lips open, and my cheeks go slack. My muscles are melting. The pain in my crotch and wrists float away, but he is there, touching me. My whole body jerks. I am moving, but there is no feeling. Nothing but the thrusts of my body on a mattress. Until that, too, drifts off with the darkness…

CHAPTER FORTY-NINE

"Owww...What did you do to me?" I roll over and nuzzle into Brian's chest. His hairs tickle my nose. "I think every knob of my spine is bruised."

"Sorry, I got carried away."

"I think we both got carried away." Whether it was the fear of getting caught or the relief that it was Brian and not Bobby Byrd standing there, I don't know—but it was hot, and it was what we needed.

"Roll over."

I roll onto my other side, and Brian runs his fingertips down my back.

"Yep, you got a few scrapes there. I'm sorry." He puts his lips to my skin and plants little kisses all the way down my back. "You're going to need some doctoring. Wait right there."

He returns with a half-crushed box of bandaids and a yellow tube of ointment.

"They need bandaids?"

"Just to keep the Neosporin from wiping away...unless you're going to lay there naked for hours."

"Okay, I'll lay here naked."

"Nice try," he says, squeezing the ointment in spots all down my back, "but you have work today."

The wrappers crinkle as he pulls them off the Band-Aids. The mourning dove coos its throaty sound right outside the window. It is half open, letting in the damp smell of the juniper and sage.

"Oooh." I flinch as he presses a Band-Aid onto my back. "I didn't expect that."

"What do you think I've been doing back here?" His voice is light and teasing, and he kisses the back of my neck.

When the rafting season is over, Brian and I can go back to snuggling in bed until we feel like getting up and then wrapping ourselves in blankets to eat our meals on the couch.

The Band-Aid box clunks to the floor, the entire bed rocks with Brian's weight.

"You're done?"

"With that part."

His arm reaches around my waist, and he pulls me against his body. His erection is hard against my back, and he whispers, "I wasn't worried about the ointment getting on your shirt…"

Just then, popping up into the window like a jack-in-the-box, Skid's face appears.

"Ahhhhh," I scream and start grabbing at the sheets to pull something over me.

"What the fuck?" Brian yells.

"Oh, Dude. Bad timing." Skid does not look away. With the light behind him and his scraggly hair, he looks like a damned creeper.

Where are the damned sheets? Our entire bed pitches back and forth, and before I know it, a pillow flies at the window, hits it and drops to the floor. Brian throws our blanket over me. When I peek out, Skid's face is gone.

We dress and head into the kitchen, where Skid is already sitting at our table. "Sorry about that. It surprised me, and I just froze. I couldn't move."

"Why would you look into someone's bedroom window this early?"

Skid shrugs and looks at us with his pathetic Eeyore eyes. "I knew that's where you would be?"

"Yeah, well, if you ever do that again, I'm going to beat the shit out of you."

"I'm sorry." There is a tiny drop of silence then he turns toward me. "What happened to your back? Were those Band-Aids?"

Before I know it, Brian's big hand flies through the air and knocks Skid across the top of his head. "Can you just stop being a dumbshit for once in your life?"

He puts his hands up in surrender. "Sorry…"

Brian turns away toward the refrigerator. He opens it and grabs hold of the milk jug just as Skid whispers to me, "Nice ass, though…"

In a blur, the entire half-filled, one-gallon jug of milk hurls toward Skid. He ducks, and it hits his shoulder, then the floor. The lid pops off, and the milk gurgles onto the linoleum. We all stare at it for a second before Brian yells, "You're done, get the fuck out."

"I was just giving Emmy a compliment…trying to make it better."

"Out!"

The chair scrapes back, and Skid heads toward the door. "Sorry," he says before pulling it shut behind him.

"Whenever he gets flustered, he tries to fix it but ends up making it worse," Brian says to me. "He's done that his whole life."

The milk is still gurgling onto the floor.

I don't agree with Brian's explanation. There was a spark in Skid's eyes like he knew exactly what he was doing.

Skid pops his head back in the door. "Oh...I forgot what I came for. No rafting trips today. Another girl is missing."

CHAPTER FIFTY

"You're going to be late for work." Brian stands in the doorway and watches me dress.

The whole thing with Skid peeping in the window and then telling us another girl is missing has pulled the air from my lungs. I feel heavy like I am filled to the throat with water.

"The girls are not drowning," I say and slip my arms into my uniform sleeves.

Brian's eyebrows pinch together, and he gets that, *Do we have to deal with this again?* look on his face. "Emmy…"

"I know they literally drowned, but they are not doing it on their own." I turn around. "Will you zip me?"

Brian slips his hands around my waist and puts his mouth to my neck. It tickles and sends a cold shiver across my shoulders. As I bend down to pick up my apron, he grabs my hips and presses himself hard against my ass.

"Mmmm…I can't stop thinking about last night by the river." His voice is deep and throaty.

"Yes," is all I can say. How can he think of his own pleasure when a girl is missing? I stand up and try to tie my stupid white apron around my waist, but my hands tremble, and I cannot make a bow.

"I'm right here, and you're going to be okay," he whispers and slips the ties from my hands. "Let's not freak out until we know what has happened."

He is right. Maybe it is a mistake. Maybe it is not the blonde who is missing. Maybe one of the other girls hooked-up with someone and crashed in their room for the night. She could be hungover and sleeping, completely unaware that she is missing.

Brian cinches my apron.

"Uhh…too tight."

"You don't want it falling down."

"It won't." I take the end of the tie and pull it loose. "That's why girls have hips."

"I got you." He plants little kisses on the back of my neck as he reties it. "This has got to be the ugliest uniform in the world."

"I could return it and quit…"

"Nice try."

We walk, hand in hand, toward the Whitehorse with our fingers intertwined. I have a death grip on Brian. The air is still, and everything floats in slow motion. It is as hot as hellfire. The cicadas' electrical buzz is so loud that I keep looking up at the power lines expecting them to snap. Everyone looks at us as we pass. Even the dogs pause and turn or look up from their naps.

The smells of oatmeal and bacon come from the cafe at Carl's Cabins. Several guests sit at tables eating while a child stands at the patio rails, gripping the bars with both hands and staring through the gap at us. Matt is sitting outside the market, hand-feeding Lieutenant Dan and kicking at other dogs who approach.

The one and only Lodell police car is parked on the side of the hotel at an angle. The chief gets the car, and the rest of them usually walk or drive their own vehicles.

Mary has Officer Green, all beefy and stuffed tight into his uniform, trapped between the chief's car and the wall of the hotel. He must have been called to duty, away from his plumbing work. As usual, Mary's face is barely moving or showing expression. I can imagine her telling him about the evil spirit in room 114 and how she and I both feel it. I know that my name is slipping from her mouth.

Brian squeezes my hand.

The girls from the soccer mom car huddle together on the patio with their arms wrapped around themselves or interlinked. They are talking with Officer Rubio and Officer Jemmy Bell.

One, two, three...there are only four of them. And the one missing is the blonde who burst into the stall with me. Oh, God...I knew it. I felt it, and I should have done more. I could have followed them, but how did I know that her selfish ass friends would leave her alone in her condition.

Chief Unger leans on the rail, close enough to listen as he scans the area. He spots something in the bushes, leans his arms on the rail, and stares at it.

My feet stop moving before Brian's, and I try to slip my hand from his, but he tightens his grip. "You're going to be late."

"I don't care. Who gives a shit about cleaning when another girl is dead."

"You don't know she is dead." Brian's voice is clipped, and he is annoyed.

"I saw her last night."

"When?" Something flashes in Brian's eyes. Something I have never seen. Maybe fear or panic, but it quickly disappears.

"She was throwing up in the bathroom...and her friend said she hardly drank anything at all."

That expression returns to Brian's face, but this time it stays.

"I watched her friends walk her out of the Buckskin, right past Darryl. You don't think..." I clamp my lips tight. The words stick between them, and a lump rises in my throat. Something is wrong. The fabric of my dress catches against one of the Band-Aids, and I remember the shadow by the river.

"There she is!" I look away from Brian and over to the Whitehorse patio. One of the girls is staring at me and pointing. Everyone turns to look at Brian and me.

Two of the girls nod their heads, and Chief Unger slowly steps off the patio. He comes toward us, all pigeon-chested, with his badge catching and flashing in the sun. I reach back to take Brian's hand, but he is not there.

CHAPTER FIFTY-ONE

CHIEF UNGER WALKS TOWARD ME IN SLOW MOTION WITH THE four girls and the two officers following behind him. Where the hell is Brian? My heart thumps so hard I can feel it pumping against my ribs. I am alone. Exposed with nowhere to go. His badge flashes on his green and white uniform shirt.

There is nothing wrong. I did not do anything. Breathe in through the nose and out the mouth.

The girls walk stiffly with narrowed eyes. One has an orange ball cap and a white sports bra. Another, I think the one who first came into the bathroom, is in a pink tank top, and her hair is a mess. The third has dark hair and a cut-off football shirt with a huge red number forty-two. And the fourth is wearing a gray wife-beater and short shorts.

"That's her. She's the one."

"Yes! She was acting like a jealous bitch and threatening us," the fourth girl says. Her hair is back in a ponytail, and her shorts are tiny, barely bigger than bathing suit bottoms. "She told us to leave."

"Maybe she did it," the girl in the pink says in that tone I remember well from the mean girls in high school.

"Hold on there, girls," Chief Unger says. "Emmy's friend drowned in the river. She…"

"Well, maybe she did it. Maybe she drowned her own friend."

"And Crystal. Where is Crystal? What did you do to her?"

Officer Bell takes hold of the girl's arm and pulls her out of my face. *Breathe. Do not punch her in the throat. They are scared, and they are worried. Remember how you felt when Amber was missing.*

"Shame on you all." Someone takes my arm. "You, of all people, Russ."

I turn and see Mary right beside me with her eyebrows lowered and finger pointing right at Chief Unger.

"Hold on," Chief Unger says, "We have a missing girl."

"Can't you see you are traumatizing Emmy?"

"She was threatening…" the girl in the orange ball cap says.

"You need to get control of these girls," Mary says. "You cannot just let them attack people. You know Emmy has nothing to do with this."

"She threatened us last night," the girl with the number forty-two says.

The one in the pink shirt nods. "In the bathroom."

"Girls, I am sorry your friend is missing, and I don't mean no disrespect, but I know Emmy, and she is just as upset about this as you."

"Oh no, she isn't. She was jealous of Crystal and did not even help her when she was sick last night. She just stood there with a strange look on her face."

"Like a crazy bitch."

The cords on Mary's neck stand out, but her voice is slow, controlled, and focused straight at Chief Unger. "Emmy and I have work to do. Give her some air. Get these girls' stories straight, then send one of your officers, preferably BJ, to talk with Emmy. You know where we will be."

With that, Mary guides me toward the hotel, which is the last place I want to be.

CHAPTER FIFTY-TWO

HIM

The house is a sweatbox. When I finish this fly, I will go to the river and wade in, deeper and deeper until the current pushes against me. Extinguishes the fire. Cools me, Hugs me. Envelops me, and I am reborn. The flesh is flawed. The river is immortal. Even when it takes a life, it is not judged—it is respected even more.

From the other room, she is screaming against her gag. The flesh is messy. I should have bound her to me last night.

"It's okay," I call to her. "I will be with you soon."

I will show her that she is loved as I run my hands over her body. She is a nymph, naked, tied to the mattress, and waiting for me.

I take his hat from the rack by the door. The inside brim is stained with his sweat, and an entire Caddisfly hatch is hooked around the brim. The whole life cycle is like a halo around his head—larva, pupa, emerger, adult, cripple, and spent. His hat is stiff and elongated from hanging on the rack for so long. I press it onto my head, forcing it to conform and reshape.

The door squeaks as I open it to watch her, naked and stretched out with her tits like perfect mounds, with her pink nipples soft and flat. She knows I am here. Her entire body is quivering in the heat, and I want to enter her, but I will wait. I need a single fresh strand of her hair.

Her muscles twinge with each of my footsteps on the hardwood. A low whistling cry starts in her throat, but it only bubbles up to the gag, unable to escape. I lick around her nipple and pinch it between my lips to wake it up. I do the same to the other. She thrashes her head side to side, and the word *no* groans in her throat as I pluck a single long strand from the crown of her head.

Crystal is wet with sweat and shivering. Dirt brown mattress stains surround her, and she is splayed out with red tie-downs. She is flesh and blood, still of the earth and not the water. Crystal will be better than Emmy. She is more beautiful, and her hair is the color of the whitewater as it crashes and foams against the boulders. And just like the whitewater, I can tell that she will roar and thrash as I channel her.

I will tie a blood worm and wrap it with a strand of her ash blonde hair. A pack of Camel's is lying in the top drawer of his tying desk. My chest aches as I tap out a smoke, light it, and set it in the ashtray like a stick of incense—to fill me with his scent as it burns itself out.

I slide a number ten nymph hook from its tray and clamp it in the vice. My breathing slows as I unravel a strand of red velvet chenille from the cardboard and run it across my lips.

Her muffled cries are a deep and throaty coo. She will have to wait.

I tie the chenille to the hook and wrap the body with black thread. Binding it around and around, I build up a bulbous head behind the eye. The chenille is soft like the red slit between Crystal's spread legs. I wrap it and tie it down, then add a crystal thread and a crystal ash blonde hair for some ribbing and flash. I twist them up to the head and bind them down. Her ash-blonde strand will appease the river and call to the fish like a siren.

The cigarette is consuming itself and already has a quarter-inch of ash. Someone is coming toward the house. Their shoes crunch on the dirt and snap the scrub beneath them. Crystal's cry turns into a muffled scream. She heard them too. The footsteps stop. Shit! She needs to be silenced.

The room is sweltering and now smells of fresh urine. I reach for the syringe and vile of Ketamine I left on the dresser. I need to get it into her now. Into her vein. How much? I have never injected it before. I pull the plunger and fill the syringe. As soon as I come near, she bucks and screams and will not hold still. I shove the gag tighter and press my knee onto her arm, looking for the vein. It bulges, turns blue, and I pierce it with the needle. I squeeze all of it in. In seconds, she is still.

I pull the bedroom door closed and head back to my tying. More steps, now on the porch. Whoever it is pounds on the door.

CHAPTER FIFTY-THREE

It's as hot as hell—at least a hundred and five degrees with heat waves rippling across the pavement. My pits and under-boobs are all sweaty in this damned uniform. Whoever invented polyester should be shot. The moment I get home, I'm dropping it to the floor, taking a cold shower, and eating my lunch in peace. I'll have forty-five minutes of no vacuuming or touching other people's filth.

Our electric fan oscillates side to side, swirling the hot air around the room.

"Brian?"

No answer.

I leave a trail of shoes, socks, uniform, panties, and bra, all the way from the front door to the shower. Brian replaced our old nozzle with a handheld showerhead that sprays wherever you need it to spray. I turn on the cold and step in, letting it rain down my head, spray beneath my arms, and between my legs. I focus on the feeling of the water over my skin and put the head on power massage. It pulsates against my scalp, causing every nerve to tingle. I finally turn it off, wrap a towel around my hair, and leave my body dripping wet.

The front door and screen open. Thank God Brian is home, and I do not need to worry. I step out of the bathroom, and a shiver runs across my shoulders and up my neck. It is not Brian.

"What are you doing here?"

Big Doug, the *flash me your boobs* bartender, stands in our living room with his arms wrapped around a giant air conditioner box and sweat dripping down from his mass of hair. For someone who is used to seeing girls' boobs, he stands there like an idiot, unable to say a word.

"Get out of here," I say.

"Uhhh…Uhhh. Brian asked me to put in an air conditioner." He sets the box on the floor and lifts an envelope from the top. "This was on your porch."

He holds out a large eight-by-ten white envelope with my name written across the front. The handwriting looks familiar, but I'm not sure why. It wasn't there when I came home.

I reach for the envelope and catch a whiff of vinegary B.O.

He looks down to the trail of clothes, then back up at me. "Shouldn't you get dressed?"

"Oh shit." I run into the bedroom, pull on a T-shirt and shorts, then run around picking up all my panties from the floor. What the hell. Couldn't Brian have told me?

Back in the living room, he still stands in the same spot.

"Did Brian say where he wants it?" I ask.

"Uhhh, yes. In the bedroom."

"It's all yours," I say, then drop the envelope onto the kitchen table and open the fridge.

The screen door squeaks, and Brian steps in. He has a terrible look on his face, and his lip is split and bloody.

"What happened?"

"Nothing." He licks the blood from his lip, streaking the end of his tongue with red.

The knuckles on his right hand are scraped red and clotting with blood. "You got in a fight?"

"It's nothing."

The sound of tearing cardboard comes from the bedroom.

"You're putting in an air conditioner?"

"You don't sound happy about it."

"I...I just didn't know, and I..."

His jaw tenses, and he shakes his head. "I'm tired of sweating my ass off while we sleep."

He is annoyed with me, so I change the subject. "Who did you get in a fight with?"

"It's nothing. Drop it."

Brian is silent. The house is filled with nothing but swirling hot air and the squeak of styrofoam from the bedroom.

"You want a sandwich?"

He nods and says, "Thank you."

I fix us each a bologna and cheese sandwich. Brian's with mayo and mine with mustard. I also crack some ice cubes from the tray and drop them into a baggie.

I set the paper plates on the table and sit across from Brian. The blood seeps up from the cut. He licks it, and I wrap the ice in a paper towel and hand it to him. He puts it to his lip.

Every time he takes a bite of his sandwich, the bread soaks up the blood. Brian holds the ice to the corner of his mouth as he chews.

"What's that?" He nods his head at the envelope.

"I don't know. Doug said it was on the porch."

"Open it."

I unclasp the metal brad, lift the flap, and find a folded cardboard photo frame. I slip it out. Printed on the cover in red letters is *Shooting the Rapids Photography* and a black silhouette of rafters paddling through a rapid. Every nerve in my body is telling me not to look inside.

"What's wrong?"

My words get caught in my throat. I look up at Brian. "I can't..."

He reaches out, and we both have hold of the cardboard frame. His hand is big and tanned and bloody. Mine is small and dry, with the nails chewed down to the quick. I do not let go, so he yanks it from my fingers.

Brian sets it on the table and opens it with his bloody knuckles. Inside is a giant eight-by-ten photo snapped at the exact moment Amber fell from the raft. Brian stands at the rear, firmly braced, with his paddle planted in the water—while I lean away from Amber, holding the chicken line and keeping myself inside the raft. Amber's arms are out, reaching, as she falls back with her mouth and eyes wide open. The water rages everywhere, swallowing her, just like the tattoo on Darryl's arm.

As Brian and I sit at the table, it feels like a gaping hole has opened between us, widening and widening, until I feel like I will fall into it and drown. I still have the same bite of sandwich in my mouth that I took before Brian opened the cover. No matter how much I chew, it will not go down past the lump in my throat.

CHAPTER FIFTY-FOUR

HIM

FLESH IS WEAK. WATER YIELDS AND FLOWS UNTIL IT DECIDES TO rage. I am becoming more fluid than flesh. He may have wounded my flesh, but he has enraged the fluid. He suspects me, but he did not find Crystal. Emmy is the problem. It is time to fill her lungs and bind her to me forever.

CHAPTER FIFTY-FIVE

BACK AT THE WHITEHORSE, PEOPLE SIT ALL OVER THE LOBBY, under the dead animal heads, on the couches, the chairs, and slouched against the wall, trying to stay cool. They all turn as I enter, hoping for the beautiful missing blonde to come sweeping in the door in her white dress and golden shoes. They are waiting to take a breath. Waiting for a happy ending. But there is no happy ending when she is the fifth girl gone—and four of them have been found in the river, nothing but flesh and bone.

Behind the front desk, Becky leans against the wall, pressing her ear to the seam of the closed office door. Crystal's friends are in there. What else could it be? They are sitting in the room that smells like cigarettes with hundreds of origami birds hanging like a string of rainbow-colored fish. They probably sit, all huddled together on that ugly yellow couch surrounded by all the photos tacked to the wall. *The butcher, the baker, the candlestick maker. Rub-a-dub-dub there was a girl in the club.*

Becky's head turns toward me, and she points her boney finger at my face. Without moving away from the door, she beckons me over. Her llama lips are pursed tight and smug, about to spit some hate from her mouth.

I do not want to go into that office. I get it. I totally get it. They are scared, but I cannot face the girls. It is more than that. Their fear smothers me like a hand over my mouth and makes me want to scream.

Becky moves away from the door and leans toward me, resting her forearms on the glass-covered counter. Her arms frame the area where Amber's missing poster used to be. "Officer Green is in there. He was looking for you. Don't go far."

"How far can I go?" I'll be tied to the cleaning cart for the rest of the day, and she knows it.

When I turn back toward the people, all their eyes are still on me. They are always on me, ever since I came to this town. Last year, I was the hysterical girl who ran around in a hospital gown with her bare ass flashing and screaming that her friend was not in the river.

Now, I am the crazy jealous bitch who warned the girls and told them to leave town just before one of them went missing.

The upstairs cart is packed heavy and rolls slowly on the carpet. I park it next to room 209 and tap on the door. "Housekeeping."

No answer. I count to ten, then put the key into the lock.

The room is dim, with the only light pushing in through the cracks in the curtains. It smells like sex, stale, and yeasty. It is not empty. I start to back out but stop. A girl is passed out, all naked, and sprawled on the bed with her blonde hair spread out over the pillow.

"Hello?"

She does not move or moan. I move closer.

"Hello?"

My foot hits a wad of clothes on the floor. White clothes. Crystal was wearing a white dress. She still does not move. I reach out to make sure she is warm and breathing. My scalp starts to tingle. Don't touch. Get help.

I hurry out the door, past the cart, and to the stairwell. My heart is spastic, and my foot slips, sliding down as I grab the handrail and end up on my ass. Breathe. In the lobby, people stand, and I hear, *What is it? What's wrong?* Becky straightens up and takes her ear from the door. I go around the front desk, into her sacred space.

"What are you doing?"

I reach for the doorknob.

"You can't..." Becky says as she takes hold of my wrist, but it is too late. The door swings open to all four girls packed on the couch. Officer Green is standing, and Doc Unger sits in his dead wife's chair with Chief Unger and Rose, half sitting on each corner of the desk.

"I found her," is all that I say and turn to run back. Behind me, I hear, *Who?* and gasps of *Oh my God*. I take the steps two at a time, dragging a whole hoard of people behind me. Mary is standing next to the open door with the cleaning cart behind her.

"Move aside. Move." Chief Unger comes pushing through the crowd. Crystal's friends follow in the wake he leaves behind. Everyone is silent, waiting, and breathing.

"Hello," he pokes his head in. "Police."

Nothing. We all hold our breaths.

He steps in. Crystal's friends crowd the doorway, pushing me aside with their elbows and shoulders.

"Police."

"Crystal..." one of the girls calls into the room.

The people in the hallway are clumped in and whispering, *Is it her? Is she okay?*

I squeeze between the doorframe and the girl with the orange ball cap. Something groans, deep and male, from the bed on the other side of the room. "What the hell?"

He sits up, and a girl rises behind him, slinking up and using him as a shield. Her dark curly hair is in tangles all around her face. The guy reaches for the bedsheets and pulls a corner over his naked lap.

The blonde girl on the other bed rises to one elbow.

"Crystal?" The girl in the sports bra says.

She sweeps her hair aside and stares at the crowd, groggy and blinking.

"Are you Crystal Rhodes?" Chief Under asks, standing in the middle of the two beds.

"It's not her," two of her friends say in unison before they start to cry.

"Sorry to have bothered you," Chief Unger says. He turns around with both hands in the air. "Everyone back up."

Once out in the hall with the door shut, the girls turn on me. Their eyes narrow, and they stare at me with tight jaws, crossed arms, and twisted mouths.

"What is wrong with you?"

"Crazy bitch."

"I…I thought…" I back up but hit the cart. I am trapped. The girl in the orange cap steps so close I can feel her breath on my face. She grabs my arm and digs her fingernails into my skin.

"That's enough." Officer Green comes through, sweeping the girls aside. "Everyone go back downstairs."

"She knows what happened to Crystal. She is trying to mislead you…" the girl in the cap says.

Officer Green turns his back, creating a giant wall between the crowd and me.

"Downstairs. Everyone down," Chief Unger's distinctive and throaty voice says on the other side of Officer Green.

Grunts, complaints, and shuffling feet echo in the hall as the crowd funnels back down. The massive back of Officer Green is so close I can smell his sweat and aftershave. It is hard to believe he is the same man who stood in our bathtub, replacing the showerhead just a week ago.

The door to the room creaks open, and between Officer Green's shoulder and the wall, I see the head of a guy poke out. "What's happening."

"We have a missing girl."

"Oh, dude. That sucks."

"The housekeeper thought one of the girls in your room…"

"She came into our room?"

"Nobody answered when I knocked…" I say.

He looks past Officer Green, and we catch eyes. I remember him from the Buckskin last night. He had two girls hanging all over him. The guy combs his hair back with his fingers. "You guys need help looking?"

"We can use all the help we can get."

"I'll get changed," he says and shuts the door.

Officer Green leads me into the utility closet and pulls the chain on the light before shutting the door. It is stuffy and smells like bleach. We stand under a bare white bulb like the interrogation in an old black and white movie. He is so freaking tall that it feels like I am sitting. He is clean-shaven with beads of sweat on his upper lip, small white tiles of teeth, and kind squinty eyes.

"The girls think you know where Crystal is. They say that you threatened them and told them to leave."

"I didn't threaten them. Something is going on. I think girls are being drugged and drowned." He does not stop me, so I keep going. "Too many girls have drowned in the middle of the night. They are dizzy and wasted without hardly having anything to drink. Ask her friends how much she drank. She was puking in the toilet, and I was scared it was happening again. I told them to leave. I was trying to help them. I know my friend Amber would not have gone near the river no matter what. As long as she had one single brain cell still firing, she would not have done it. She was scared of the water. Someone drugged us. I remember the room started spinning and blurring and...and...I didn't remember anything after that, but Brian said he and Matt walked us to our room and locked the door. Our door was locked. I think someone has a key to that room. All the missing girls are from there."

The lightbulb is warm. Sweat runs down my cheek and between my boobs. He stands there listening, like a giant teddy bear.

"Not only the missing girls. One night, it happened to Erin, and we had to take her home. And then Jake came to get..." I pinch my lips together. I sound like a lunatic, but I know that something is happening. I don't know who I can trust. I am the outsider in this town. I cannot accuse Jake. He is an Unger, and the Ungers run this town.

"Why didn't you report any of this before?"

I cannot say that Brian asked me not to. "Who would believe me?"

"Do you have any proof at all? Did you see anyone putting something into a drink?"

I shake my head. I have nothing but hunches. Except... "Someone left a photograph on Brian's porch for me."

"Of someone drugging a girl?"

"No. It was from *Shooting the Rapids*. It was a photo of when my friend Amber fell out of the raft."

His eyebrows pinch together like he cannot see a connection.

"That was a year ago, and it suddenly shows up? I think it is a threat or a warning to scare me."

He nods and writes into his notebook. "I'll check on that and see who delivered it."

I cup my hands around my mouth, and he lowers his ear toward me. "I think there is a serial killer."

He straightens up and looks down. He doesn't believe me.

He has listened, but this was too much. I have to do something. I need to make him believe. "The shoe tree!"

He cocks his head sideways and waits.

"The shoe tree. I bet her shoes are up there. I think he kills the girls and throws their shoes in the tree." For all I know, Officer Green has hooked up with girls and tossed their shoes up. "I mean…not all the shoes are from him. Amber and I would not have thrown our brand new Converse into a tree. Never. We just bought them…I know that the boys do that. They hook up and steal the girls' shoes…"

"Who does that? Which boys?" He seems genuinely concerned.

"All the boys…" I thought it was common knowledge.

He writes in his notebook again.

"We can go look. We can see if Crystal's shoes are there. She was wearing gold heels. They were sparkly and had ankle straps."

He opens the closet door. The hall is empty, and the only sound is the high-pitched hum of the vacuum from an open room. I lead Officer Green down the back hallway, down the empty wooden stairs that echo with every step. He is so heavy it sounds like the wood will snap beneath his weight. We make it to the outside door. When I open it, a blast of heat stings my face, and I squint from the glare and the sun reflecting off the windows of cars.

The shoe tree drips with clumps of shoes like swarming bees. We circle around to the river side where two dogs lay panting with spots of wet dirt below their long tongues. It is so hot I can smell the warm rubber of the soles mixed in with the juniper. Toward the top, a pair of sparkly golden heels are strapped together and hanging like two dandelion seeds caught and unable to rise.

CHAPTER FIFTY-SIX

A STRING OF CARS AND SUVS WHIP UP A LONG LINE OF DUST ALL the way from the railroad trestle, past Old Lodell, and into the Whitehorse Inn parking lot. They are all new BMWs, Hondas, and Cadillacs now coated in dust.

The Rhodes family and friends arrive in town like a swarm of ants, all in matching red t-shirts with a photograph of Crystal's face. In white letters above her photo, it says, Missing and below it is Crystal Rhodes. They all have their names printed on the back, just like a baseball team. Janet, Scott, Carrie, Caleb, Eric, Ashley, Miranda, Tom, Tom Jr., Grandma Louise, Grandpa Ray, Cassie, Christy, on and on.

There are about thirty of them, and they all funnel into the lobby.

"You better get back to work," Officer Green says, taking hold of the door to the rear stairwell, but it is locked.

I do not want to go into the lobby. I do not want to be pointed out to these people. We go around, and I walk in, half-hidden behind Officer Green's bulk, ready to slip back upstairs and find a bathroom to throw up in. Crystal's family looks as if it has been ripped from the front page of a magazine with their upright posture and cheerleader, football captain, and tennis mom good looks.

Three men stand at the front counter, all facing Becky and demanding rooms that we do not have. The back of their shirts say, Scott, Uncle Brent, and Grandpa Ray.

Becky points in our direction. "There is Officer Green."

I slip out from behind him just as the men swivel around. "Who is in charge of the search for my daughter? Where is the command post?"

Nobody tells them that Crystal's friends are just behind the door, talking with the Ungers who run the town. Nobody tells them that four girls have already been found dead. Now with the wave of red t-shirts in the lobby, nobody pays attention to me, a housekeeper in an ugly blue uniform. I follow the hardwood planks until I come to the red carpet on the stairs. My scalp tingles, and I feel that someone is watching. I turn around to see the tiny head and beady eyes of Bobby Byrd.

CHAPTER FIFTY-SEVEN
HIM

EMMY IS ON HER SIDE, NAKED AND HALF COVERED BY THE SHEETS with her hair flowing across the pillow. I want her. It is time to tie her hair and bind her to me forever. The needle slides right into the hole of the vial, and the liquid rises against the black lines as I pull the plunger. Not too much. Not too much. Crystal took too much. Emmy's arm is extended as if she has been waiting for me. Her thick blue vein waiting for my needle. I lift a sock from the floor in case she screams. Of course, she will scream. Girls before the Ketamine are messy. Just like Crystal, they thrash, and they scream. I prefer to spare my nymphs from the panic and the fear. That is not my thing.

Emmy's eyelids flutter, and her lips are parted, waiting to fill her lungs with my water. Later. Later. First the Ketamine, then I'll do as I please. I will bind her to me with peace and serenity. I will slip her below the surface in my arms with a slight smile on her lips, the last exhalation, and a shudder before she takes me into her body.

I kneel beside her. Her vein is there, waiting below the surface of her skin, too deep for me to see. She will fight me. My best option may be to inject it into her bicep and hold her down until it takes and her muscles go slack.

I slide into bed behind her, pull her to me, and slide one arm beneath her. She lets out a satisfied coo and wiggles her ass against me. Her hair is soft and tickles my nose. I want to wind it around my finger, but I will wait. I guide the syringe between my fingers with my thumb on the plunger. Quick, into her muscle and press. She flinches and pulls away from me, but I curl my bottom arm and pull her tight.

"What are you…"

I keep pressing until the liquid is pressed in.

"Brian?"

She tries to pull away.

"Let me go," she screams. The panic is rising. "Stop!"

I press her mouth shut with my hand, and she tries to bite. She kicks. Where's the damned sock? Pain shoots through my shin. Fuck. I throw my leg over hers and pin her to the bed. Three minutes. I only need to hold her for three minutes. Then she will be mine. Her entire body thrashes and squirms. She is strong. Before I know it, she has rotated beneath me, and her eyes are on me, wide with panic. Her mouth is free and open, but instead of a scream, she inhales—gasping for air.

The front door squeaks. Fuck. He's home. Fuck. Fuck. I wind her hair around my finger and yank. She lets out a horrible scream. I jump off of her, off the bed, and out the window just as the bedroom door opens.

CHAPTER FIFTY-EIGHT

"Emmy, Emmy." Brian's voice comes through a tunnel.

I try to open my eyes. My lids are heavy.

"Emmy. What did you take?"

I shake my head.

"Emmy."

I'm rocking. Heavy muscles.

A face. Not Brian's.

"Oh, God. What is it? What have you taken? Why is your lip bleeding?

A hand over my mouth. "No! No! No!" I grab at it. No hand there.

A cold cloth. A face. Not Brian's.

CHAPTER FIFTY-NINE

The room is bright, and I feel like shit. There's a damp washcloth on the pillow next to me. What happened? My lip. I touch it with my tongue and feel a lump. Brian is behind with his arm around my waist. My head throbs, and my arm aches. My ribs…oh God, it hurts to take a breath.

"You all right?" Brian's voice is groggy.

He pulls me closer until his warm body is fully wrapped around mine. The curtains are gauzy with light and hang flat over the open window. No wind. The new air conditioner still sits beneath a hole covered in cardboard and duct tape.

"What did you take last night?" His breath is warm and damp on the top of my head.

"Nothing. I was sleeping."

"You were hallucinating and screaming. Did you take some sleeping pills and have a bad dream?" He runs his hand over my hip.

A train chugs and screeches in the distance. Brian strokes my hair. His hand comes to a spot above my ear that sends a wave of pain across my scalp. "Ouch."

Brian gets to one elbow and moves my hair aside. "You have a chunk missing."

"What?" I touch where he is looking until my fingers find the sore spot. *What the...?* A shiver runs through my body. A touch that was not Brian's. And a hand over my mouth. Oh my God.

I roll over face-to-face with Brian. His beard stubble is long and brownish-red. "Someone came in last night."

"Who?" His face tightens.

"I...I don't know." A dark face.

"You let someone in?"

"No. I was sleeping. I thought it was you, but his body was skinny..."

"His body? What the fuck?" Brian sits up. "Who was it?"

"I...don't." It's there, foggy and floating like a dream.

"Who was it? You got high with him?" Brian's entire body is tense. "Who was it?"

"Give me a minute. I'm trying to..."

"What the hell, Emmy?"

"Please...I can't think" He is quiet, but every inch of his body is clenched and jumbling my thoughts. I lean away from him, and something hard presses against my ass. I reach back and feel something thin and plastic. I close my fingers around it and bring it between Brian and me.

A syringe.

In the moment of silence, as we both look at it, I remember the face! Oh my God! "It was Skid!"

CHAPTER SIXTY

BRIAN IS CLENCHING AND UNCLENCHING HIS FISTS. "I'M GOING. To beat. The living shit. Out of him." The knuckles on his right hand are still red and swollen. I still have no idea why. He jumps off the bed starts pacing. He runs his fingers through his hair and grabs hold like he will pull it out by the roots.

I have never seen Brian angry, and he is scaring me. "We should call the police."

Brian stops and stares at me like I'm an idiot.

"You mean his father? Skid is an Unger. I need to handle this myself." Brian lifts a pair of shorts from the floor and pulls them on without underwear.

"Now? You're going there now?"

His entire body is tense. I don't know if he hears me. "Don't go. Let's talk."

As I scoot to the edge of the bed, a sharp pain shoots through my ribs and chest. Brian rips up the velcro on his water shoes and shoves his foot in. His eyes scan the room, and he kicks at clothes and towels on the floor. "Where the fuck is my other shoe?"

"Don't leave me here. What if he comes back?"

Brian kneels at my feet, then puts his hands down to look under the bed. I want to stay here curled into a ball with his arms around me. If Skid is the killer, what would he do to Brian?

I grab hold of Brian's arm. It is thick and strong. "Please don't go. I don't want anything to happen to you."

He rises up with the other sandal in his hand and sits back on his ass with a sarcastic glare in his eyes.

"That pussy couldn't do shit to me." He rips the velcro up on that shoe. "Thanks for the confidence."

"Maybe he is the one killing the girls. Maybe he came here to kill me."

Brian stops and turns to face me. His jaw is tight, and his nostrils are flared. "What made you jump to that?"

"Someone is killing girls."

Brian takes a deep breath like he is trying to control his anger. "You always think the worst."

"Girls don't just drown themselves, drunk or not. Not that many of them." My mouth is dry, and I taste something coppery. I put my fingertips to my fat lip and see that it is bleeding. I realize that I am sitting there butt-ass naked with nothing but a fat lip and sore ribs.

Brian stands, with his chest heaving and his nostrils flaring.

"What if he has Crystal? Maybe she is still alive."

"I've known him his whole life. He is not a killer. Skid's the biggest pussy I know."

"We can call Officer Green. He is not an Unger. He thinks there's a killer too."

Brian narrows his eyes at me. His face flushes red, and the vein in his forehead bulges. "I told you not to tell your stories. You cannot go around accusing people..."

"I didn't accuse anyone. He thinks it's suspicious too."

Brian takes hold of my shoulders like he wants to shake me. I jerk away. "Ouch!"

"I barely…"

I rub my left shoulder. That must be where Skid put the needle.

Brian turns to the door and punches the frame as he passes through. I jump off the bed. I don't want to be alone. I don't want Brian facing Skid by himself. The front screen door screeches as I pull on a pair of shorts. I shuffle through the mess of clothes on the floor. The screen closes with a bang. I lift a T-shirt, but it is Brian's. I don't care, and I slide it on.

Outside, the morning is already heating up. Because of Crystal missing, few people are on the street, and the dogs are still nosing around the trash cans. I turn toward Skid's house. I have never been inside. We never party there. I run, and when I turn the corner, I see Brian walking, barebacked with heavy steps and clenched fists.

I catch up to him, and without looking at me, he says. "Go back home."

"No."

He stops and looks like he wants to strangle me. "Go home. This is none of your business."

"Like hell, it isn't. He tried to rape or kill me last night."

"Go home."

I cross my arms. Maybe if he has to drag me home, it will keep him from Skid long enough for me to talk some sense into him.

He sticks his finger in my face so close that it touches my nose. "Damnit, Emmy! Go home."

I lift my chin and stare directly into his eyes. "No."

"Uhhhhh!" His eyes are hard, and his jaw is clenched.

"If I go, I'll head straight to Officer Green and tell him what happened."

Without a word, Brian turns and leaves me to my own decision. Of course, I stay with him. I love him so much it hurts, and I could not bear it if anything happened to him. If Skid is the killer, he could have a gun. After last night, he knows Brian is coming for him.

Skid's front yard is surrounded by a white picket fence with peeling paint. Brian opens the gate and steps through without turning to look at me, but he leaves it open. My heart pounds. I look at the windows, waiting to see the curtains flutter, but there is no movement. With every breath, my ribs ache, and I feel the ghost of his bony arm around me and his hand grinding my lips into my teeth. Skid's yard is filled with junk cars, a rusty lawnmower, scrap wood, and a pile of bent screens. Three cement deers stand around a dried-up old pond by the front window. The buck's antlers are broken off on one side, and they all are sun-bleached and chipped.

Brian climbs up onto the porch that's piled with wood and warped cardboard boxes. He does not knock. And it is not locked. I want to yell for Brian to stop. It is a trap, and I picture Skid in there, waiting calmly with a gun pointed right at the door. There is no shot, and all is quiet, so I climb up the steps.

A huge whiff of something putrid comes from inside the house. Maybe he is dead in there. Maybe someone else is. Every nerve in my body tells me to turn around and run, but Brian is already inside. What if I was wrong? What if it was not Skid? Maybe I imagined his face. Maybe the drugs confused me.

A wall of stench stops me at the front door. It is so bad, I can taste it. It reminds me of a diaper that has been left in the trash for days or lumpy and spoiled milk. I pull the neck of the T-shirt over my nose.

The house is a junkyard of crap with pathways leading to the couch, the kitchen, and the hallway. His fly vest is on a hangar and hooked to the curtain rod. The couch is one of those beige-flowered ones that grandmothers love, and his coffee table is piled with pizza boxes and beer bottles and cans.

A birdcage is filled with empty cans of Rainier and Coors and sits on an old pink beauty salon chair. A desk, with a vice clamped to the edge, is stacked with bins of what looks like feathers and fur and an old green tackle box. I cup my hand and press the T-shirt tight over my nose. A pain shoots through my fat lip, and I taste blood.

Brian stands at the entrance to the hall, scanning the living room, peering around the piles of boxes. He does not call out to Skid. We move through the filth with our arms close to our bodies, careful not to brush up against the crap or knock things to the ground.

As we pass the brown and beige retro kitchen, the table is piled with mail and advertisements. Plates and pans are stacked in the sink. The cabinets with no doors are filled with plates, trash, and off-brand boxes of mac and cheese, cereal, and snacks. Empty tin cans, with their lids pried open, litter the counters.

A mouse pokes its head out of an open can of beans and stares at me with beady little eyes. A parade of glue traps line the baseboards—all with decomposing dead mice tacked down to the glue in unnatural poses. One is nothing but a skeleton, with its inner workings visible, like a steampunk mouse. My throat stings, and I feel like I'm going to throw up.

I follow Brian down the hallway. I am so overwhelmed with the house that I forget why we are here—until Brian pauses at a door and listens. Turning toward me, he presses a finger to his lips, slowly turns the knob, pushes the door open, and steps in. I can see the heel of one of his shoes, and it does not move. He backs out, leaves the door open, and walks toward a different door down the hall.

I peek into the bedroom as I pass. The walls are covered with dark brown paneling, and the bed is piled high with clothing, blankets, old shoes, boxes, and a bright red Tickle Me Elmo doll. At the foot of the bed are stacked plastic bins filled with Legos, Beanie Babies, Hot Wheels, and K'Nex pieces. On top of them is an open shoebox filled with a rainbow of Nano Pets,

Giga Pets, and Tamagatchis—the cyberpets we all had as kids. I had a Nano Kitty that I always forgot to feed. I step in and lift the box. There is a neon green Nano Kitty in the bottom, just like...

"What are you doing?" Brian takes hold of the shoebox and pulls it from my hand.

I mouth that I am sorry. This house is filled with distractions and the smell...it is like walking through a bad dream and knowing it cannot be real.

I peek into the bathroom. It is filled with towels draped over the shower rod and wadded up on the floor next to all the trash of empty toilet paper rolls, Q-Tips, and wads of tissue paper. The toilet lid is open with a thick mustard-yellow ring just above the water level.

We reach the last room in the house. Brian stops at the door with an ash white face. I cannot tell if it is because of the stink or because he had no idea that Skid lived in such filth. He waves me aside and puts his hand on the knob.

Brian cracks the door open, waits, then steps inside. In what feels like forever, he finally backs out, pulling the door closed without letting me in.

"He's not there."

I can tell he does not want me looking inside. "Is Crystal?"

"No. Nobody is in there."

Brian puts a hand on my shoulder, trying to turn me around. I don't know why, but I need to look. I need to see for myself. I resist and stand my ground.

"You don't trust me?" His lips are tight, and his look is hard.

"You know I do."

"It doesn't fucking feel like it." He stands there like a wall. "Let's go."

"What if he came in? I'm afraid to go first."

Brian takes a deep breath and slides by me in the hall. Once he is past, I turn around and push the door open. It looks like a teenager's den of disgusting and perverted crap. A giant golden chandelier hangs low over the bed, draped with women's panties and bras, coated in dust and clumps of cobwebs.

A hand circles my waist and pulls me backward.

"You don't trust me." Brian's voice is filled with disgust.

I grab hold of the doorjamb and do not let him pull me through. "I'm not a child, and you do not tell me what I can and cannot do."

"Fine." He lets go, and I almost fall on my face.

The room is wallpapered in torn-out Playboy centerfold girls from what looks like the eighties, mixed in with two movie posters of Home Alone and Space Jam. In a bra and thigh-high stockings, a full-size and armless mannequin sits with her knees up on top of a desk. She has shoulder-length black hair with bangs and a fishing hat on her head.

On a shelf along one wall are the action figures of Batman, Robin, Spiderman, Dr. Doom, and Wolverine, alongside fishing trophies and a row of naked barbie dolls sitting with straight legs and bare boobs.

An armchair faces an old boxy television with a Nintendo 64 hooked to it. Next to a stack of game cartridges, a controller sits on top of the television. A guitar leans against the wall next to the nightstand with a giant bottle of lube and two little girl hand puppets, one with blonde yarn for hair and the other with red. A shudder runs through me, and I feel like I will throw up.

"You had enough?" Brian asks me. He sounds half angry and half-mocking.

I nod and turn toward the door. Just as my gaze sweeps past the mannequin, I freeze. Her bra. I cannot breathe. It feels as if a sledgehammer has hit against my chest. She is wearing a pink bra with embroidered stars, just like Ambers. A cold shiver runs through my entire body.

"What's wrong?"

"Amber's..." A cry comes gasping up, and I cannot talk. "Amber's..."

The room is spinning. I force myself toward it. Amber's bra broke, and she had a safety pin. I steady myself on the desk and feel Brian's hand around my waist.

"What is it?"

I keep stepping forward and circle around the mannequin. She stares at me with deep blue eye shadow and coats of red lipstick smeared around the edges of her mouth. My entire body is shaking.

"I got you," Brian says. "Take my arm."

I step around her, and there, on the left strap, is a large silver safety pin.

CHAPTER SIXTY-ONE

BRIAN STANDS IN THE DOORWAY AS I PEE. WE BARELY MADE IT home in time. I am not sure if he is mumbling to himself or to me. I can still taste Skid's house and feel it on my skin. I want to shower and scrub it off, but we don't have time.

Brian rocks back and forth with his fists clenched. "What the hell? The little shit. Fucking little shit."

I was right. The girls are not drowning themselves, and we are wasting time. I go to the sink, pull my hair up into a ponytail, and splash water on my face. "Okay, let's go."

Brian looks at me with a frown. "Where?"

"To the police. We need to report it."

"No!" He blocks the door. "We need to think. Not the police."

"Let me out."

He does not move. "Goddamnit, give me a minute to think."

"Crystal may not have a minute."

I push. He is solid and does not budge. His skin is clammy, and his heart pounds against my palms.

"Please," I beg and put my hands to his cheeks. "We need to do something."

He is a good man. He is just scared.

"We need to get help."

"You don't understand. Skid is an Unger. They will do anything to protect him."

"What about the sheriff?"

"I know where Skid is. If he's not home, he's at the old Unger homestead, at his grandfather's house." Brian palms my head like a basketball and presses it hard into his chest. "No police yet. Let's go check, then we will decide."

I am pinned to him and cannot move. "Okay. Okay. Let me go."

"I was there yesterday." Pressed to his chest, his words resonate from deep within.

"Where?"

"The Unger homestead. I saw Skid, and we got in a fight. I didn't look through the house. What if she was there and I didn't even look? I knew that he…" Brian shakes his head but does not continue.

"He what?"

"Nothing."

"Is that what happened to your knuckles?"

Brian nods but does not explain. He releases me. "Let's take your car."

We run to the kitchen, and I pull open the junk drawer. I dig through all the crap, but I cannot find the keys. Did I put them back? Shit.

Brian shoulders me aside, pulls the drawer out, and flips it upside down over the table. Everything spills out. We both sift through the junk until I see the little black remote and the damned dog whistle. I was so stupid.

I have not driven my car since Amber went missing. Brian and I both run for the driver's side. We stop at the door and lock eyes for a moment. I run back around to the passenger's side, open the door and get in. The last person to sit in this seat was Amber. My chest feels tight like I do not have enough air.

Brian slides the key into the ignition and turns. It clicks and clicks but does not start.

I remember Amber with the window down and her hair whipping in the wind as she sings, "Let's straighten our hair and line our eyes. Don't ever go back, don't ever go back." She glances over at me and smiles.

"Emmy." Brian's hand is on my leg. "You okay?"

I nod, and the tears break loose in gasps.

He turns the key again, and it does not start.

"Shit! Come on." He opens his door and climbs out.

My body is heavy, and I cannot move. I brought Amber right into the hands of a killer.

My door opens, and Brian is there with his hand out.

I shake my head, sobbing like a child.

"She might still be alive," Brian says.

He finally believes me. I take his hand, and we start toward Old Lodell on foot.

Crystal's family, still in their red shirts, mill around the picnic tables of Carl's Cabins, waiting for word. At least a dozen dogs lay around, already panting under porches or in the shade of trees. Lieutenant Dan hobbles behind a pack of kids heading toward the river. Nobody pays any attention to us as we slip right out of town.

As soon as we are clear of downtown, we pick up our pace. The pavement ends, and our feet crunch on the dirt road. Up ahead, a train chugs over the trestle with rumbling wheels.

We pass by the trail to the cliff, where I stared down the rock ledge and watched men searching for my Amber. Where I refused to believe she was there unless someone put her there. Now, everyone will know that I was right.

The homestead is an old yellow two-story house with the downstairs windows boarded up. It is surrounded by an old tumble-down barbed wire fence and a graveyard of old cars with a wooden sign that says "Rust in Peace." There are two bare wood outbuildings. One is a barn with the roof caving in, and the other is a shed with a tall windmill next to it. On the other side of the shed, and almost out of view, is a red tailgate—just like the one on Skid's truck.

Brian tries the front door, but it is locked, and all the downstairs windows are boarded with plywood. Before I know it, Brian plows his shoulder into the door, splintering the casing. It flies open, and Brian falls in, catching himself with a step. I climb up and into a creepy old living room with yellow-flowered wallpaper that is peeling off in strips. It is still furnished and dusty. An old fishing hat hangs on a rack, and a rolltop desk is filled with fly tying materials—threads, feathers, fur, scissors, and a vice.

A door creaks open, and we both turn toward it. Skid slips out in nothing but a pair of shorts and pulls it shut behind him. He blinks at us like he has no idea why we are there. His left eye is black and blue, and his cheek is red and raw. "Hey, what's up?"

"You know what the fuck is up." Brian points his finger straight at Skid and takes a step toward him. "You broke into my house, you little shit."

Skid puts his hands up. "I didn't, I swear. I was here all night."

All I can think of is the filth and the stench of his house—and his perverted bedroom with hand puppets and Amber's bra.

"Like shit you were. Who's in that room?"

"Nobody. It's just me."

Brian takes another step forward, and Skid grabs both sides of the doorframe with the door closed behind him.

"Move."

Skid's knuckles turn white, along with his face, but he does not budge.

Brian's elbow comes back, and he plants a fist right into Skid's gut, forcing all the air from his lungs. Skid doubles over, and Brian shoves him aside. He opens the door and freezes.

"Oh my God…"

As I hurry toward the open door, Skid grabs my ankle and pulls to me the floor. The wind is knocked out of me, and I cannot scream. He grabs me by the hair. "I should have killed you both that night. Amber was such a nice piece of ass."

I kick him in the shins and try to scream for Brian, but his hand covers my mouth.

"You were a nice piece of ass too."

Something superhuman comes over me, and I thrash and kick, and before I know it, I am on top of him clawing and scratching and punching. All he does is flail his arms at me, but I feel nothing. He finally brings his arms in front of his face, unable to do anything but cower beneath me.

Through the pounding in my ears, I hear. "Emmy." And a hand touches my back.

I look up to see Brian standing there with a red tie-down and a smile on his face. "That's good. I'll take care of him."

Every nerve in my body rages, and I want to keep thrashing him. I want to scratch out his eyes and cave in his face. My entire body starts to quiver, and a scream that I didn't know I had in me rises up and comes out, echoing off the walls.

The next thing I know, Brian lifts me off of Skid, and I feel his warm breath in my ear. "It's okay. I got him. Crystal's alive."

I wiggle out of his arms and turn toward him. "She is in the room. Go untie her, and I'll take care of this piece of shit."

The room is dark and paneled and smells like pee. A stained mattress lies on the floor with Crystal naked and spread-eagle across it. One of her arms is loose, and she is touching her face. Her other arm and ankles are restrained with the same type of tie-down that Brian had in his hand.

"You're safe," I say to her.

She lies there, all skinny and sweaty, with her blonde hair spread out across a dirty pillow. I kneel down on the hardwood.

The tie-downs are knotted through thick metal eyebolts screwed into the floor.

"Oh, thank God," Crystal says, barely loud enough to hear.

As I work at the knots, it feels like my body is filling with water, weighing me down. Was Amber still alive as I watched them search the rapids? Was she tied to this mattress, and I never came to save her?

"You're going to be okay," I say to Crystal.

"He drugged me and kept pulling out my hair."

"I know. You're going to be okay."

I slip the last tie-downs from the bolt and release the clip at her ankle. Beneath it, her skin is red and raw and bleeding.

"Your family is here in town. In Lodell."

At that, she starts to cry, but it is so weak she sounds like a mewing kitten.

Once she is free, Brian comes into the room with a long flannel shirt and khaki pants.

"Where is he?"

"Tied up. We need to get her to the hospital."

I slide one of the sleeves over her bony arm and around her shoulders. I remember her over the toilet with the nobs of her spine poking up. I slip her other arm in and button it closed over her breasts, belly, and crotch. Brian slips his forearms beneath her armpits and steadies her while I get the pants onto her bare legs. Her head is down, and she is not responding.

"Crystal...Are you okay?"

She lets out a small moan that sounds like, "Uh-huh."

As we take her through the living room, I see Skid tied to the desk chair, bound with the red tie-down.

"She is mine. She belongs to the river. It is the fluid, and I am the flesh."

Crystal lets out a high-pitched moan. He starts thrashing so violently the chair tips over, and he crashes to the floor.

"You need to get her straight to the hospital."

"Me? By myself?" She is so weak. There is no way I can get her there.

Brian holds up and jingles a set of keys in the air. "In Skid's truck. I need to make sure he doesn't go anywhere."

It feels like forever by the time we get her to the truck. The door squeaks as Brian opens it, and a beer bottle rolls out onto the dirt. He lifts Crystal in, lays her across it, and pulls the seatbelt over her. It's an old truck with empty candy and food wrappers all over the floor.

I grab the handle to pull my door shut, but Brian grabs it and leans his head in.

"I'm sorry I didn't believe you. I love you." His voice is sad, and his eyes are filled with tears.

He gives me a long and tender kiss.

"As soon as you drop her off, call the sheriff and do not let Russ Unger know we are here."

"I'm scared. Will everything be okay?"

"If you can get the sheriff here, it will be okay. If you can't, then…then I don't know." He looks down at Crystal. "You need to get her to town."

"What about Doc? Do you think he will hurt her?"

"No, I don't. And she needs a doctor now."

He must see the look on my face.

"And he won't know it was Skid." He gives me a quick kiss. "You need to go."

I slip the key into the ignition, and it starts on the first try.

CHAPTER SIXTY-TWO

HIM

THE RIVER RAGES AND CANNOT BE CONTAINED. MAN CAN DIVERT me but cannot conquer me. I surge and thrash and loosen my bonds. My arms are free, and so are my feet. I shrug off my tethers and rush for the door.

CHAPTER SIXTY-THREE

The truck jostles over potholes as I steer toward the dirt road. Crystal isn't moving or making a sound. No, no, no. I cannot lose her now, so I reach down and put my hand on her cheek. She flinches and lets out a frightened cry at my touch.

Oh, thank God.

"You're okay. I'm taking you to your family."

Her muscles relax. "Thanks…" she says barely in a whisper.

We should have found her earlier. Please let her be okay. The old truck bumps and squeaks over the ruts, and we bring up a rooster tail of dust. If only the people in town knew what was coming. The missing girl is found. One of their own is a killer. Nobody will ever be the same. Their sense of safety and trust will be gone. My mouth is dry, and my throat feels thick.

Our ride smooths out as we hit the pavement. A mob of town kids sit outside Happy Cow sharing a single soda and basket of fries. They are surrounded by a mangy pack of town dogs begging for food. These poor children will forever shy away and mistrust, not just strangers but the people they have always known. And I am the one bringing it into town. They will forever remember the red truck with me at the wheel.

This will be that moment when they realize that life was never as they had thought it. Evil people do not live in caves with permanent sneers on their faces like in the cartoons. They will feel lied to and realize that evil can grab them at any time.

A lump comes to my throat, and I think of little Willow and Susan at the group home. Amber and I left them on the verge of losing all their innocence to Ed. We never called Child Protective Services to report him. I wonder where they are right now. I could have called all these months since…no, a year since. Maybe it is not too late for them. I need to make the call.

Crystal's family is still on the lawn of Carl's Cabins, gathered around Chief Unger, Officer Rubio, and his dog, Pistol. They all turn or look up to see who is driving by. Chief Unger stares and follows me with his eyes. He knows his son's truck. He knows I should not be driving it.

I keep my head straight and take a deep breath. Act normal. Keep driving. I need to call the sheriff before I am detained for questioning. He takes a step toward the road, but it is too late. I am past, and I keep driving. I wish I could hang my head out the open window and yell to her family that Crystal is alive. That I have her in this truck. I want to stop their suffering, but I roll past them and turn toward the hospital. Just the sight of it makes me feel sick to my stomach.

I pull up to the handicap ramp, lift the fingers of my right hand from the wheel, and shift it into park. I did it. I got her here.

"Crystal?"

She does not move.

"Crystal?"

Please, God. I put my hand on her cheek. She is still warm, and her eyelids flutter.

"We're at the hospital. I'm going in to get you help."

I have not been inside the hospital since they released me to Brian. I feel sick and swallow, trying to keep it down. The moment I open the door and see the cheap plastic blinds and black padded armchairs, it all hits me. My head feels thick, and my ears pound. Just like the throbbing of the helicopter that sucked all the air from the room. The 1980s decor with a row of dingy mud-brown triangles on mustard-yellow walls. The dingy green hospital gown with my bare-ass sticking out the back. A lump rises in my throat, and my mouth is too dry to swallow it down.

"You gonna just stand there and let all the cool air out?" Tina Stewart sits behind the receptionist's desk glaring at me. She still has her puffy lady mullet hair and llama face.

I try to swallow. "I have the missing girl."

It takes her a moment to process. "Here?"

"Yes. In the truck."

She jumps up from her chair and runs down the hall. "Doc, Doc! We have an emergency."

She immediately returns, pushing a wheelchair, with Doc right behind her. Everything is a blur. I follow them down the ramp to the truck. Tina opens the door and starts rambling. *Oh dear Lord. Poor girl.* She steadies the chair, and Doc reaches in with his strong arms.

Crystal's head appears over the dash and flops to the side. Her blonde hair is a mess and falls over her face. Her knobby knees poke up in the khaki pants, and her shoulders are so bony it looks like the flannel shirt is on a hanger. Tina leans forward and pushes her up the ramp.

"Where did you find her?" Doc asks as he passes by.

I look up into his face. My mouth opens, but no words come out. He keeps walking up the ramp and into the door behind Crystal and Tina.

I stop at the door, unable to put my foot onto the linoleum.

Doc looks back. "Call the police."

I nod and make myself take that step, past the door, past the black leather chairs, around the desk, and to Tina's chair. I do not sit. I pick up the receiver. A dial tone. I do not know the number. 911 may get me straight to the city police. There's got to be a directory. I look around for a phone book. Something. Nothing. Until I see one of those old flippy things with address cards. The phone starts beeping, so I hang it up. I turn the dial until the "S" comes to the top. Sanders, Sawyer, Sayers, Scott, Seeley, Shaw, Sheriff! I put in the number, and someone picks up.

"Canyon County Sheriff's office." A pleasant woman's voice.

"Hello. I need to talk to the sheriff."

"Can you speak up? I can barely hear you."

I cup my hand over my lips and the mouthpiece. "I need the sheriff to come to Lodell. Send everyone you have."

"Have you tried the city police? I can put you through."

"No. No. I need the sheriff."

"We do not have jurisdiction…"

I glance down the corridor. "Please. You do not understand. Another girl went missing. The fifth girl. We found her."

"Take a breath, dear…"

"We found her with Chief Unger's son. He is killing the…"

"Oh, dear. Oh, dear. I will go directly to Sheriff Briggs. Where are you?"

"Rimrock Health Clinic. Hurry before Chief Unger gets here."

"Okay, you hold tight, dear. I will do everything I can."

"Oh…don't send them here. Go to the old Unger homestead. Skid…I mean, Dylan Unger is there. Tied up. With Brian. Don't hurt Brian. He has him tied up."

I hear her gasp. "Are there any weapons?"

"No. I don't think so."

"Okay, you hold tight."

I do not hold tight. There is no way in hell I want to be here when Chief Unger arrives. What can I say? They will ask where I found her, and they will know. I run down the ramp, jump into the truck, pull the door shut, and stick the key into the ignition. If I take the truck, they will find me. I pull it into a parking spot and drop the keys onto the seat.

On the floor, and poking out from beneath a grocery sack, is the corner of a black plastic box. I pull it out, and a chill runs up my spine and over my scalp. It is a fly box with Brian's name scratched into the top, just like the one someone left for me. I lift the lid, and inside is the chunk of hair missing from my head.

CHAPTER SIXTY-FOUR

HIM

THEY CANNOT BIND OR CONTAIN ME, FOR I AM THE RIVER, AND the river is free. The sun shines and warms me, but I am cool in my depth. I flow over the dirt, the rocks, the scrub. The scrub snaps beneath my feet. My flesh is bleeding, but there is no pain. I am already transforming.

I am almost to the sacred spot where grandpa took his last breath. Where he taught me to fish and revere the river that springs from the earth. Where I will finally join him.

I climb up onto our rock, just above Steelhead Rapids and where we used to lay on our bellies to watch for trout. I pull down my shorts and step out of them. My bloody feet stain the rock with the last of my footsteps upon the earth. The flesh is weak. The river is eternal. Water gives life and takes life. It is the fluid, and I *was* the flesh.

"Skid!"

Brian is back and has found me. He stands there like my savior, always playing the righteous role. "You are not better than me."

"Come back, and let's talk this out."

"There is no talking it out. They took all my nymphs from

me, and you think you have released my last one. But you are wrong. Once I am the river, I will take all the nymphs I want. I will hold them in me until they shudder and breathe me into their lungs."

"You are not thinking straight. This is not you."

"No. This is me. You never knew me. You and Jake and Erin always thought you were the powerful ones. Now everyone will know it was me."

Brian starts toward me, thinking he can stop me. Thinking he can save me. "Stop, or I'll jump in."

He stops.

"You and Jake are no better than me. Just because you didn't take the girls' lives, you still took from them and left them empty and broken. At least I did not leave them to suffer and live in fear."

It is time to wash away the pain and release my soul. I slide off the rock and wade into the flow. Brian is nothing but a blur of flesh as I hold out my arms and fall back. I release my body and let the river cradle me. I let it take me where it will rage and churn and slam my soul from my flesh. It is time to wash away the pain, for I am the river, and the river is me.

CHAPTER SIXTY-FIVE

It feels like I've been gone from Brian forever, like in one of those nightmares where you need to get somewhere and cannot. I drop off the fly box with my hair, slide it beneath the shorts in my drawer, and head straight toward the Unger Homestead. Please, God, let the sheriff be there before Chief Unger realizes what happened and that his son is involved. I slip behind Whiskey Dicks, Happy Cow Hamburgers, and Tortilla Flat, back with all the dumpsters and a rusty old frier and rack. Chief Unger saw me in Skid's truck, and it won't be long until he follows up on that.

There's a sound behind me. I jerk my head around and see two town dogs following behind. One a shepherd mix and the other some sort of a matted poodle.

"Shoo. Go away." I wave my hand at them and stamp my foot on the ground, but they do not care. A white one with pink skin comes from behind a bin, and I have three. I peek between the buildings before running across with my long tail of dogs.

Soon, Crystal's family and the entire town will know that she is found. I wish I could be there to see the excitement on their faces at that moment. A moment that will only last until they know what she has endured. They look like a loving family, like the type of family I wish I had.

Nobody came for Amber, and nobody would ever come for me. Amber's death only lightened the load for the state. The only tribute paid to her would be moving her file and burying it somewhere in an archive.

I pick up two more dogs between the firehouse and community church—a white pit bull and a lab mix.

"Where you going?" A child calls out.

I look around and don't see anyone.

"Up here," Dustin calls down from a tree behind the church. He is with two girls, one with scraggly brown hair and the other with a messy ponytail. "Where you going? And why do you have the dogs?"

Good God. I will never get out of this damned town. "Oh, I'm…" I don't know what to tell them.

Dustin shifts his body, and before I know it, he is dangling from a branch by his arms and drops to the ground.

Think. Think. "I need your help."

His eyes widen, and he nods his head. "Sure."

Behind him, the girls wriggle down and drop to their feet.

The scraggly-haired girl drops to a knee. "Ouch." She dusts if off with a grimace but no tears.

"I will give you a dollar each if you lead the dogs away from me."

Dustin's eyes narrow, and he assesses me. "Why?"

Come on. I need to go. Think. It needs to be something fun, or they will follow me. "I also need you to deliver a secret message."

The girl with skinned knee tugs at Dustin's shirt and nods. "Okay."

They all hold out their hands.

"I don't have the money on me."

Their shoulders droop.

"Come by my house before dinner. I will give you the money, and I have some popsicles in my freezer."

Dustin looks at the girls, and they both nod. "Deal."

"You know the family that is here in the red t-shirts? The ones with a girl's face on the front?"

They all nod their heads.

"Go to one of the older ones. A man or lady who looks like a parent or grandparent and give them a message...you have to remember it exactly, and you cannot tell them who told you."

"Okay." Their eyes are wide.

"Tell them, *Crystal is at the Rimrock Health Clinic.* You got that?"

"Yes," the girl in the ponytail says. "Crystal is at the Rimrock Health Clinic."

"And make sure nobody else can hear you when you tell them."

The kids call to the dogs and run off.

When I finally get to the homestead, it is deserted with no sign of life or sheriff trucks. Just the rusty old cars with their "Rust in Peace" sign. I run to the door, where it is still open and splintered. I want to call Brian's name, but when I step into the living room, I see the chair on its side with loose red tie-downs and no Skid. *What the?* Every nerve in my body starts to tingle, and I cannot breathe. The house is silent except for the buzz of cicadas outside.

What if something happened to Brian? What if Skid got loose and grabbed a gun or a knife? I step toward the kitchen, and the floorboards creak beneath my feet. I freeze and listen. Nothing. The kitchen is empty except for the mess. The door to the room where we found Crystal is still open. Please, God. Please let Brian be okay. Terrible images of him on the ground flash through my head. I peek in, and it is empty.

There are two stories to this house, and the deeper I go, the more I will be trapped. Skid may be waiting for me.

I hear the sound of tires rolling across the dirt. Lots of tires. Please let it be the sheriff. I hurry to the living room. The windows are boarded, so I go to the door. My entire body feels light, and I start to tremble. Two unmarked black cars and two white sheriff trucks with blue flashing lights come bumping over the ruts and toward the house. Thank God. I step out onto the porch and wave my arms. "Here! Over here."

The sheriff, wearing a tan and green uniform and cowboy hat, steps from his truck.

"Oh, thank God. Thank God you're here."

"Calm down, ma'am. Take a breath."

"My boyfriend was here. They were here. He was tied up right there. We found a girl. The missing girl, Crystal. I took her to the hospital and…"

"Take a breath."

"We didn't want to call Chief Unger because it's his son. His son kidnapped Crystal. We had him tied up right there, but he's not there. I came back, and he's not there, and I don't know. I don't know where they are. Brian is gone, and I didn't search the whole house because I was scared. What if he is here waiting? He tried to kill me last night. He shot me with drugs. Please don't let him hurt Brian. Please, please." I sound like a raving lunatic. I need them to believe me.

"We're here now. Have a seat."

He makes a motion with his hand. The men behind him pull their guns and filter into the house. Two are in tan and green uniforms with bulletproof vests, and the other two are in jeans and t-shirts with vests and badges clipped to their belts. I hear them stop at the front bedroom, where we found Crystal.

"Sir, you may want to come look."

The sheriff nods then glances over at me. "Stay here."

Oh, God. Footsteps echo throughout the house. The floorboards creak upstairs, and I hear doors opening. Breathe,

breathe. What if they find Brian up there? Please let him be alive.

The sheriff returns. "Where did you find the girl?"

"Her name is Crystal, and we found her in that first room. On a mattress and tied to the floor."

The men come down and shake their heads. It's empty. Oh God, where are they? "Outside. Did you look outside?"

"Check the outbuildings," the sheriff tells his men, and they leave. "Can you tell me what happened?"

I tell him all about Crystal. I tell him she's at the hospital with Doc and Tina, and I feel like I'm going to throw up. "Doc is his uncle. Can you send a man there?"

"Doc is who's uncle?"

"Skid's uncle. The killer."

His eyebrows pinch together.

"Skid is Dylan Unger. He is the one who kidnapped Crystal and the one who broke into my house last night. He is Chief Unger's son and Doc Unger's nephew. What if Doc lets her die to protect him? Can you send a deputy there?"

Sheriff Briggs talks into his radio. "10-S-2, do you copy?" Someone responds, and he asks them to come into the house.

"Crystal's family is in town. In red shirts with her picture on the front. Don't hurt Brian. He is wearing a white T-shirt with *Rimrock Outfitters* in red letters."

"Sir? A uniformed deputy steps into the doorway."

"Go over to the hospital and guard the girl. Her name is Crystal."

He turns to me. "Do you know her last name?"

"Rhodes. I think it is Crystal Rhodes."

The deputy leaves just as *Ten-A-One* comes over the Sheriff's Radio. "Go ahead," he says. *Police vehicle approaching at high speed.*

At the sound of another car coming toward the house, my heart pounds, and I jump to my feet. "I don't want to talk to Chief Unger."

The sheriff holds his hand out. "Wait here and don't touch anything."

There is yelling outside. "Where is my son? Get off my property. Not your jurisdiction. Get the hell out of my town."

What if he comes in? I don't want him to see me. I hurry over to the corner and duck between a desk and the wall.

"Step aside." Chief Unger's voice shoots into the house like he is right at the front door.

I scrunch into the corner and pull my knees to my chest. My heart pounds in my throat. Please do not let him find me.

"The house is clear. We're checking the outbuildings. Do you know where Dylan may be?" There is a moment of silence before the sheriff continues. "A missing girl was found here in the house with your son."

"What the hell? Who told you that?"

"Do you know where he could be?"

"Goddamnit," Chief Unger says. "Tell your men to stand down. I think I know where he is."

There is silence and retreating footsteps. My head is light. I don't think I took a single breath the entire time they were at the door. I rise up on shaky legs and peer over the desk. It's a fly tying desk covered in bits of feathers, fur, thread…and something that looks like a hair color chart. I move to the front of the desk, and sure enough, it is a hair color chart with a chunk of hair that looks like Crystal's lying across it. Several of the colors are crossed out.

I'm going to be sick. My hand goes to the spot where he yanked the hair from my head. My hair is in the fly box with Brian's name. And the black box given to me…do they have Amber's hair tied into the flies? Oh my God…

There is a commotion outside, and I hear Chief Unger's voice yell, "Dylan!"

Not Brian? A cold chill runs through my body, and I run out the door. The plainclothes detectives, uniformed deputies, sheriff, and Chief Unger move toward the barn. Just beyond it is Brian! Oh, thank you, God. He is stumbling through the scrub with Skid in his arms—Skid is completely butt-ass naked. Brian stumbles as he comes toward us. His wet hair and shirt are plastered to his body.

Two deputies run toward him, but Brian keeps walking. Two paramedics hurry toward Brian with a red padded stretcher and medical bag. When did they get here? Chief Unger and the sheriff start toward them, and I follow.

As soon as the medics get to Brian, he stops. They place the stretcher on the ground, and Brian lowers Skid onto it. The medics kneel down and start working on him with everyone gathered around and Chief Unger barking questions and calling out to his son.

Brian steps aside and keeps walking toward me.

"Oh, thank God you are okay. I was so worried when..."

He wraps his arms around my shoulders and pulls me into a full-body hug. The wetness of his clothes seep through mine and cool my skin.

"What happened after I left?"

"He got free." Brian holds me tight, and his words vibrate between us. "He ran for the river to kill himself. He is not right in the head. Something snapped. He took all his clothes off and sunk into the current toward Steelhead Rapids."

I try to pull away, but he is holding me tight.

"And you saved him? After what he did to Amber and Crystal and the others?"

"That's what I do, Emmy. I save people."

I want to say, *Like me?* Like you saved me from the river and from the nothingness of being alone?

"And Skid is like my brother. We grew up together." He presses his lips to the top of my head. "I'm sorry, so sorry, Emmy."

"You're alive, and that's what matters."

"I'm sorry I have done this to you."

"It's all right. I'm fine now that I know you are okay."

"I'm not okay, and it's not over. I'm sorry."

I try to pull back, but he holds me. I push away hard and look up at him. His eyes are so pained that I want to go home and cuddle together in the nest of our bed.

"You don't understand. There are more things that you don't know. I'm sorry. They will take me to jail, and what they say will be true."

"What is it? You're scaring me."

"I am ashamed to even tell you."

Out of the corner of my eye, I see the sheriff looking toward us. "Tell me. Tell me now while you can."

He turns his head toward the sheriff, then back at me. "It's a long story."

"Please. I want to hear it from you."

He stares down at the dirt and takes a deep inhale. "Jake came up with the idea to date rape party girls from the Buckskin."

My heart sinks. Please don't let…

"And we did. He took some drugs from his father's pharmacy. I only did it once. I was drunk and went along…but that is no excuse. It was horrible, and I cannot get away from the guilt." His voice is barely a whisper, and he won't look at me.

Oh my God. The shoes in the tree. My stomach feels sick, and I want to punch him. I remember how sore my crotch was. "Was it me? Me and Amber?"

He shakes his head but does not answer. I put my hand to his cheek to turn his face to me, but he closes his eyes.

"Was it?"

"No." When he opens his eyes, it scares me. There is something on fire in them. "No. It was Jake and Skid. It fucking pisses me off every time I look at either of them near you."

A trembling starts in my body, and I take a step away.

"I've tried to stop them…"

"You could have turned them in."

"To who? Skid's dad is the chief of police." He looks over at the sheriff, who starts walking toward us. "I could have gone to the sheriff, but it's not as easy as it seems. This is my town. These people are my family. I thought I could stop them."

"I tried to tell you someone was killing the girls."

He nods his head. "I didn't think Skid or Jake could do such a thing. I've known them my whole life. Maybe I just didn't want to believe it, and even if I did, they are Ungers. I should have been stronger. I should have stopped them."

I feel like dragging my fingernails across his face, and at the same time, I want to cling to him. I love him so much that I cannot breathe or swallow. My words come out choked. "You saved Crystal. Maybe they will let you go since you saved her. And you can testify…"

"I am still guilty. I need to take responsibility for what I did."

I cannot live without Brian. He is all that I have. My cries come out in gasps. "Please…"

"You don't understand. I need to pay for it, or I will never get past my guilt. I still may not, but at least I will get what is coming to me."

Brian pulls me to him and kisses the top of my head. I cling to him and dig my nails into his back.

"You need to get out of Lodell before all hell breaks loose," he says.

My heart pounds against him, and I do not want to let go.

"There's a box in the back of my closet. Inside is my birth certificate, diploma, my mom's documents, and all the money I have saved." He looks toward the sheriff, who is walking slow, but closing in. "Get the box, my mom's ashes, and Otis, then leave town. Those are the only things I care about—other than you. Use the money and get us a place in Silverdale. There is enough to get you started, but you will need to get a job. After this is over, we'll start a new life together. Just us."

He kisses the top of my head and pulls away from me. I cling to him. Brian grabs my wrists, peels me off, and walks to the sheriff until they are face-to-face. Beyond them, the paramedics carry Skid strapped to the red stretcher. Chief Unger walks beside them, holding his son's hand.

By Brian's posture and drooping shoulders, I can tell that he is telling the sheriff everything. I stand alone with every nerve quivering in my body. I want to throw up. I want to scream. But all I can do is stand there with my heart pounding against my ribs.

Above me in a twisted juniper tree, the mourning dove that has haunted me since the day I arrived coos his pillowy sound. The cicadas are buzzing like electrical wires, and the ambulance beeps as it backs up then pulls away.

I am alone in the middle of nowhere. Brian turns around and puts his hands behind him. He stares at me with a sad smile and mouths, *I love you*, as he is handcuffed. The sheriff puts his hand on Brian's arm and turns him toward a truck. I cannot move. A deputy opens the back door, and Brian climbs in.

The deputy's truck circles around toward the road with Brian in the back. Brian stares out the window at me as they drive away. I am alone. Completely alone.

CHAPTER SIXTY-SIX

"You need to come into the office to give an official statement," Sheriff Briggs says to me as the men rope the area with yellow tape.

"With you?"

"Yes, ma'am."

My body feels empty and drained, and I shake my head.

"I will have you back before dark."

"I'm afraid of the Ungers." I picture Rose pounding on the door and forcing her way in. Or Chief and Doc coming to question me.

"Can we go pick up my things? And get my car? Then I won't need to come back."

He takes off his cowboy hat and runs his fingers through his sweaty hair. "How long will it take you?"

I think through my belongings and what Brian asked me to grab. "Fifteen minutes."

"I can do that."

"My car battery is dead. Can you give me a jump?"

He looks hesitant. I'm sure he has better things to do.

"It's all I've got in this world," I say.

His face softens, and he agrees. We head over to his truck, past two unmarked black cars, where he opens the back passenger door, and I climb in. It is sweltering hot inside and smells like Big Red bubble gum. He cranks up the air conditioner, and it blows out a bunch of hot air as we bump over the ruts and toward town.

As we make it to the dirt road, an ambulance without it's lights on comes toward us, whipping up a cloud of dust. And behind it is the entire convoy of Crystal's family in their SUVs, BMWs, Hondas, and Cadillacs, all coated in dust. Through the windows, I see their red shirts.

"There were no lights. Is Crystal..." My mouth is dry... "Is she dead?"

"No. She'll be fine. They're taking her to a hospital in Bend."

Thank God. She will be away from this town and away from the Ungers. That is what happens when you have people who care.

As I direct the sheriff to Brian's house, a terrible sadness washes over me. He puts it in park, and I grab the handle, but the door will not open. Sheriff Briggs comes around and lets me out. My entire body feels heavy as I step up onto our porch for the very last time.

Sheriff Briggs stands in the doorway to the house, not coming in but looking around. I bet all he sees is a one-bedroom house with mismatched and cheap furniture with stains on the wood and a blanket for a curtain in the living room. He does not know the love that was here.

Our bed is unmade, and I do not touch anything on it. After I give my statement about Skid and how we found a needle beneath the covers, our house will be a crime scene with strangers bagging things up and taking pictures of all our stuff.

I take my suitcase from the back of the closet, unzip it, and lay it on the floor. I find the box Brian told me to grab and untuck the folded flaps. Beneath the documents and certificates is more money than I have ever seen, mainly in wads of hundreds and twenties. I take five of the twenty-dollar bills and tuck them into my pocket before closing the box and setting it next to my suitcase.

I pull my clothes from their hangers and drop them inside, then pull open the top dresser drawer. As I scoop my clothes out, Otis stares at me. His fur is coated in dust, and a single string of cobweb stretches across his ears, from tip to tip. The box with Brian's mom's ashes is just below his chest as if he is guarding her.

In the second drawer, I feel the hard lump of the fly box from Skid, which makes me feel sick. My name is gouged into the top in child-like letters. I should turn it over to the sheriff for evidence since the flies inside are probably wrapped with Amber's hair, but it is all that I have left of her, so I set it next to Brian's mom.

I take the new box, the one with Brian's name and the clump of my hair, and set it aside. I will turn that one over. Brian did not tell me to pack him any clothes, but I do. I stuff his duffle bag full, which still leaves enough for him if he returns.

I slide Brian's mom and Amber below the lump of clothes in my suitcase, zip it shut, loop the strap of Brian's duffle over my shoulder, and walk out to the sheriff.

"That everything?"

"Almost. Will you take these to my car?"

After grabbing the money box, Otis, and the fly box with Brian's name, I look around. The white envelope from *Shooting the Rapids* sits on the kitchen table. I take that. It is evidence, but it is mine. I think they will have enough without it. We are about to leave when I remember one more thing.

I set everything on the table, fish out an envelope from the junk drawer, and take three dollars in coins from Brian's change jar. I write *Dustin and girls* on the front and slip the money in. I also write *The popsicles are in the freezer. Take as many as you want.* I place it on the porch chair on my way out.

I throw my suitcase, the envelope, and Otis onto the passenger seat and pop the trunk for the money box. The sunlight shines on something black beneath the passenger seat. I sweep my hand beneath it, and the Magic 8 Ball rolls out and onto the floor mat. I turn it over. The white triangle rises up in the blue liquid. Before it has a chance to touch the surface and reveal my fortune, I flip it over and back out of the car.

Sheriff Briggs comes toward me with a set of black and red jumper cables.

"Can I show you something before we go?" I ask.

He hesitates. "I need to get back to…"

"It won't take long, and it is evidence."

He agrees, and I lead him toward the Whitehorse Inn. We circle around the side and to the shoe tree. It stands there, leafless and dark and dripping with shoes.

I point to a pair of golden heels. "Those are the heels Crystal was wearing the night he took her."

Before the sheriff has a chance to answer, I point to one of the pairs of faded green Converse. "And those were Amber's, taken the night she went missing."

I point to the black cowboy boots, "And those were Kate's, the girl they had to lower the river for."

The sheriff is silent and staring.

I scan the tree until I see the turquoise tennis shoes with rhinestones. "And those were Mandy's…the girl whose body floated all the way down to Mullin's Falls. And there may be more."

"Are you saying the girls did not throw them up there themselves?"

"I know Amber and I didn't. It's hard to believe that any girl would throw their best shoes into a tree." I can see that he is skeptical. "I also know that some of the guys in this town steal the shoes of drunk girls after they have sex with them. They throw them into the tree like trophies."

"How do you know this?"

I do not want to throw anyone's name out to him, especially Brian's. "It is common knowledge to the guides."

He puts his mouth to his radio. "10-D-15, do you copy?"

"Go ahead."

"Are you still in town?"

"Just leaving."

"Come to the south side of the Whitehorse Inn. Bring a camera and some caution tape."

"Copy."

Sheriff Briggs takes a deep breath and rubs his chin across his clenched hand. "As soon as he gets here, we'll leave."

"Can I go say goodbye to my friend while we wait?"

"I don't think that is a good idea."

"At her cross. It's just there, by the river."

He nods, and I head toward the spot. Amber's name is stenciled in black on the white wood. I kneel beside it, and every last bit of my energy drains into the dirt.

"He is caught," is all that I say. Amber knows that I love her like a sister, and I will never forget her. This is her only marker to signify that she had lived. It is all my fault, and I wish we had never come. I kiss my fingers and press them to her name.

A brown horse with a black mane stands in the long grass across the river. He dips his head in the water for a drink. *If wishes were horses, then beggars would ride.* I lift the Magic 8 Ball up with its giant eight sideways like an infinity symbol.

I will never put my life in the hands of fate again—whether through fortunes or wishes. It is time to do something with my life, and I will start it by giving my statement against Skid and reporting Ed to Child Protective Services. Maybe I can get a job helping foster kids or become a cop so I can take down pedophiles like Ed. I want to help people and make their lives better.

I hurl the Magic 8 Ball into the river with a plunk. The horse lifts his head and whinnies as the ball sinks, then pops up and bobs in the current—drag-free and untethered in a perfect dead drift.

I hurry back to the shoe tree where Sheriff Briggs is snapping pictures. He hands the camera to the deputy. "Rope off this entire area, and I will send Hodges to come and take a look."

On our way back to my car, Sheriff Briggs is quiet and has that faraway look people get when they think.

"There's something else," I say.

He stops and turns toward me. Behind him, a pack of town kids sit on the edge of the porch at the Mercantile, sharing a bag of Doritos.

"I need to report a pedophile."

"Now? Is a child in danger?"

"I don't know. He lives at a foster home. It's a group home."

His eyebrows pinch in like he is trying to put it together.

"Not here in Lodell. It's been a while, but I need to report it. Can I call when we get to the station or talk to someone about it?"

"Yes, we'll get everything down with your statement."

The pack of kids must have finished their chips because one of them stuffs the bag into a trash bin, and they all run off toward the boat launch.

Back at my car, Sheriff Briggs attaches the clamps of the jumper cables to his battery and then to mine. After revving his engine several times, he signals me to turn the key. It clicks but does not start. I try again, and my engine comes to life. Thank you, God. I have money and a car to start a new life for Brian and me. I close the door and roll down my window to let out the heat.

I put my car into drive and pull away with all Brian and I

need. I follow the sheriff through town, past Lou's Hardware, Whiskey Dicks, Happy Cow Hamburger, Tortilla Flat, the town hall, and Lodell Community Church.

As we pass by Jake and Erin's house, several white sheriff's trucks are parked in front, all at angles and blocking the street. He comes out the door with his hands cuffed behind him and a deputy gripping his arm. He looks up and sees me driving by.

"Fucking bitch." Jake screams. His face is all red and raging. "Brian should have let you drown."

Every nerve in my body burns, and I want to yell back at him, but my air conditioning is starting to cool, so I roll up my windows and follow the sheriff out of town. When my car hits the dirt road, it whips up a dust cloud that grows bigger and bigger until it envelops Otis and me, and we are nothing but shadows inside it.

As I drive beneath the railroad trestle and to the mouth of the tunnel, I pause. My heartbeat quickens. My entire future starts once I am through it. I take a deep breath and lift my foot from the brake. I pass by the graffiti that says *DEATH*, *Jason loves Candie*, and a giant red penis and balls right next to *Becky sucks dick*...and I come out on the other side.

HIM
I AM THE RIVER, HAND-TIED FLIES

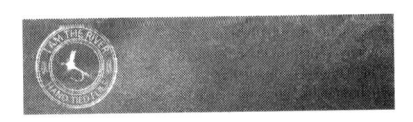

I AM THE RIVER, and the river is me. It is the fluid, and I am the flesh. Each fly is hand-tied with high-quality and carefully chosen materials.

SHOP NOW

https://www.etsy.com/shop/IAmTheRiver

ACKNOWLEDGMENTS

Nothing in life is done in isolation. This novel would not be possible without all the love, support, instruction, and feedback from the people in my life.

Thanks to my biggest supporters: My children, Brittany Romo, Brennan Romo, and Ryan Romo. Brittany spent countless hours sitting with me in coffee shops from when she was in elementary school until now as a graphic designer. She helps me with my marketing and creates my beautiful cover designs. Brennan and Ryan are always willing to let me bounce ideas off them and help me work through things when I feel stuck.

Thanks to my mother, Sandy Folk, for being a kind and loving mother and an avid reader who instilled in me a love of literature.

To my father, John J. Folk II who left this earth far too early. He always encouraged me to do what I love in life, and I have.

To my newest family members: Chris Jungenberg and Cathy Cogliano—thank you for putting up with my craziness and especially for accepting me into your hearts.

To Mark Overholtzer for offering his perspective and challenging me—especially about my titles, which I struggle with.

To Randy and Kiki Hopp, thank you for all the encouragement and for always caring and believing in me. Also, for giving me space at your dining room table as I try to write like Kermit.

I am also blessed by the rest of my big and loving family and my friends. All of you have helped shape who I am and have given me many experiences to draw on for my writing.

To my content editors: Craig Lesley, Serina Savage, Mica Fish, Corey Talbott, and Jayson Janes, for their expertise and feedback so I feel confident putting my novel out to the world. To Diane Peters, my beta reader, who isn't afraid to tell me like it is in a very constructive and encouraging way. And to my copy editor, Mark Overholtzer, who finds errors even after twenty other people read it.

I am grateful to Pacific University's MFA program, especially my advisors: Craig Lesley, Pete Fromm, Ann Hood, and Mary Helen Stefaniak. I especially appreciate the continued friendship with Craig Lesley. A special thanks to Deborah Reed for giving me the jump-start on my career—there are just not enough words.

A very special thank you to Mica Fish, a beautiful and inspiring whitewater guide. She helped me immensely in the beginning stages of this novel and at the end as one of my content editors. She also took me down the rapids for my first of many whitewater rafting trips.

ABOUT THE AUTHOR

Kelly Romo grew up in California but, currently lives in Oregon where she teaches writing, literature, and social studies. She is the mother of three grown children: Brittany, Brennan, and Ryan. She is an avid outdoorswoman who loves to kayak, hike, and fish. *Dead Drift* is her third novel. Her debut novel, *Whistling Women*, was published in November 2015. *When Sorrow Takes Wing* was published in May 2021.

Thank you for reading my novel. I hope you enjoyed it and will give me a review.

If you would like to be part of my VIP Reader club, please sign up on my website, www.kellyromo.com. My VIP Readers get updates on my writing, exclusive offers and promos, free entry into drawings for books, and other fun items.

- facebook.com/kellyromoauthorpage
- twitter.com/KellyAnneRomo
- instagram.com/kellyromo.author
- amazon.com/Dead-Drift-Kelly-Romo/dp/B0B37W54ZY
- bookbub.com/books/dead-drift-a-whitewater-thriller-book-1-by-kelly-romo
- linkedin.com/in/kelly-romo-a49a256

ALSO BY KELLY ROMO

Historical Fiction:
When Sorrow Takes Wing
Whistling Women

Thrillers:
Whitewater Thriller Series book 2 is in the works

Made in the USA
Columbia, SC
24 September 2022